RACER

New York Times **bestselling author**
KATY EVANS

Copyright © Katy Evans

First paperback edition: August 2017

Copyright © 2017 by Katy Evans
Cover design by Sara Hansen at Okay Creations
Interior formatting by JT Formatting

10 9 8 7 6 5 4 2 1

Library of Congress Cataloguing-in-Publication Data is available

ISBN-13: 978-1635763546
ISBN-13: (eBook) 978-0-9972636-6-4

table of contents

To the fire inside us, may it always burn

playlist

"Fast Car" by Jonas Blue (feat. Dakota)
"Don't You Need Somebody"
by RedOne (feat. Enrique Iglesias)
"Love Drunk" by Boys Like Girls
"Sound Of Your Heart" by Shawn Hook
"Favorite Record" by Fall Out Boy
"Believer" by Imagine Dragons
"The Other Side" by Jason Derulo
"Jet Pack Blues" by Fall Out Boy
"Battle Scars"
by Lupe Fiasco and Guy Sebastian
"Come and Get It" by Selena Gomez
"Walk" by Kwabs
"Undisclosed Desires" by Muse
"Unwell" by Matchbox Twenty
"Redbone" by Childish Gambino
"Your Guardian Angel"
by The Red Jumpsuit Apparatus

"Remember When" by Chris Wallace
"Maps" by Maroon 5
"Let Me Love You" by Ne-Yo
"XO" by Beyoncé
"The Best" by Tina Turner
"Whatever It Takes" by Imagine Dragons

the best

Lana

There's something about being the last child born in a family. Something about being the only daughter. I'm the youngest in the family, the fourth child born after my three brothers. My whole life I've been coddled, protected, bullied, bribed, and all of that is all fine, because I love my brothers, I love my family, but sometimes I wish I were the eldest, so I wouldn't be underestimated the way I am now. My name is Lana, but to them and my dad, I'm their *Lainie baby* even at twenty-two.

My brothers and dad stand by our tent at the side of the track. Dozens of cars zoom past. Blue, black, yellow colors flying by, helmets with rainbow visors, sponsor logos, and testosterone galore. Other than the fact that they are all Formula One race cars, they have one other thing in common: none of those cars are ours. None of those cars are being driven by one of our drivers.

I sigh and carry the lemonade cups back to our tent. The autumn cold air cuts into my cheeks and steals under my ponytail to freeze the back of my neck. This fall, while testing possible drivers, I've gained two bright spots on my cheeks, thank you wind-chill combined with sunlight, and judging by the way my face is stinging now, I'll bet the red is spreading to my ears and nose.

There's a whistle as I pass our neighbor's tent. "Lainey, that for me?" one of the mechanics calls.

"Sorry I've only got two hands and they're both spoken for." I don't even glance his way—it's true that everybody is always nice to me, but I try not to get too friendly with the other teams. We're opponents, after all. Let's keep it real.

HW RACING TEAM, our logo stares back at me as I reach our tent—black as background, red and white on the logo.

The cars are rumbling past in practice and we already know this will be our last, and worst, season. We used to be the team with the smallest tent, the lowest budget, but the greatest talent. Now we have a small tent, low budget, and no talent. And next year, without my dad ... I glance at my dad and he's in a pullout chair. He's got his face in his hands, exhaling deeply.

At the side of the tent, the only driver out of three who still meant to race is puking. The car is smashed. He's shaking, pale and pissed at himself. The driver was physically unharmed, but we all know, if you smash the car in a test drive, you're not going to get the gig.

I bring the guy one of the lemonades. "Sugar," I coax. "Could help."

He keeps staring at his racing boots, his shoulders bent in defeat. "Only chance I get to test and blow it."

I set the cup at his side and give him my most comforting smile, though my three brothers and my dad want to murder him.

"It's gonna take hundreds of thousands to fix this fucker," my oldest brother, Drake, grumbles as I head over to my dad.

"Hundreds of thousands we barely have," Clay grumbles back.

I stroke the side of the smashed car. Dad has three cars. My favorite is Kelsey, and I'm relieved she was out. I'm still sad for Moira though.

The day you think about a car as a friend ...

"Might be time for me to admit, I'm waiting for something that isn't going to happen," I hear my dad say.

I head over to him with the other lemonade cup. "It will, daddy, it will."

I'm the assigned team PR. I feed them, organize hotel stays, interviews for our drivers (not that that's been a big part of the job lately). I get their clothes cleaned, pick up the dry cleaning. Basically, I make a home for them an ocean and a thousand and one miles away from where we grew up in Ohio.

We uprooted after mom left us, all dad's money going to a Formula One team. It's his dream. One thing he gave up for my mom and could never get over. And now that I know it's his last chance to get it, it's mine too.

"So what's the plan?"

"Not now, Lainie."

They're pissed. They need a pep talk, but I can see dad is fresh out of pep talks. He looks defeated.

"He's not the only guy with talent," I tell my brothers.

"We don't have money to take in anyone with talent anymore. Everyone's been groomed since they were racing go-karts at six. By the time they're in their teens they're already owned by their sponsors or their teams," Drake says.

"I'll reel him in."

I'm panicked. I've never seen them look so defeated and frustrated. When did it stop being fun? When we lost hope of winning.

"Clay, Drake, Adrian, shush. I'll do it. You set the cars, dad's head of the team, let me bring in the talent."

It's my dad's dream. Now it's mine too.

"I'll do it."

My brothers keep on talking, and so does my dad.

I grab my shoe and toss it at them. It hits Drake in the shoulders and he turns, scowling.

"I said, I'll do it."

"Did you just throw your shoe at me?"

I grab the other one, and throw it too. "No, I threw you two."

"Lainie ..."

"Don't Lainie me. Dad, you run this team, you guys fix the cars, let me bring in the talent."

"Look, Lane, just because dad made you the PR doesn't mean you have a lick of sense in determining whether someone has talent," Drake says.

"It's not hard to spot. Give me a chance. This is our life. We gave up ... *everything* for this. I don't want us to quit." I step forward. "I don't want Dad to quit."

He looks at me.

I don't mention that I'm afraid that quitting might make him give up, that quitting will give him some sort of permission to leave now that he has no dream to live for.

"Drake, it's his dream."

"It's all our dreams, but we need to be realistic here. We don't have any of the money Dad started with: no wins equals all expenses, Lainie. It's a long shot and Dad's tired, he's tired, we might as well spend it somewhere calm where he can take it easy …"

"No," I say firmly.

"Lainie," he begins.

"No. This will give him new life. This will make him happy."

He looks at me with pity, the kind of pity reserved for older brothers who are more mature, who've dealt with the news about your dad. And me? I have focused on his every dream for the past four years because tomorrow we all die. It's today that matters to me, because today my dad is right here in the tent, breathing and living and disappointed and I'm the fixer.

"You guys are being too realistic, let me dream for all of us. Give me ONE chance. Just one test. I'll bring the pilot."

Silence.

"Dad, I said I could do this."

He looks at my brothers, and I groan.

"Who do you have in mind?" Drake finally asks.

"You'll see," I lie.

"Whoever he is, you think you can just convince a guy to come with a team on its last legs?"

"How hard can he be? He's a man, isn't he?"

I shoot them a look that speaks volumes, then kiss my dad on the cheek and tell him, "I'm going to have to travel. Hang tight, Daddy. I'm not coming back until I find him. I'm not settling for anything but the best—someone who loves the wheel and doesn't have a ride."

That same night, I take a red-eye flight from Australia to Atlanta, then another from Atlanta to St. Petersburg, Florida. My plan is to try to catch the Indy drivers during practice before their season starts, and I know they're practicing in St. Pete right now. So I run through the list of pilots during my flight, researching their pros and cons.

I'm uncomfortable in my seat, shifting as I try not to bother the two people next to me. I booked my flight last minute, and therefore ended up with the very coveted (not!) middle seat.

By the time I land in Florida, it's afternoon, and I'm badly slept, dehydrated from the flight, and completely exhausted—but I have three days not only to find a driver, but to take the long flight back to Australia in time for the first F1 race of the season. Speculation about our team pulling out of the race must already be in full bloom, and although I can't control what others think, I'd be damned before I let my father retire with anything less than a gold star. So even sleepless, dehydrated, hungry, and worried, I'm clinging to all my determination to prove myself to my family as I drive my rental to the track. My stomach growls every time I drive past a restaurant, but I know that food needs to wait.

I circle around the track where the drivers are testing before race day. I'm searching for a place to park, struggling because of the blocked streets due to the temporary street circuit set up for the St. Petersburg Indy-Car race.

I spot a space, but I have to slam on the brakes when a red car turns with a screech before me.

I frown, annoyed, and press the accelerator again toward one of two empty slots. The mustang in front of me swoops in and steals the first vacant slot and, panicked that someone will jump out of the blue and take the only remaining one right next to it, I gun it into the second slot. The car stops with a jolt.

Oh fuck!

I just crashed the guy.

"Ooops, my bad," I say, putting the car in reverse and then back to drive, carefully parking it in place.

The door of the mustang swings open, and a guy clad in black exits the vehicle. I nervously hurry out of my car and head around to stand next to the guy.

He inspects the damage.

I inspect the damage.

"You need driving school," he gruffs out in a very deep voice.

Aghast at the insult, I grit, "You need driving manners." I raise my head to glare at him, and my breath stalls in my throat when I look into his face.

Because ...

No one.

In this *world.*

Should own such a masculine.

Hot.

Terribly handsome *face*.

His eyes have a gleam that makes me feel as if he wants to devour me. They're irresistible, raw, intense and challenging, completely animal and fiery. The rest of him is absolute beauty. That's really the only way I can describe him. The floor under my feet tilts a little bit when he smiles, and one lone dimple appears. Oh god, I'm a sucker for dimples.

"Really?" the guy says, lips now curving in amusement as our eyes meet.

"Yes. Really. I'm not in the mood for this. You took *my* slot." I feel a frown pinch my face as my anger over his driving manners mingles with my anger over his handsomeness, and his eyes begin to twinkle.

I try to suppress my reaction to that twinkling eye; but the truth is, I don't think I've ever seen blue of this shade in real life or *anywhere* but in pictures of beautiful oceans somewhere far away like Fiji.

"I haven't eaten in hours, or slept at all. I'm really not in the mood," I say, and when he only glares down at me, something inside me starts to heat up under his intense gaze.

His eyes keep glued to me.

I don't think anyone has ever stared at me so thoroughly.

Not just with annoyance, and interest, but almost ... amusement along with ... confusion?

Exactly the way *I* feel. Staring up at *him*.

There's a slight darkening in his eyes as he keeps staring at me. I don't know what that something is, but it's something that makes parts of me tickle and squirm.

"Watch out next time," he then says, after a long moment, his voice gentler, his eyes sort of sliding hungrily all over my body as he takes a step back, grabs a cap from inside the car, slams the door, and locks it with a little beeping sound.

I look at the scratch and tiny dent in it, realizing he's just spared me by not insisting we call the insurance company. "I'm sorry," I say belatedly.

He stares at me past his shoulder and clenches his jaw, comes back to tower over me, glaring. "What's your name?"

"Um ... Alana," I lie. It's close to Lana, but not exact. I'm too nervous.

"Alana. You crashed my car," he growls, shooting a pointed look towards his gorgeous cherry-red mustang.

"I ... I'm sorry? I just got out of a sixteen-hour flight and it's been a never-ending day."

He laughs to himself, as if he can't believe my excuse.

He shoots me a pointed look, and I stare at his midnight-black hair as he leaves, resisting the urge to fan myself a little.

Whoa.

I stare at his backside in jeans, the black T-shirt hugging his chest, my irritation sort of falling away as a nearly over-whelming wave of lust hits me.

I discreetly brush my hands over my breasts to try to get my nipples to stand down.

Going out with guys with my four men in my life isn't an easy option. Nobody is good enough for me, and all of the men I meet are drivers. The last thing I've wanted is get involved with a driver. When I was seventeen, I had a boyfriend. He died. David was everything to me. I would never want to date anyone who put his life on the line like car racers do. But boy, I really need to get laid.

Hurrying into the stands, I'm glad to find that because it's testing day, not racing day, the stands are somewhat uncluttered.

At the far end of a set of stands, there's a man in jeans and white shirt, his dark hair peppered with salt at the temples. I head over and take two seats before him when my heart stops as the man behind me calls, "Son!" and I watch the guy I crashed into head up the steps.

My heart starts beating so hard when I see him again that I duck my head, and yet even through the noises of car motors, I watch him through the corner of my eye as he takes the steps up to his father.

Clearing my throat, I pull out my list of drivers and my marker. I've got eight drivers on my list that I want to watch, but I've got the rest of the Indy drivers' names on the bottom of the list too. Just in case.

"You weren't at the gym today," I hear the man behind me say.

"I don't get off on getting my face rearranged. Jesus, Dad."

There's a low laugh from one of them, and once again the voice of the guy I crashed into. He's got a very deep voice. "Where's Iris?"

"Getting some water."

A girl of about eighteen takes the steps up the stands to where they sit. Glancing back to see, my stomach tumbles when she hugs the moody hottie and the moody hottie hugs her back, and then she sits right next to him.

She looks tiny compared to him.

He's all big and muscly, and too gorgeous to name.

Okay so he has a girlfriend. Big deal. He's terribly beautiful, and so is she. Both of them dark-haired and model-looking. But so what? Good for them. I'm not here for romance. I'm here for work.

But suddenly the idea of having a fling before going back starts to appeal. Nothing serious. I don't want anything like that. But maybe something … to get me relaxed. Get my mind back on racing and off the body-hunger things.

I can't help but be curious about him, though. I can somehow feel his eyes on the back of my head, boring into my skull like lasers as I study my list.

Inhaling nervously, I steal a look past my shoulders.

The young man shoves his hands in his pockets as he locks eyes with me, his eyebrows raising, his lips curving as he catches me staring.

His dad is staring at him now too. Frowning.

He says something to his son, but his son doesn't reply. He smirks at me.

I don't smirk back; I can't think straight.

The son stands and takes the steps down toward me.

Oh shit.

I turn back to my list. He comes over and leans behind me, his body warmth somehow suddenly too close to mine as he starts reading my list over my shoulder.

He smells like soap. Not cologne.

Just clean and soapy and male.

Something about that natural scent makes my mouth salivate and I swallow nervously.

"He's too slow on the straight." He taps the top name on my list. I try to shove the page under my bag but a part of it still peeks out from underneath.

"You know a lot about cars, do you." I scowl and try to suppress the way my body warms under the effect of his smile as he comes over to sit beside me.

"Too bad you don't have any driving manners," I add.

He smiles wider as he settles down beside me, all lean and fluid, and he looks at my paper again. "Bucket list?"

Huh?

"No!" I laugh then. "It's ... *no*," I say, realizing what he's implying.

"Can I make a suggestion?"

"You can, but it doesn't mean I'll take it."

He reaches for my list and slides it out from under my bag, and then he plucks the pen from my hand and scratches a line down the list of names. Then he sets the page on his jean-clad thigh, a very hard-looking thigh, and writes down one word. Racer.

"Is this ... what does this mean?" I ask, confused.

He winks as he hands it back. "You'll be smart to keep him on top of that to-do list."

I laugh. Blushing. OMG is he asking me to do him? Is that his name? No way, it can't be. "It's not my to-do list. I'm looking for a driver," I say.

"I know the best driver in the world. Actually."

"Really."

"Yep."

"I'd like to meet him. Then see him drive to see if I agree."

"You'll agree, all right." He stares at me. He looks very cocky right now, lips curved. "Tell you what. If you agree he's the best driver in the world, you fix my car," he then says.

"And if I don't?" I dare.

"I'll get you a brand new one."

"Oh wow, that confident of you."

He just smirks, those damn gorgeous eyes twinkling again.

I laugh, my tiredness evaporating. "So who's Racer. Is that you? Or is it this driver?"

His smile fades, and his eyes drink in my whole face again. When he speaks, his voice is lower. Husky. "Come to dinner with me, and we'll talk about it all you want."

Oh god. Is he staring at my mouth?

Am I staring at his mouth?

"I can't. Well, I suppose I could but … I'm here on work. I don't have time for dinner. Even if I'm starved."

There's a change in his expression as he regards me in unnerving silence, then he gruffs out, "I'll be right back."

I watch him head down the stands, a part of me hating to watch him leave, knowing I'll probably never see him again. I don't know why he has this effect on me. Maybe it's the fact that I've been around my brothers and father too long. Maybe I really do need to get laid before going back.

The blue-eyed hottie appears about ten minutes later, and he's carrying the best-looking hotdog I've ever seen, a bucket of fries, and a bottled water.

For a moment I gape at the food as he extends it over, his eyebrows low over those brilliant eyes as he smiles down at me, saying nothing.

"I …"

Usually I'm the one bringing food and drinks to everyone. I'm so unused to it I don't even know what to say.

When he keeps his arm out, I force myself to take it.

My fingers brush over his, and a current shoots down my spine.

I try to hide my reaction by bringing the food to my lap and lifting the hotdog immediately to my mouth. I take a large bite, then realize he's settling down next to me, watching me.

"Thank you," I say, gulping it down.

"You're welcome." His eyes twinkle again as he shifts his thigh, his body lean and big and yet remarkably agile in the easy, stealth-like way he moves. "You said you hadn't eaten or slept. It was either this or a pillow," he says, his eyes glinting amusedly.

I bite the inside of my cheek to keep from smiling.

"Let me pay you." I reach into my wallet, the hotdog in one hand as I try to open up my wallet with the other. "How much was it."

"Don't worry about it, I get free food here," he says.

I think he's joking, because his eyes are doing that wicked thing they do, but I'm not sure because he's not smiling.

Relenting because I really need to watch my expenses during this trip and he looks stubborn enough that I'm pretty sure arguing won't work, I slowly eat it, aware of him watching the track as I do. I hear his father and girlfriend walk down the steps. "We're heading home," his dad says.

The guy keeps his eyes on me, absently nodding as he looks at me thoughtfully.

I see his dad frown at him, and his girlfriend also seems confused as they shuffle out.

"Your girlfriend seemed concerned that you're sitting here," I say, once they leave.

He chuckles a low, rich sound, shakes his head. "Don't you know? I've got no driving manners, but I'm not wishing

me on anyone." He grins when I only stare. "I've got no girlfriend." He leans over, brushes a little piece of bread out of my
lipstick. "But you're pretty."

"Thank you."

I glance at the track, the food almost stuck in my throat as
he lifts his thumb and licks off the piece of bread from his
skin.

Oh my god.

I just came—*almost.*

There's a silence. His eyes so blue I feel like they're an
angel's eyes, or a devil's in disguise.

"I don't have one either."

"You don't have a girlfriend?" There's a twinkle in his
eye and a smirk on his lips that I find irresistible.

I laugh. "No! I don't have time for a *girlfriend.* I had ...
well, I had a boyfriend but ..." I shake my head, look down at
the hotdog on my lap. "I don't mean to go through that again."

After David nobody has touched me. I suppose that's why
my knees feel weak, why my cheeks burn as his finger brushes
my hair, and why staring into his eyes makes me breathless.

I suppose I didn't expect ... that face.

I mean.

Who in the world could expect that face staring back?

Chiseled to perfection. Perfect nose, high cheekbones,
hard jaw, glinting narrowed eyes, straight eyebrows, and
fringed among the darkest lashes I've ever seen, those electric
blue eyes.

I almost choke out, after I swallow my most recent bite of
the hotdog. "Do I have more food on my lipstick? Your staring
is making me nervous."

His soft chuckle seems more amused than apologetic as he shakes his head. "You know what they say about people who wear their emotions on their sleeves."

"Yeah."

"You wear yours in your eyes."

My eyes widen. He peers down at me intently, a smile on his lips.

"Really? How am I feeling now?" I laugh at that, feeling flustered as I clutch my hotdog.

"Now? Or before you asked?"

"Now."

"You're happy."

"Really?" I say, and I *do* feel carefree, happy, and a little flirty too.

"It's the hotdog," he says, though I can tell by the mischief in his gaze he's not buying that.

"Oh. For sure. You have no idea how long it's been since I had one," I say, biting into it again, a big bite to prove my point.

His smile widens for a second, and then it fades, and we sit in silence, watching the track as the cars zoom past.

I feel self-conscious now.

About my stupid, expression-filled eyes.

"Are you traveling on your own?" he asks.

I nod.

"How long are you staying here?" he asks again, sounding intensely curious.

"Not long," I breathe, unsettled by his implacable gaze. "You? Do you live here?"

"I do. Not my family. They're visiting." He smiles lightly, one dimple appearing.

"Oh."

Just then, he leans forward, taking the idle hotdog from my hand and lifting it to my mouth.

I open my mouth to protest and he inches it closer, and I end up taking a bite. My stomach tightens as he lowers it, watching me eat it, his eyes really blue, really observant and unnerving, and really, really close.

"What about him," I ask, pointing at the guy currently out on the track.

"Awkward on turn four," he says, sparing him a second's glance.

I pay attention, and realize he's right, he loses speed on turn four.

"Is it true you know the best driver in the world?"

I know I sound dubious, but I know there's no such thing. All of them have qualities and flaws, all of them depend on the car, the weather, hell their lucky stars.

His eyes darken. He nods.

His body is delicious, I need to fight my eyes to keep them from dropping down to his thick thighs in those black jeans, and his shirt hugging those muscles.

"Will you introduce me."

He reaches out and takes my pen again, scribbling a street address on the back of my list. As he bends down to write, I stare at his profile and at his mouth, and I wonder what that mouth would look like after being kissed by me. After kissing me.

He lifts his head and catches me staring, and looks at my lips too. I snap out of it and smile as I take the paper he extends out. "Nine p.m. tonight. Be there," he says, almost a warning in his tone.

I notice he wrote another word after Racer too. It says Tate.

I gather my things, and say, "You better not be a serial killer," warningly too.

"Not yet. But this guy ... you should stay away from him." He shoots me a meaningful look, and I shiver all over.

I walk away and hurry to my car, not knowing what the hell I'm doing. I wasted the Indy drivers' practice session ogling this guy, and now I've literally still got no driver, only an address, and the word Racer on my "to-do" list.

And though I should be worried about this situation, I'm smiling as I pull my car out, my whole body feeling oddly untired now. Maybe it's the prospect of him being right. Maybe it's the prospect of him being *there*.

I shouldn't even want him to be right because I'd owe him a very expensive car fix. But a part of me still wants him to be.

I arrive at my hotel room and settle down before taking a bath to change for tonight, and I call the concierge for a complimentary Wi-Fi code and decide to type in

Racer Tate into the Google search bar.

I'm fucking mind-blown with the results I get.

FAMOUS SEATTLE ILLEGAL STREET RACER, RACER TATE, SAID TO BE HEATING UP THE STREETS IN ST. PETERSBURG ...

car trouble

Lana

The thing about lying is you never know how to stop. One lie requires another and another and another. I've got a flat tire, am on the outskirts of St. Petersburg, heading to what I assume is a street race happening around here, and having to walk the rest of the way there isn't exactly my idea of smooth sailing.

My brothers don't know I'm here. They know I'm scouting for talent. I didn't tell them I ended up with nothing from Indy today, except I happened to meet the most fucking popular street racer in the whole damn world. He's a veritable legend in those dark, secret forums I ended up squirming into, where all they talked about was Tate and how he never loses. I should've totally shut my computer down and taken my flight straight home. Who in their right mind would put a freaking illegal street racer behind the wheel of a million-dollar Formula One car? My dad's F1 car?

But here I am, on my way to the address the man himself wrote down on my page.

You should stay away from him ...

Why do we do the opposite of what we're told?

And why is it true that when it rains, it pours? I got a call from Drake checking in on me and to let me know my dad is in the *hospital.*

"But is he all right? Are you sure?" I peer straight ahead at the cars in the distance.

"Yeah, they said it was dehydration. Hang on. You're on speaker."

"Daddy, please take good care of yourself!"

"You take better care of me than I do," I hear my dad's soft, amused voice on the other end, a little tired. My eyes well.

"Well yes but I'm doing other things for you, please take good care of yourself for me."

I can hear the smile in his voice when he replies. "Only because you asked nicely and didn't throw a shoe at me."

"See? You're my favorite dad," I tease.

I don't get a reply. I hear Drake's voice closer to the speaker and I know I've been taken off speaker. "So how's it going?"

"I told you to trust me, I said I'd do it and I will," I say, double checking the tire I just changed to make sure it's on right.

"I also said I don't trust you."

"Asshole." I'm not too mad because the fact that I just changed my own tire is only thanks to my mechanic brothers.

"Lainie ... " He sighs exasperatedly. "Just come back to Australia. We'll—"

"I'll be there in time for the start of the season. With the best driver in the world," I bluff, hanging up. Oh god. Fuck.

I glance ahead as car after car drives past me, probably all of them heading to the race. I put the tools back into the trunk of the car and then climb behind the wheel, turning on the car and easing onto the street, pulling into the parking lot straight ahead.

About two dozen people are already parked here, waiting by a small hill on the sidelines of the parking lot.

There's a blue Camaro near what I assume is the start line, and the other slot is empty. I lock my car and head closer to where the people are.

The crowd is deafening, and it smells like armpits.

For a second my stomach knots up as I wonder if I'm really this desperate.

If I'm really out of options.

On my flight, I did my research. I've searched the Daytona serial, the IndyCar, and I even was at the track today, and found nothing to blow my mind.

Now it seems all I have is watching this race and then going back to my hotel to sulk about how expensive flying across the world back to the US was, as well as coming back with my tail between my legs and proving to my brothers that I'm as useless as they thought I'd be.

I feel a prick at the thought of coming back empty-handed.

Which explains why I'm still here.

What other choice do I have?

It's not like I really think I'm going to bring any of these guys back home, though I suppose the little candle of hope burning inside me hasn't been fully extinguished. Or maybe

I'm just not ready to come back home a loser yet. If I'm going to fail at this, I still need one more night to brace myself for the familial humiliation I'd be sure to endure.

I'm intrigued about Racer Tate. I won't lie.

According to the comments of dozens and dozens of fans, he's the best street racer anyone has ever seen. He shies from nothing. He's one with the machine, as if the machine were a part of him. So here I am, sitting here, waiting for an illegal street race. Two minutes to the race, and he's nowhere in sight.

Wow. What a dick.

"I get to fuck him tonight," one woman breathes excitedly behind me.

"What do you mean?" her friend asks.

"The guys asked me to show him the winner's treatment."

Wow. So apparently he's a bit of a manwhore too.

My stomach clutches.

The crowd cheers.

His competitor motions to his car, a shiny black thing with fire drawn on it and everything.

Then points at the vacant space, and turns his thumb down.

People cheer even *more* and that seems to make the guy get a little upset, shaking his head.

I stand to leave. Really I shouldn't even be here, *near* here.

There's silence as a cherry mustang comes into view.

"Ohmigod, it's him," I hear someone whisper as the mustang roars into the parking lot and screeches to a halt right at the starting line.

My heart stops, and I sit back down.

And there he is.

The guy leaps out of the car through his open window, and one guy greets him with a slap of the back. He's changed into blue jeans. He's got a ton of muscles, those jeans, and a long-sleeved white shirt.

Racer rakes a hand through his mussed-up, just-woke-up black hair, grinning, and then his eyes start to scan the crowd of people.

I have an urge to hide—but somehow don't act fast enough and before I know it, his blue eyes find me in the crowd.

He just stares, his hands idle at his sides.

He looks very interested to see me here, and as he stares at me, he narrows his eyes and his lips curve ever so slightly as if he's pleased to see me here.

They're all saying his name. "Racer."

The girls' fingers are glorying over his chest and I clench my hands at my sides, not liking it and I don't know why. I wonder what he'd do if I told him who I am.

He doesn't really look like he wants any of them. But their neediness vexes me. I'm jet-lagged and impatient and a little bit jealous that these women seem to have no trouble reaching out to touch him.

He jams his hands into his pockets, and he looks at me subtly between dark lashes, so subtly I can't believe how overwhelmed I am by feeling his eyes on me.

Doubt creeps in as I wonder if this guy is really what I need. I'm gonna need to watch his diet; he's all muscle but he won't be able to add an ounce of muscle if I want him to fit in our Kelsey.

He starts shoving his way for me.

I tug my shirt a little, feeling undressed, needing a reminder that there's actually a pretty decent amount of fabric covering me.

His intense eyes drop down my stomach, and a bevy of butterflies go off there. *This is so not appropriate, Lana* ...

The testosterone around him is so off the charts that if we'd been in a closed space, we'd all grow muscles.

He starts smiling as he approaches.

"What is this? Role-play today? School teacher slut—" someone is saying about my cropped top and long skirt.

"She's not a whore," he breathes, angry.

He comes to stop before me, frowning because of the comment, but his eyes devour me.

Flat out devour me with a single look.

I take a hesitant step forward.

"You ready for the race of your life, Alana?" he asks. So gruff, so male.

His eyes ... I feel the urge to look away, but I can't, as if his eyes just trapped mine. The color is a swirl of blue and grey and specks of black, but mostly blue, mostly electrifying blue. I'm still as uncomfortable as I was a nanosecond ago. It's just an eye-connection, nothing really. I glance away, and he eases back, and so do I. He's leaning back, watching me.

"You're late," is all I can say, already feeling as if I won't stand for tardiness if he works on my team.

He stares at me wordlessly, then smiles in amusement and heads to his car, giving me a look before he climbs inside and slams the door shut.

My breath is all but gone, and so is obviously my mind, because I react really strangely to this guy, and he's a manwhore and a law breaker, and here I am. *Still.* Hearing him fire up his car and wondering what he's doing to fire up something in *me*.

purring

Racer

5 minutes ago…

I hear the siren well before the cop car lights flash red and blue in my rearview mirror.

I'm a damn idiot thinking I'd get away with it this time.

Exhaling with a growl, I pull over to the side of the road on the outskirts of St. Petersburg. Turn down the music, then drum my fingers as I watch through the rearview mirror as the cop straightens his belt and walks over. *Fucker, get over here already.*

The guy probably knows I'm in a hurry (hint: I was going 29 mph above the speed limit) and is taking his goddamn time. Rankled and intent in rankling him back, I take my time too as he stands out the window. Then, after a while, I slowly click the button and lower the window. I suppose a smirk's not the way to greet a cop but I can't fucking help it when he stops me every damn time my wheels are spotted around here.

"License and registration, Tate," he says.

"You already know I've got both."

"Yeah well I want to see them again."

"For the twelfth time? Must look pretty in my license picture."

"Don't be a smartass, Tate," he growls.

I pull my hands from the steering wheel, reach into the glove compartment, then my wallet, and hand them over.

"You up to mischief again, Tate?"

"Not especially." I grin.

He does the same dance we always do—checks the paperwork, clucks as he shakes his head.

I pull out a hundred-dollar bill, place it between my index and middle finger, and shove it out the window. "You might want to catch a beer for the next half hour. In fact, make it an hour. Invite a few buddies. On me."

"Man ... you're really pushing it." He pockets the money. "Don't be so eager to go to the grave."

"Nah. I'm immortal." I grin.

He laughs, then shoots me a scowl and walks away. I fire up the car and screech away, switching gears as I speed off the narrow road, hitting it hard as I glance at the time. Two minutes to the race, still a couple miles to go.

I push on faster—never wanting to be in a race like I want to race this one. Because she's fucking there. I can feel it in my bones, and I want her to know who the fuck the best driver in the world is.

Fucking *me*.

I pull into the parking lot where the crowd of usuals snap up at attention when they watch my car pull in.

They squeal and wave.

Preston's car is already lined up—ready.

I park mine and leap out through the window.

Adrenaline courses in my veins.

I crave this shit. It's in my DNA, in my very damn bones. I need it like air. I need it like I need a heart.

"Tate?"

I scan the crowd for her. Fucking couldn't stop thinking about her. I wanted her here as hard as I wanted to race. Where the fuck is she?

I hear Henley approach.

"Tate? You ready?"

I spot Preston across the street, surrounded with girls, drinking.

"That's gonna be his third," Henley says to me.

I keep my eyes out for her, and suddenly I see a speck of light brown hair and green eyes.

She's gaping at me.

I kinda like it.

Female hands are on my abdomen, stroking. Wanting. Purring in my ear.

"A little tension release before the race, Tate?" one of the girls whispers.

I feel my lips hike up at the corners. Yeah, I don't reply. My mind is on racing now.

But my eyes ...

My eyes are on *her*.

Honey hair, light-green eyes, a fucking wet dream. My muscles tight, I'm ready. But I can't keep from walking over, my heart pounding as I envision claiming her as my prize, feeling her melt beneath me, tasting her mouth beneath mine, letting her show me all the favorite places of her body while my mouth shows them all some TLC, Racer-style.

"What is this? Role-play today? School teacher slut—" I hear some asshole say.

"She's not a whore," I growl, angry, shoving my way to her as she watches me, wide-eyed, in both interest and concern.

I warned her to stay away; she should've. But she's here now, and I'm so ready to blow her fucking mind off, I can already taste her on my lips. Feel her with my goddamn hands.

"You ready for the race of your life, Alana?" I ask, my voice gruff.

I've got a hard-on, and it's for her.

My dick swells with speed, yeah I get hard when I race, but it's never swelled like this before.

She narrows her eyes as she thinks about it.

"You're late," she says with that princess-like, bossy tone that somehow turns me on.

I just smile and make her watch me head to my car.

I'm testosterone-laden and as pumped as it gets every time I begin, and I'm high on my own power when I end.

I'm going to fuck her like she's never been fucked tonight.

Soundlessly I walk to my mustang. It's nicked by her, and I suppose that's why she got off with it. Because it'll have a thousand more nicks by the time I'm done tonight. And because she looked tired, tired, beat-up, and about as lovely as a bird with a broken wing.

Dozens of footsteps hurry behind me as I reach my mustang.

"Holy shit!" the girls cry.

"Bring your camera," the guys say.

Yeah, they're pumped about it.

Because I'm good. Because nobody is as good.

I grab the door, climb in and take the seat, waiting for it to fuel me, fill the void that keeps growing in me no matter what I do—pissing me the fuck off. Nothing satiates me, nothing fills me, it's the curse of being a Tate—one I inherited from my father.

But I've got this.

And suddenly, I'm wired up because tonight, I'm going to have *her*.

Preston fires up next, and we let the engines steam.

I eye my car not only because she's beautiful, but because of what she can do.

She's all red body, black seats. Four hundred horsepower. (I did some modifications to take her to this level.) A beauty. She's raring to go.

I shift, pull up an inch closer to the starting line—line up next to him.

I feel him glancing at me, I glance back, giving him my best eat-shit smile. *Ten* ... the count begins.

Nine...

Eight...

Seven...

Six...

Five...

Four...

THREE...

TWO...

ONE!!

The squeal of tires on asphalt. Pedal to the metal, the seat vibrating beneath me as I step it. Easy first—and she's purring. Shifting gears, I head down the narrow road, and pick up speed, my foot down harder as I shift again.

We're neck to neck.

I'm hitting 100 mph. 120 mph. 150 mph.

We're fucking fast now. Trees flying past my window. Preston bumping up against my side. I swerve lightly and lock our wheels together. Shove him off the road. Destabilized, I swerve and straighten with a screech. He loses seconds.

Up ahead, there are headlights, like beady red eyes coming at me.

I keep my feet on the pedal, swerving right as the truck passes, dust piling up in a cloud behind me. My heart is racing a thousand miles an hour, and I want it to race even more.

Preston comes up, attempting a pass. He gyrates and bumps me to the side, sending me spinning.

"Fucker." I let go of the wheel, let her spin before I grab her back in my hold and recover control.

I'm fucking pissed now.

I pull up behind him and kiss his bumper. We meet eyes through his rearview mirror, and I smile menacingly, pressing the last way into the pedal to kiss the fucker harder.

He swerves—I swerve the other way and pass him until he's eating my dirty air. I push harder to get away so he can't use my draft, my eyes up ahead, where I pull up the parking brake and spin to turn.

I release it and speed back to the parking lot, my mind on that finish line—and on fucking sexy crash-into-my-cherry-mustang Alana waiting in the crowd.

Is she like my fans who watch me? Whose pussies get wet from the excitement? Whose nipples turn hard as fuck by the time I climb out of the car and give them a glance?

My cock is thick again. It's been acting up since I met her, and it's only been intensifying with each second she breathes even in my zip code.

Yeah my dad is a man who goes after what he wants. You can say I'm cut of the same cloth.

I want her beneath me tonight.

I screech to a halt. I turn her off, then ease out of the car, breathing hard. I hear the shuffle of feet as girls scramble to get closer, meanwhile the guys shove their way forward too, including Henley.

"Insane, you're a ridiculous beast!!" Henley yells.

I raise my arm and slap his hand. He also places my bets, and the wad of cash he shoves into my hand is 30,000-dollars thick.

Yeah it feels good to stuff that money in my back pocket, but not even winning feels as good as the drive.

The moment I hit that pedal, I'm alive.

And tonight I feel drunk with it.

I scan the crowd and look for her—my eyes finding her in the same spot I left her, her mouth gaping wide open. I don't think I've ever wanted anything as much as I want to fucking kiss the shit out of that mouth. Tonight my prize is her.

My eyes stay on her, my gut roiling with hunger. I smile at her; her eyes widen a little bit, and she blinks.

"We've got you a prize … show you what champions …" I'm hearing Henley say.

I start walking forward, feeling crazed like I've never felt crazed in my life, my eyes, hands, mind, even the hot, adrenaline-buzzed blood pumping in my veins, all pumping for her.

racer effing tate

Lana

'm still reeling. While people approach him, he cuts a path straight to me, his gaze penetrating and target-like; making me want to bolt.

His lips do that little upward tilt they do that seems so sexy, and for a second, I feel like I'm lightheaded.

I gulp, and then feel mad at myself for acting like some idiot as fucking devil-Racer Tate reaches me, throws himself into a seat next to me, and turns to look at me expectantly with the most gorgeous grin on his face.

I don't know what to say.

This guy has left me sort of speechless.

"So ..." I say, staring in the distance at his beat-up mustang, then at him.

"So ..." he says too, in his deep voice, his smile a little more wicked than it was two seconds ago. He glances at my mouth.

Oh god.

Why am I licking my lips?

It only made his eyes narrow and darken.

I open my mouth to speak, failing to find words. He smells like sweat and soap and shampoo, and I feel my traitorous nipples push up to my top again. Why do they do that when he's around?

"This is illegal," I state.

His voice is husky from exertion, and his eyes glint with laughter. "That's why it's fun."

I look away from his eyes, trying to focus and clear my head. He leans over and peers into my face, his face shadowed by the moonlight and his jaw now carrying a little scruff. "Are we in agreement?" he presses.

"No." I glare and shake my head, meeting his cocky gaze. "You're reckless, Racer."

"So are you, Alana."

"It's just … Lana."

His brows fly up in surprise. "And a bit of a liar too."

I purse my lips, still glaring as my gaze goes back to his car. Girls are rubbing against it as if it were him, and I find it disgusting. Why are women always acting so slutty around race car drivers and bad boys?

"You crashed your car," I say flippantly.

"You crashed *my* car," he contradicts, amused.

I laugh, then scowl in his direction. "You crashed it more. I can't believe you were making such a fuss about me crashing into you when it was just a little kiss—"

He leans in to peck my lips—fast but firmly. "That's a kiss."

I lose my breath.

My eyes wide.

He eases back, lips smiling as he comes to his feet and stretches his hand out to take me by the elbow and help me to my feet.

"Let's get out of here." He starts walking, leading the way.

"And go where?"

"Anywhere I can get my hands on you." He's serious. His hand is sliding into the back of my neck and I feel tiny as he guides me forward by the nape.

"I don't know what to do with you," I breathe, looking sideways at his profile.

He smirks, shooting me a sidelong glance. "I know exactly what to do with you."

I gulp.

He studies me with a growing smirk, his eyes fierce and savage as he tugs me closer and closer to him with that hand. He's guiding me to the parking lot. To my car. "Have your keys?" he asks.

I nod dumbly and unlock the car.

He eases me into the back of my car, following me in and shutting the door behind me. Suddenly I can smell sweat and warm guy, all too close to me.

He pulls me up a little close to his very hard, muscled side, his eyes trekking up my neck, to my jaw. "I wanted to taste you the second I saw you," he husks out as he runs his big palm down my arm.

"Why would—"

He leans his dark head, and his tongue is in my mouth.

He touches my lips lightly, moving and parting them beneath his, and I'm going to stop him any second now, except oh my fucking god!

He kisses me for ten seconds, and when we pause for air, I try, I really *try*, to grab some while I can.

His eyes are really blue, really dark and really beautiful. He's looking at me in ways I've never been stared at before, his eyes trekking my whole face, and for just a second I want to pretend I'm just a girl. I missed the parties, the make-outs, the guys, and suddenly here is this guy and I feel so drawn to him I'm trembling.

He drags me to his lap, and he's so hard I'm turning to putty in his hands.

He leans over. I stutter when he reaches out and takes a strand of my hair, leaning in. To give me ...

The most ferocious kiss I've ever been given in my whole life.

"Who the fuck are you, huh?" He covers my face with one hand, and stares down at me, smiling against my mouth, inhaling hard.

"Who the fuck are *you*?" I breathe.

My wet dream or my worst nightmare?

He presses his mouth to mine, a little more tenderly, sliding his fingers into my hair. He starts to kiss me again, tonguing me really hungrily, as if he needs me to live.

I feel myself melt, my whole body respond and vibrate in the most pleasant ways.

There's a knock on the window. "Dude. The prize is ... ahem. Outside."

As we hear a guy speak outside, Racer glances past my shoulders at that someone who knocked, then at me with a curl of his lips. "We've got spectators. Want to take this somewhere more quiet?" he asks.

"Where?" I ask, breathless.

Horny.

Out of my goddamned *mind*.

"Somewhere I can have my hands on you nonstop," is all he says.

I blink, sort of woozy at the idea of it.

He pulls me close, and plants a soft kiss on me—again our tongues hungrily meeting. My eyes shut as I feel myself float in his hot embrace and demanding mouth, then I open my eyes and stare into those gorgeous blue eyes of his.

I need this so much I can't even breathe. But I manage to whisper, "I have a hotel room."

His voice is also low, husky with arousal, and his eyes look heavy and half-lowered as he looks at me. "Works for me. I can't wait to see you in bed, crasher." He cups the back of my head, nuzzling my face with his nose and jaw before he eases back and looks at me with hot eyes.

He reaches for the door.

We step out of the car and he shelters me from the crowd as he takes my keys, ushers me to the passenger door, then goes around and slides behind the wheel. He ignites the car.

"You still need to fix my car," he says warningly, eyes straight ahead as he drives to my hotel, a smile curving his mouth.

"No, I haven't agreed you're the best driver in the world yet."

"Best kisser too."

"Really."

"Baby ..." he rolls his eyes.

"I don't agree on that either," I lie, shaking my still-woozy head. He laughs quietly, and then we ride in silence with my mind going a thousand miles a minute wondering if

I'm going to regret this. Why am I doing this? My mind still on the cherry-red mustang—and the motherfucking, crazy-ass *devil* behind the wheel.

He's the best street racer I've ever seen. My heart is still wanting to leap out of my throat.

How long has it been since I've seen driving like that?

Have I ever—ever—seen driving like that? Certainly not in the streets. And if this guy—the guy I found on the internet, Racer Tate, can do what he just did with a mustang, I can't even begin to imagine what he can do with an F1 engine.

On my flight here I couldn't sleep for fear I wouldn't find anyone good enough. Promising enough.

Now I doubt I'll get sleep tonight wondering if I've found him and whether I have balls enough to actually go get him.

Street cars aren't like F1 cars. They drive differently, and while one guy can dominate one kind of car, he can totally fail at another.

And not only that, but …

There's some sort of weird chemistry leaping between us that I can't deny. Yes, maybe I need to get laid, but maybe working with a guy I'm so attracted to isn't the best idea.

He's so damn good I can't imagine not asking him to come with us. I'm nervous when he asks for my hotel name and drives me there, and still nervous as he parks my car and comes open the door to my side. I rub my clammy hands together as I step out, aware of his eyes raking me hungrily, top to bottom.

"Come here." He reaches out to shut the door behind me and tug me towards him with his free hand. "Come here," he rasps again, his gaze intense and so hungry he looks down at me like a lion as he reels me in, looking so hungry I'm shaking in my knees. "Come up on your toes and kiss me."

"Why," I breathe.

A brief smile. "Because I asked you to."

"You're arrogant and self-centered."

"You've seen nothing, baby. Come on. Do it."

I hesitate.

He smiles, grabs my ass, lifts me, sets me on the hood of my car in the hotel parking lot, devours my mouth visually with his eyes as he leans over and brushes my mouth with his, and then proceeds to devour it with his mouth too. "I wanted to let you take it easy, do it your way. So you don't. We do it my way now," he rasps menacingly, locking his mouth with mine again.

He kisses me for a whole minute.

Hotly.

Perfectly.

Completely.

I like his way better but I'll never admit it out loud.

His smile fades as he eases back to let us catch our breaths; his eyes shadow darkly as his gaze trails my face slowly, almost in amusement but also with something really sober there too. "Fuck, you turn me on." His eyes gleam brilliant as he helps me down, takes my hand, and leads me toward the lobby.

He laughs to himself and shakes his head. "You had to be staying in this hotel, didn't you?" he asks me with a small frown.

I frown, not understanding what he's saying.

He clenches my hand in his and leads me toward the revolving doors. And I can feel the *gut* he put in his driving in the way he's commanding me, in the certainty of his stride and the way he holds my hand as if it's his to hold.

He leads us to the elevator bank when out of the corner of my eye I see the young girl who was with him at the IndyCar track.

She runs over from the end of the lobby while her father—*his* father—follows more calmly.

"I thought you'd meet us after dinner with her!" she says, eyes wide.

Racer looks down at her, his eyes sliding to his father, and then back at her.

"We ran late." He looks at me, and I realize his family maybe doesn't know about the illegal race tonight. He told his family he was ... having dinner with me?

"Iris, this is Lana. Dad. Lana, my sister and my dad," Racer says in an exasperated tone, as if he knows there's no getting around it.

"Nice to meet you." I smile at his sister and then his handsome dad. "We're done though," I quickly add, smiling as I pry my hand free of Racer's hold.

This was insane—what I was about to do.

Seeing his family look at him in concern, and me in interest (as if they want to know who I am to him) only makes me remember my own.

"Thank you for dinner," I tell Racer, and I can see the shadows in his eyes as I step into the elevator alone and hold his gaze as the elevator door closes.

His angry

Lust-filled

Possessive

Gaze.

I lean back on the elevator mirror and exhale.

"Fuck," I groan.

I was about to go to bed with the guy and then what? I didn't come here for a fling, I came here for a driver, and Tate is a damn good one too.

I pull out my key and head to my room, then shut myself inside and pace the shit out of the carpet.

Focus, Lana! I scold myself, trying to calm down my body.

After a few minutes, I feel more sane and go through what I found.

Racer Tate. He reportedly started street-racing when he was eighteen ... his talent blew everyone out of the water. But he was difficult, and he didn't play well with others. Off the track, he got in a fight with one of his competitors when he took Racer out on the first curve. Racer didn't like it. It was all over the news—he was arrested—his parents intervened—he moved from Seattle to St. Petersburg and "cleaned" his act. Until he was spotted racing and the rumors began.

Apparently he now travels the country, looking for races, and keeping some home races very tight and secretive.

All I know is that this guy is not just a star, he's a comet, someone with rare talent that is near impossible to find. Sometimes there are drivers that when you watch them drive, you know they are destined for greatness. This guy is one of them. Sometimes, some people just have it, and it hangs over them like a bright light that makes everyone else stop and take notice.

But does he have it to shine in F1?

He's ballsy. A little bit of extra ball, but that makes a good driver, and he's so damn smart and fast. If he did this with a mustang … but am I really thinking of putting this guy behind the wheel of one of my father's cars?

Yes. Yes I am.

But for a hot little second I wonder if I'm thinking with my brain or with whatever's tingling between my legs.

Before I know it, I call the concierge and say my friend Racer Tate's family is staying here and I need to return his cell phone. They give me the room number, and nervously, I dial. Hoping he'll be there.

His sister's voice answers.

"Yea?"

"Is … Racer available?"

She groans and I hear her march across the room and whisper out in a hiss, "One of your damn groupies."

"Why the fuck did you say I was here, Jesus," he growls in complaint, picking up the phone. "Yeah?" He sounds exasperated.

"Racer?"

There's a silence.

"Where are you?" he husks out.

"I … um …"

"Give me your room number," he growls quietly into the receiver.

"No. If I give it to you, you'll spend the night, and that can't happen. I've had time to … collect myself." I exhale.

Silence. Then, "It'll take me one second to uncollect you, Lana."

Oh god. This man will be the total explosion of my ovaries.

"That's why I won't tell you and even if you found out, I'm not opening the bolt so don't even try," I warn, still feeling hot inside and unable to quench the way my hormones respond to his voice on the other end of the line.

"I want to talk to you seriously," I add. "There's a … I've been in town before. I knew someone who lived here. Would you meet me at the museum of Seth Rothschild tomorrow morning?"

"I'll be there," he growls.

trophy room

Lana

I tossed and flipped around in bed like a worm, unable to find sleep. I guzzle down two cups of coffee as I shower and dress the next morning, nervous about what I'm going to do.

Slipping into a pair of jeans and a navy-blue T-shirt, I pull my hair back in a ponytail and reach for my purse. There, beneath it, is my IndyCar drivers list. I pick it up and read the name he wrote on it.

Racer

Tate

I exhale, fold it in four, and tuck it into my bag.

Am I really doing this?

I march out of the room and take the elevator downstairs, keeping my eye out for his family. But they're nowhere in sight.

Racer Tate may be a very hot, very male guy, but my personal crazy reactions for him don't need to get in the way of business.

In fact I won't let them.

My dad, his dream, comes above it all. It has for a long time, and the more time passes, the more important it becomes.

I drive with this new determination to the Seth Rothschild Hall. It's a small museum that was made for one of our pilots. It sells F1 memorabilia, and offers coffee and "cars"—which means everyone can bring their cars into the parking lot on Saturdays for what feels like an adult show-and-tell.

There's a gazillion cars parked there, but no red, banged-up mustang.

I'm hurrying inside and hoping to head to the ladies' room to be sure I look my best when I spot a tall, dark-haired guy inside the main hall display. He's looking at a trophy. The trophy Seth won for us, a long time ago.

He lifts his head towards me as if there's some sort of built-in alarm inside of him to alert him that I'd arrived.

I'd arrived and was standing a few feet away, staring at him.

Our eyes meet—and his eyes slide from mine toward the wall behind the trophy, where a photograph of HW Racing Team hangs. Framed in black oak, my father, brothers, Seth, and I stand with his trophy. All of us smiling. I was about eighteen then … it was our first year racing, and the first smile I'd felt on my face since David died.

I watch the expression on Racer's face as he seems to register what he's seeing, and then one of his eyebrows starts to rise, ever so slowly, as his gaze slides to lock on mine.

I approach with a very fast-pounding heart, and all the nerves in the whole goddamned world.

"What is this?" he asks.

My flesh pebbles.

It's his damn voice.

I can't help it.

I feel myself tremble inside, when I start to wonder; what if he's not interested? What if he's not the one we need?

My fingers feel quivery as I point to the image, and then trophy case. My voice is surprisingly level, as firm as I can make it.

"That's my dad, that's our team, and that's the last trophy we've ever won since we started racing. Third place in the last race of the season. My family's dream is to win the Formula One championship, and you're the only one who can help us achieve this."

Racer leans back on his heels, crossing his arms and frowning as he listens. Today he's wearing shorts which display his muscled legs and calves, a form-fitting Under Armour T-shirt on his muscular chest, and his hair looks extra messed-up and is standing up cutely on the top of his gorgeous head.

"I'm not going to lie. Our team is on its last legs, but this is my father's dream, and so it's mine too, and you're the only guy that can get us this—make us win again."

Racer is silent.

"Street cars and F1 are a whole other beast," he gruffs out, looking slightly bemused.

"I know. But I'd love for you to test, and if it goes well …"

"When's this test?" he cuts me off.

"Yesterday." I grin. "*Now*. As soon as possible. The season starts in two days."

He looks at me, then laughs softly as he pushes off the wall and we start walking again. "Fucking F1?"

"Yes."

"You're talking about F1."

"Yes." I laugh, feeling giddy because of the way his blue eyes start to glint.

His lips curve mischievously, and he drags a hand across his face before he turns sober. "When do we leave?"

Oh god. He said yes?

He looks thirsty for it; his gaze feral all of a sudden. Competitive.

"Tonight? Can you make it?"

"I'll make it," he assures.

I smile and reach out, embracing him. He wraps his arms around me too and I feel him inhale along the back of my ear before we step away—my heart beating fast.

He's seriously god's handiwork. The natural selection process of evolution couldn't be enough to produce something like him. He's illegal.

His only law is breaking the law, and a flicker of insecurity slithers inside me. Do I have the ability to control a guy like him?

Drake, Clay, and Adrian … all three of my brothers together plotting in some way or another against me have never made me as nervous as this guy on his own.

The last thing I want is get involved with a driver. I cannot keep feeling like this around him.

"It won't be a problem with your family—"

"I'll handle my family." He chuckles over my worry and reaches out and grabs my face, smiling down at me. "You're too gorgeous for your own good." He brushes my mouth with his, causing my whole body to awaken and to tingle, his eyes twinkling, and he walks away. "Send me the flight information and I'll meet you at the airport."

"Good but if we can keep this professional I'd be really— grateful."

He stops walking and turns, looking at me.

I close the distance between us, breathless. "Last night we almost went too far."

"I'm not letting you get away." He looks uncompromising. Determined.

I wring my hands. "This is more complicated than I thought."

He looks at my face, and I lick my lips, lean over, and kiss his cheek. I found him. He's the one driver I've chosen to believe in, to bring into our fold and try out, and this cannot happen, especially with my family around.

I ease back, but it's like something unleashes, and he growls, takes my hands and pulls me up, pinning me against him.

"Are we in agreement …" he says, his eyes starting to twinkle as his lips curve mischievously.

"Agreement of what?" I breathe.

He's got a big ego, I can tell.

"I'm the best driver in the world."

I shake my head. "Nope."

"You don't want to fix my car, that's the only reason you won't admit it."

"No. I'm not in agreement. I haven't seen much."

He's breathing hard, smells freshly showered and feels so warm as I try to pry myself free and we head outside, walking side by side.

"What do you get when you win your street races."

"I get laid."

"Oh. You got laid."

He shakes his head. "My prize walked away on me last night."

"Oh really? I wasn't your prize. Obviously you had a real prize somewhere and she must feel very rejected."

"She's paid to feel happy no matter I fuck her or not."

My smile fades, and I clear my throat and decide this is too intimate. Feeling jealous over him is not the thing. He's not mine; I'm not his. We're nothing to each other but business partners now. "Okay so. We leave tonight. I'll get us tickets."

He narrows his eyes, as if confused that I shut down so fast. "I said I'll be there and I will. I don't lie."

He tightens his jaw and it looks square as he flexes a muscle in the back, looking frustrated as I simply nod and add, "Racer. Tomorrow this never happened. What almost happened between us—never happened."

He grins and hikes up one eyebrow, then just says, "Understood." He nods, and I watch him head toward a black Jeep Cherokee, and I assume his mustang is getting fixed after the thousand kisses he gave it during his street race.

He'll be driving Kelsey, I think mournfully, praying he doesn't leave those sorts of marks on her too. We have no money for that—no room for error.

God, please let me be right about him.

family

Racer

"You weren't at the gym today."

First thing my dad says when I meet them for lunch at a restaurant by the gym I usually visit.

"No." I meet his irritated gaze. I'm like a carbon copy of the guy, except he's got two dimples, and I've got one. He's also hard for fighting. I'm hard for cars. Not that he knows what I still do with my cars.

Leaning over to kiss my mom on the cheek and rumple my eighteen-year-old sister's hair, I glance at my mom while she sips her tea. "Tell Dad to cut me some slack, huh?"

"Cut your son some slack, Remy."

He grins and leans back in his seat. "I will when he stops being a pussy."

"I like speed, all right. Wasn't that the point of you giving me this lame-ass name."

My mom gasps. "Your name is beautiful. It's unique."

My dad shoots me a glare. "What did you want us to call you? John?"

"Tate. Just Tate."

He smirks. "Baby, tell John here that I expect my son to train daily. No excuses." He levels me a look. "Take something serious for once."

"I pulled weights this morning and ran 7 miles before you even woke up. That would make most of my friends' fathers ecstatic."

"What would make me ecstatic is for you to fight a fight. Fight a fight, and I'll get you your dream car."

I raise my brows. "You don't mean that. A white Aventador?"

He nods.

My cock gets thick thinking about it.

"Bribery?" my mom asks, raising her brows.

"It works." I can hear the grin in his voice.

I grin too.

Iris groans and sets down her napkin. "I need to go to the restroom."

"I'll go with you," my mom says.

My dad regards me for a moment.

"I know that look," he says, after a long while.

"What?"

"There's a woman in your life, not a girl."

I sip the glass of water the waitress sets before me, aware of Dad watching me. "She's the one."

Dad looks at me, laughs softly.

"Don't fucking laugh about this."

"It's amusing."

"The fuck it is." I scowl, then grin and chuckle, shaking my head. "I just met her and I know it sounds crazy but I know it somewhere here." I punch my gut.

"When I met your mom, I knew from where I stood in the ring. No such thing as too soon to know."

I drag a hand along the back of my neck. "Right thing to do would be to stay away. But I'm not going to. She just offered me a try on an F1 car."

"What?"

"You heard me." I hold his incredulous stare. "I want you to be okay with me racing F1."

Iris and my mother return to their seats, and I can tell from the look in Mom's eyes that she heard me crystal clear.

"You know I don't want you racing," Dad says.

"You want me fighting; I don't want to do that." I lean back and drape an arm along the back of my chair, eyeing him in silence. "Her name is Lana, she's with HW Racing Team."

"That team still exists?"

"Barely, from what she says."

"Racer …" Mom interjects. "You'll be away from home, with nobody you know, putting your life on the line—"

"I'm going."

My mom's eyes widen.

"You going because you want to race, or you want the girl?" Dad asks.

"Both. I'm racing; and I want the girl." I look at him. "Tell me it can happen for me like it did for you. That I can find someone to get me. To take me, as is."

Iris blinks at that, just staring at me. "Did I miss something?" she asks out loud, but I keep staring at my dad until he replies.

"I wish nothing more."

I exhale. "This is the girl. The one I'm going to marry. The one whose life I'm going to completely ruin." I chuckle, he laughs, then we both fall sober.

"Let her get to know you. And then she can decide what the 'right' thing is," Dad says.

I exhale, standing up as I look at Mom and Iris. "I need to pack." My eyes focus on my sister's. "Come to one of my races?"

"I don't know if I can watch."

I scowl but rumple her hair. "Wuss."

"Bully."

She stands and hugs me goodbye, and I hug her back, not saying anymore. Iris always tells me I'm emotionally unavailable. I'm just not used to expressing shit. I always tell her that she should already know. So with a smile, a hug, and a *don't get into trouble* look, I go and kiss my mother, tell her I love her, and hear her whisper, "Come home in one piece."

I nod, and my dad walks with me outside.

"Take care of Iris for me."

"Take care of yourself."

"I will."

"I fucking mean it," he growls.

I clench my jaw. I exhale, unclenching my fingers. I nod.

He part grabs, part slaps my jaw. "Good."

He smiles at me, and I can see the pride in his eyes, the pride and the damn concern that appeared from the moment I was diagnosed with bipolar 1.

I push that out of my mind as I fire up my Cherokee, pull out, and head to my apartment to pack.

I'll be working with her. Touching her is not a good idea. But I don't know that I could do that. Fucking want to do that. I can still feel her warmth in my fucking hands. Taste her in my mouth. Remembering makes me hard as iron.

There's something inside of me screaming her name. Something like I've known her my whole life. Something the moment I locked eyes on her that whispered, *you're going to marry this chick. This girl is going to own you, and you're going to own her, and that's that.*

flight

Lana

"There must be some mistake. I didn't buy us first class tickets. Our team—"

"I've got it. I'll take it from my salary." He grins as we're handed our tickets at the airport.

"You won't have much left."

I tuck my ticket into my bag and cross one arm across my chest in an effort to calm down my overreactive nipples. I don't have big breasts, but I have nipples that seem to act like twin dicks on guys. Ugh.

"Actually I will," he growls softly, "because I'm going to win this thing."

I let out a surprised laugh as we take our tickets and head to the security checkpoint. "Cocky much?"

This guy is like the Muhammad Ali of car racing; he says he's the shit and from what I've seen so far, he's got enough to back it up. But F1 cars drive differently. I've seen too many drivers be unable to handle the car, the way it drives.

He helps me take my laptop out of my bag, then seems to stare at my feet as I put my shoes on the bin. I forgot to wear socks and was wearing my sandals, and my toes are rather small and pink-painted.

He smiles to himself as if he finds them amusing and motions for me to pass through the X-ray scanner first. I watch as he follows, raising his arms while some lucky female officer is probably seeing what he looks like underneath his clothes, and I shake my head at my own lusty thoughts.

Gosh. My brain really needs to stop that.

The boarding gate is full. I head over to stand by the window when he asks a woman if someone is taking the seat beside her, where she has her bag. She grins at him, flustered. He lifts his head and winks. "Come here, Lana."

I swallow nervously and because I don't want to argue, I take a seat, keeping my eyes on him as he stands by the window and checks his phone.

"Your boyfriend?" the woman beside me asks with an I'm-swooning look on her face.

"No." I feel myself flush because for some reason the thought alone makes me heated, and I pretend to be busy with my own phone for a while.

Forty minutes later, we finally board the plane, and I'm short enough that I have trouble raising my carry-on. Racer grabs it from my hand and slides my bag over my shoulder, and slides them both next to his backpack.

Sending him a wary look because I'm not used to anyone doing anything for me, I drop down on my seat, strapping my seatbelt as he lowers his body to the seat beside mine.

He's so wide-shouldered that our shoulders are about a hair from touching. I feel the panicked sensation that I should move away, but I don't—it would be too obvious.

It feels a bit overwhelming to sit this close to him—next to him without remembering that his hands sort of touched me only yesterday. That his lips sort of mischievously tasted mine and I liked it so much.

We're offered refreshments. I decline, he orders an apple juice.

"So when we arrive, I'll introduce you to the team, get you set up—then we need to get your seat fitted. You'll need a physical, I'm sure you'll be fine."

He just looks at me for a moment.

When he looks into my eyes, I feel like he's dissecting me, as if he's reading into me—as if these stupid expressive eyes he claims I have have some sort of silent language for him.

"Also if you would stop doing that, I would appreciate it."

"What am I doing?"

"You're staring, Tate. You're unnerving me." I swallow, laughing when he smiles in confusion. "My dad ..." I shake my head. I'm not here to be his friend, really. "I just want to prove to him I can be reliable to bring in the talent. Don't make me look bad." I frown.

"Sounds like a plan."

"Thank you."

I exhale as we take off.

His hand is on the armrest as he pulls out his phone, plugs in his earbuds, and listens to music. I wonder what he's listening to. I wait for the seatbelt button to turn off, then ease out of my seat and feel a little self-conscious about my butt sort of being in his face as I step out and search my bag for my own earbuds. I can't seem to find them.

I sit back down. He raises his eyebrows. "No earbuds?"

Flustered because of his intent blue gaze, I motion to the flight attendant. "Can I purchase some earbuds?"

"I'll bring them right away."

He pulls off one of his earbuds and hands it over. "Here."

"No, really …"

He reaches out to put one on my ear, and an unfamiliar song is playing. He grins and it's irresistible, a part of me seems to be sinking, deep, deep, DEEP into his eyes as he smiles and watches me.

"What's that song called?"

"Believer. Imagine Dragons."

"I like it. You can learn a lot about a person based on the songs he or she listens to."

"So what's on your playlist?" he asks.

I shrug. "Normal stuff. A few oldies but goodies."

"Let's have a look." He peers at my phone screen and sees my song; *Elastic Heart* by Sia. "Fucking love this song." He taps my phone screen with a smile of approval.

"Ohmigod, me too!" I say, and he just looks at me, Believer still blasting in my ear.

"Have you ever heard this one?" I search for my favorite song of the moment—*Favorite Record* by Fall Out Boy— connect the earbuds to my phone rather than his, and play it. We just sit there, listening.

He's staring at my profile, drinking me in. He reaches out and brushes his thumb along my ear. "Do you do that on purpose?"

"What?"

"Stare at me like that."

"How am I staring at you?"

I start feeling a little breathless.

He stares at me like a predator—quiet. Waiting.

Every inch of my body seems to buzz with the nearness—the total awareness—of every inch of his body, close enough to touch.

"Is this how we're going to play it?" he asks me then.

"Huh?"

"This." He motions to him and me. "Is this how we're going to play it?"

I swallow thickly and nod. Lowering my earbud as he pries his off too, waiting for my answer. "What happened in St. Pete stays in St. Pete," I say. "We're going to be working closely together. And I really … think it's best if we don't complicate things."

"I like them complicated."

"I don't." I scowl because of his sexy grin. "Masochist," I accuse.

"Crasher."

I gasp. "I kissed your car with mine, *you* crashed your own car …"

He leans over fast and pecks my lips again.

Fast and without any advance notice.

I hear a soft moan leave me; and it makes me frown and it makes him grin devilishly.

"Stop doing that."

"Close your eyes then," he says meaningfully.

"What?"

"Your eyes make me do shit. I'm under a spell." That lone dimple appears.

Damn him, that dimple is going to be the *end* of me.

I frown. "I'm not going to argue until I sleep for a while," I say, and he lifts the armrest between our seats and slides his arm around me, pressing my cheek to his chest as he runs his thumbs over my eyelids, making me close my eyes.

I'm stiff for a second. He snuggles his head against the top of my head. "You smell good," he rasps.

"You smell different than my brothers."

"Could be because I'm not your brother." His voice rumbles under my ear.

I clutch his shirt in my fist and raise my head to look at him, and for a moment I just want this whole plane to vanish, our clothes to vanish, everything to vanish but him.

"I'm sort of your boss, Racer. You can't play games with me," I whisper, instead of frowning, I sound pleading.

His smile fades and he leans a little more forward, his voice a deep whisper, "I'm going to be your man. You better not play games with me," he says.

I can't breathe.

He leans his head, and ever so slowly, ever so exquisitely, his lips run side to side across mine.

I gasp, motionless, and shiver when his tongue slides out to lick inside of me. Just one lick, and he eases back, smiling.

I somehow stare, and he smiles, and somehow for the next seven hours until we're woken up with breakfast, I sort of sleep with my cheek sort of against his chest, and his arm sort of around me, and I should've eased away, but for the first time in days, I can actually take a breath to really start to wonder about my dad and how he's doing, and feeling his arm around me makes me stop worrying about everything at all.

Except that arm. Around me.

How delicious it feels.

How possessive it is.

And maybe how it shouldn't be there, and yet it is.

Did I turn into a slut overnight?

I don't know what's wrong with me, but I'm sure it's the jet lag and it'll all turn to rights once I'm back with my family and back at work.

We get a cab at the airport, and Drake meets us at the hotel lobby. I feel guilty that I've been kissing and touching this stranger—our driver. I feel afraid that my brothers will notice and I'll never live my sluttiness down.

I want to put some space between me and Racer as we walk down the airport aisles but at the same time I see the women passing by look at him, and I don't like it.

I stay where I am.

Drake hugs me, and I SEE Racer turn his head and stare, his eyes a little dark.

"This is my brother, Drake. Drake, this is Racer …"

Racer's posture eases, and he shakes his hand. "Tate," he finishes.

"How is Daddy?"

"Good. Waiting for you two," Drake says as he hands Racer a room key.

We step into the elevators, and I meet Racer's gaze as we head up to my dad's floor.

"My dad wants to meet you."

I smile, but inside, I'm praying that this goes well.

We step off the elevator and Drake slides Dad's room key into the slot before he lets us in. "Dad, they're here."

At the end of the room, my dad is in a large single chair by the corner. His face lights up when he sees me, and I notice that his eyes immediately drift away, to take in the large, dark-haired guy beside me.

"Racer Tate, my father," I introduce.

"Sir." They shake hands.

"Illegal street racing," Dad says.

"I see it as just racing."

"The law doesn't." He eyes him, and though his eyes look tired, there's a spark of mischief in them. "You ready for to-morrow?"

"Born ready."

I salivate a little over his confidence, and Drake frowns at me.

"Let's see what you've got," Dad says.

"A pleasure to show you. Goodnight, sir." He nods at Dad, and I leap to my feet from where I'd dropped down at the edge of the bed. "I'll settle him in—"

"I'll settle him in," Drake says. "You get some sleep. And keep him out of trouble and focused on work, Lainie. *If* he even stays."

Drake follows Racer out.

Sighing, I head over to sit next to my dad and take his hand. "Are you okay?"

"I am now that my baby's back."

I smile and hug him, trying not to think of one day ever not having him to hug. Willing him to be all right because I'm selfish, because he's my rock and I need him so much.

off limits

Racer

"My sister's off limits," I hear Lana's brother say as he follows me to my room.

"So's mine." I grin.

He smiles, then narrows his eyes. "I don't know what you've got, I don't think you've got much. F1 isn't like the streets. But my sister went through the trouble recruiting you, so we might as well give you a shot."

I know what he's trying to do: intimidate the rookie, make him walk a straight line, draw the line, set the rules.

I break the rules.

I respect no line.

I couldn't walk a straight line if I tried.

And intimidating me is impossible.

So I tell it like it is: "I don't see many other guys lined up to take my place."

He clenches his jaw, then he shoots me a look and bursts out laughing. I can't help but chuckle too, our postures easing.

"My sister's got it in her head to save this team—I hope you realize how lucky you got. I expect you out on the track at 7 a.m. Sharp."

With that, he leaves, and I head into my room, toss my duffel bags into the ground and stare out the window, crack my knuckles. Far away from home. I was fine—racing making me happy. But always fucking restless. Going from city to city, looking for the next high. Dad said I didn't take anything seriously.

Maybe it's true.

Anything except racing.

And now her.

I don't know what it is about her, but from the moment I saw her I wanted to claim, conquer, and own.

Fuck me, worst part is that I'm lying to her. I'll lie to her whole family. I don't want her to know.

I want her too much.

I want to race too much.

Be well, motherfucker, I curse myself. It's been months without an episode. I feel good—I want to be better than good. I want to pretend that's all behind me. Pull out my meds. I shove them back into the very bottom of my duffel bag.

first track day

Lana

I tossed and turned during the night, too excited for today to rest well. I heard noises in the room next to mine, and if I had to guess, I think our new talent didn't sleep either. I heard his door shut early in the morning (at around 4 a.m.) and the guy hasn't come back since.

I shower and dress, slipping on a pair of jeans, a T-shirt with our team logo, and I pull my hair back in a ponytail and lather sunblock on my face. I usually don't do anything else—this is racing, after all. Not modeling. But for some reason I impulsively grab a lip gloss, and swipe it across my lips before I head to the track.

It's a sunny day, and I can hear the car motors rumbling in the distance.

It's the last testing day, so it's not as busy as racing day, which puts some of the pressure off. And yet I've never been as nervous as I am now. I just brought a guy into our team. A very talented but a little-too-reckless guy who will be handling millions of dollars that my father invested.

Money we no longer have.

I spot my brothers in our tent. Not good to be anxious I suppose, so I exhale and I kiss my dad on the cheek and head into the motorhome to get him a coffee. I check my texts as I wait for it to brew.

Clark: dinner tonight?
Come on say yes

I'm not planning to answer—he's last year's F1 champion and one of our competitors—when the door of the room opens and my breath catches a little bit as Racer appears.

He's got his racing suit on, down to the waist, the sleeves hanging at his side. On his chest is his white undershirt, covering muscles that are lean and hard.

I swallow. "Good morning."

"Good morning," he says, smiling a little.

His eyes drift to my phone, and I tuck it away.

I pour a cup of coffee, feeling him brush past behind me and out the door.

I exhale, my hands shaking.

I step outside to see my brothers bent over the hood of our repaired car.

"Let him drive Kelsey," I say.

Drake shakes his head. "She's too high-strung."

"What's the point of bringing in talent if we can't trust them to drive our best car? Let him drive Kelsey. He can do it." My eyes find his, and I send him a silent message, *you better do it.*

He seems amused as he pulls up his Nomex and starts to zip up. Drake curses under his breath and motions for the mechanics, Clay, and Adrian, to help him work on adjusting his seat.

"She's high-strung and light on the wheels. Can you handle her?"

"Can she handle me?" He winks, then pulls on his helmet, leaving me struggling to counter the effects of his glinting, lightning-blue eyes.

What possessed me to bring in this guy? Promise my brothers I can control him? I can barely look him in the eye for a couple of seconds without feeling like he's seeing right through me. Past the front I put up. To the little girl that just wants everything to be all right.

But I cannot let my personal feelings for him take over. This is a fresh start—a new opportunity, and seeing the hope in my father's eyes is reason enough.

He climbs into the car. Slides into his seat so that only his shiny helmet and colored visor can be seen. The motor comes to life with a roar. He starts warming it. Roarrrrr, roarrrr, roarrrr.

The vibrations make even my body feel the buzz.

I watch as Kelsey, number 38, literally storms through the track—in the most perfect line you could ask for. Usually it's hard to stay on the line … for new drivers.

This guy … he's—good.

So

fucking

Good!

I'm tongue-tied after his first few laps as he pulls back into pits and straight into the team garage. He leaps out of the car and pulls off his helmet, and I take it from his hands as he walks around the car towards Adrian, who's head of the mechanics.

"She's heavy on the curve. Lighten the downforce."

"If we lighten the downforce she'll be flying, you won't be able to control her," Adrian says.

Racer restlessly pulls off his Nomex down to his waist, and grabs the water I hand him. He just waits, as if he expects them to do it.

"Thanks," he murmurs, his eyes meeting mine for a moment before he goes back to look at the car with a look of concentration on his face.

My eyes travel along the back of his neck, the way his hair is standing up a little messy—not only because he just took off the helmet, but it simply seems like that dark hair is always perky.

I can make out the darker points of his nipples under the white shirt, and his hard chest muscles.

I try not to notice his muscular shoulders, his narrow hips, accentuated by the waistband of the Nomex suit, and I'm not sure anything this blazing hot has ever been in my eyesight before him.

I realize that my brothers are arguing, and he's still there, waiting …

As tall as my brothers, but very defined and with a presence that makes you pause and stare and have trouble to stop yourself from staring.

After they work on the changes for over an hour, he suits back up, slides on his helmet, eases into the car, and roars back onto the track.

A thousand knots are in my stomach. He does one lap. A second lap, even faster. I can't look away now. He hasn't lost control, and Kelsey feels completely at ease in his hands. Hell he makes it look easy, even though I know it's hard as fuck.

"Time!" my father barks.

"One minute twenty-six point nine," Drake says with the chronometer in his hand, eyes wide.

Behind us, Clay speaks to him on the headset. "Keep it up. A millisecond from the fastest lap."

When he finally pulls back into pits and gets out, my brothers are speechless, the three of them staring at him sort of with godlike reverence.

Drake is the first to speak. "Welcome to HW Racing." Drake shakes his hand and looks at me, and smiles.

I smile back, and when my eyes slide to Racer, I realize he's pulled off his helmet and holds it dangling at his side and is looking at me with a proud, male look in his eyes.

I start to flush.

"You killed it. I don't think we've ever seen a rookie go this fast in a new car, in a new-to-him track," Clay says.

He tucks his helmet under his arm, fists his hand and smashes it into his palm. "I *knew* it."

"How did you know it?" I ask.

He smiles at me as his dimple appears. "Because I'm here to stay, crasher."

I feel my toes curl a little under his smile as he storms to the motorhome, and I realize that Drake and Clay are both staring at me while Adrian gets busy with the motor fixes.

"Lainie, he's an illegal street racer, okay. Don't get too attached to him, you hear?" Drake starts to ramble. "Not personally, and not because he's in our team. The moment the other

teams catch onto him, they'll be offering more money than we
could ever compete against."

"Don't say that, Drake."

"I'm being realistic."

"You're being a pessimist and I'm too happy today to
come down from my party in heaven. Cut me a break. This is
good. We had a good day."

"Lainie …"

I watch Racer come over from the motorhome, taking the
steps down two at a time, running his hands over his sweaty
head. I leap to my feet and feel a little unsteady because my
heart leaps a little too. "You thirsty?"

He just nods and grabs the bottle I pull out of the cooler,
taking less than a minute to down it all. He gasps as he finishes
it, exhales and looks at me. His nostrils flaring. "Car felt
good."

I nod, breathless. "You looked pretty good out there."

"Yeah?"

I nod fast. "Yeah."

And I realize all my three brothers are staring, frowning. I
look away and head to the motorhome, aware of Racer following me inside, where it's a little less windy and we can get out
of the sun.

"Your brothers wanted me to do better?" He drops down
on one of the couches, and he's frowning. Clearly puzzled.

"No, they're thrilled with qualifying."

He raises his brows as if he's confused about their way of
showing it.

"Really. They love it. They don't know that you're here
to stay."

He pulls his Nomex out of his arms and lets it drop at his waist, and the white shirt under his suit is plastered to his chest so much I see his small brown nipples. I pull my eyes up, gulping when I realize he asked me a question. "Where do they think I'm going?" he asked.

"They don't want me spending time with you."

He laughs at that, then looks at me quietly, his blue eyes twinkling.

"Because they don't feel you're a good influence and want us to keep things professional at all times."

He reaches out to touch a strand of hair with one finger. "What's wrong with having a little fun?" he asks, his voice a little guttural as he looks down at me intently.

"It's not the fun they're worried about, it's you and I having fun. Together."

He grins, I'm laughing, can't believe I said that.

Heat spreads over me when his eyes fall to my chest, and I see him checking out my breasts before pulling up his gaze, his lips curving sardonically at the corners—a dimple popping out in a half-apologetic, half-not-apologetic smile.

I pull in a long breath, breathing in his scent and wondering why I find it addictive, why it makes things inside of me ball up with wanting. Wanting to smell him from up close, to taste him, feel him, touch all of his male-scented body.

There's a rap on the door before it swings open.

"Tate. We're working fast on it and we can fit in another session."

I see the heat in his eyes before he comes to his feet. I follow him outside, and there it is, that heat in his eyes as our eyes lock before he lowers his helmet, lowers his visor, and he's back out again.

I feel my cheeks burn and am aware of my brothers still fucking staring.

I hum softly, as if there's nothing going on, and go take a seat next to my dad as he holds his chronometer.

Okay so obviously my brothers are concerned about Racer, and maybe I've been staring too much. I really need to work on that.

And maybe it wasn't that good an idea to commission me to keep the guy out of trouble, because I clearly have no control over the guy and he's as wild as they come, but I can't help a kick of my heart every time I see him around the track.

I can't help but feel myself perspire when I hear his voice around the tent, I can't seem to stop feeling the little hairs on my arms rise at attention when I feel him nearby. I can't help but feel my stomach knot up as he climbs the car, and I can't help but feel extra nervous when he's out there on the track, zooming past us in a car that—as of two days ago—he'd never driven before.

The fastest vehicles in the world.

That evening, after a successful test, my brothers stay working on the car, and while Dad heads to his room to rest, I linger downstairs with Racer, giving him a tour of the hotel facilities.

I step outside to show him the pool—it's vacant at this hour, since it's actually close to midnight—when I see his whole face just light up with devilish interest.

"I wouldn't mind taking a dip in that blue-as-shit pool," he gruffs out.

He looks really virile in his racing suit—but in jeans and a navy-blue T-shirt, his hair in organized chaos like he always wears it, he looks terribly raw and masculine. And when his eyes slide to me, my whole stomach turns to knots.

"I wouldn't mind a dip in that blue-as-shit pool with *you*. Lana."

His gaze is riveted on my face, then runs over my body slowly. It stops on the creamy skin of my midriff exposed by my top, and I have to suck in a breath.

I have to fight the overwhelming need to scoot closer to him.

He smiles, his dimple showing; I tug my top a little nervously.

He steps closer and pulls up his shirt and before I know it, he's bare-chested as fuck. Bare-chested as fuck and flipping open his jean button.

"What are you doing?"

Racer lifts his head. "What does it look like I'm doing?"

"You're taking your clothes off."

"That's what people do when they want to cool off." He starts to lower his zipper.

"I'm going inside," I croak out as I hastily turn around to do just that.

His strong arm snatches out to grab my elbow and turn me around. "Cool off with me."

He takes my chin.

And Racer looks at me with those blue eyes that seem to peer into my very soul and I can't help but squirm inside.

"I'm not that hot," I protest.

"You're very hot," he contradicts on a devilish purr, his eyes acquiring a spark that's just wicked. "But you're very wound up too, Lainie." He tsks softly, his eyes twinkling. "What are we going to do about it?"

I reach for my jeans and pull them off, the words "turn away" somehow getting stuck in my throat when I reach for my T-shirt.

He just stands there, looking at me. Not looking at me like a pervert. Just ... as a guy. As a very big, dark-haired, hot young man.

And feeling reckless, I pull my T-shirt over my head, and his eyes coast my whole body in underwear in one clean, very thorough swoop.

Hating that my nipples respond almost instantly, I purse my lips and walk, in panties and bra, toward the pool, aware of every freaking move of my butt, and quickly racing to the edge and leaping in the air, I wrap my arms around my folded legs and plunge like a ball into the water.

When I surface after my splash, I see only Racer in a perfect-position dive cutting into the water in a perfect, rather Olympian way, and surfacing—his hair wet as he slicks it back and looks at me—only a few feet away. "Stylish way to go in the pool," he says in reference to me, the pool lights revealing only a tan.

And the fact that he's completely naked in the pool.

I'm blushing, wading in the water as he starts moving under the water. Coming closer and closer. I don't know why knowing Racer is naked and swimming toward me makes him more dangerous than JAWS swimming closer. Because this shark, I want him to take a bite out of me, and I really cannot afford my father to lose the only talented driver he's ever had. It would be a recipe for disaster.

I also like my guys a little less knowledgeable of sex, like maybe I am, a little less hot or I'd be crazy jealous every time he went out, and I've been around racers too long to know that the assortment of women surrounding these men is too numerous, and even trying to compete with that would be exhausting.

I don't have the energy for that. All the energy I have is to focus on us winning.

"Relax. I'm not going to sink you," he purrs.

"I don't think you'll sink me," I whisper, feeling out of air.

"What do you think I'm going to do?"

I shrug.

"What do you want me to do?" He grins devilishly, his gaze sparkling.

"I want you to …" Kiss me again. Touch me. Finish what we started. It's all so crazy I scramble for an answer. "… get me something to snack on."

He lifts his brows, then scans around. "Think the coffee shop is open. Be right back."

"I was kidding."

"No you weren't—stay put now." He eases out of the pool, and my mouth drops when I look at his perfect male ass. A perfect male ass with a tattoo on his butt with an RT on it. Oh my god. He scours around the pool for one of the towels they offer the bathers during the day and wraps it around his waist, then he comes back with two coffee cups, and a muffin for me.

"I can't believe you brought me a muffin and coffee. Thank you," I say.

I hear him whip off his towel and slowly lower himself back into the pool, and every atom in my body seems to electrify just by sharing the water with him.

"Feels like you're always feeding me."

"Purely selfish reasons. I get hard watching your mouth do anything at all."

I nearly choke.

"Racer!"

He chuckles, his eyes dark and glowing in the moonlight, reflecting the pool lights in those baby blues.

"How did you feel in the track today?" I ask as I eat.

"I felt good. I'm fired up." He smiles, and though he doesn't say much more, I can tell he's fired up, the energy around him is so strong and vibrant, like a hum of an incoming storm.

"So the Clarks are the reigning champions. They've got the best cars, best sponsors, best budget, best driver," I explain.

He raises his brows over the best driver comment, and I laugh. "Best after *you*," I tease.

He chuckles.

After taking coffee and wading in the pool for a while discussing the other teams, we head up to our rooms. "Goodnight," I say, and Racer reaches out to slide his hand on my nape, lean down, and press his lips to my temple. "Invite me in," he breathes, taking an inhale and growling softly before he presses a kiss to my temple.

"I … I can't. It's not that I don't want to, but you're in my team, and I have to keep you out of trouble."

He clenches his jaw but nods his head, "Fair enough," he says, glancing at my lips before letting me go.

He walks to his door, cracking his neck restlessly.

I head inside and take a shower. I slide into bed, somehow acutely aware of the sounds in the room next to mine. There's a lot of noise, as if he's doing exercise. I wish I could blame that on my inability to fall asleep, but it's a faint sound, and really nothing compared to the chaos Racer has left in my body. He hasn't touched me today. He hasn't kissed me. He's not even in the room with me. But he sure makes a lot of noise in my body.

qualifying

Lana

I t's qualifying day, the first official day to start off the season. The Formula One Grand Prix championship consists of approximately 20-plus drivers, all of them competing every few weeks for a total of 20 Grand Prix races. Each race earns them points for the championship, and to be serious contenders this year, we must try to end up in the top five in every race. That hasn't happened to us in forever. Not since Seth won third place in the championship in our debut year. Plus to even try to finish in the top five of each race, we need a good qualifying, which is why today matters quite a bit.

Also, today matters because we have *never* done something like this before.

I scan the track another time, hoping to see Racer. Disappointment washes over me when I can't spot him. I check the time, then ask Clay, "Have you heard from Drake?"

"No."

"What if Racer doesn't show up?" I ask.

"That would be unfortunate."

I exhale. "Right. Thanks."

There's a dip in my stomach when I suddenly see a dark figure walking forward—next to Drake.

Racer Tate.

In all his glory.

I know everyone in the track is staring at him. He's not only the novelty, but I think the guys can tell that he's someone to watch. His presence, the way he carries himself, the way he walks, sort of lazy—like a wild cat who knows he's the king of the jungle and doesn't need to strut. His T-shirt clings to his chest and arm muscles. His gorgeous blue eyes blaze bright as he looks at me standing across the tent, sort of gaping at him. His dimple appears as he slowly begins to smile. "Lainie."

"Racer." I nod, blinking and inhaling to try to calm down the rioting in my body.

There's a tingle in my tummy when he smiles, and we smile at each other for a hot second.

He squints up at the sunlight, then down at me and playfully tugs my cap down a little.

"That's not gentlemanly to do," I say, shoving him playfully although it's as impossible as shoving a wall and expecting it to move. It doesn't.

"I'm not a gentleman." His eyes gleam as he reaches out to cup my buttocks slightly, looking down at me.

"You okay?" he asks.

I'm surprised that he noticed anything wrong. Oh god. Did my makeup not cover the circles under my eyes?

I try to keep my voice level. "Why do you ask?"

"Because I look at you." He tips my chin back and studies my face.

Sometimes I wonder if I have wanted someone to ask. So that when I say my usual answer, "I'm okay," they would know that it's not true, that I'm not okay.

He pulls me into the motorhome.

I follow, nervous.

He's scowling deeply. "Did you stay awake at night?" he asks as he pulls out his gear.

"Yes," I admit.

His stare is nerve-wrackingly intense, and I'm at a loss as to how to explain, because—although Racer makes me nervous, he also makes me calm deep where it hurts, his presence both soothing and exciting at the same time.

I crave it.

I hadn't realized how much I craved something like this.

Something personal.

Something just for me and not just racing.

Dad asked me once if I was sure that this was my dream, that it wasn't his.

I told him I was.

But how much of it being my dream is actually because it's my family's and how much of it is mine?

My chest constricts when I think about Dad. My family means the world to me. If I had one prayer it would be that I would always have them by my side. We were all hurt by my mom leaving us, but it only brought us closer, it only made us value each other more. I value my dad more than anything. He's my hero. He's taught me to work, to have a dream, have a goal, he's taught me generosity, and he's taught me how to overcome. He weathers this in silence, never once telling me anything or complaining. I worry, because he's sick and I don't want him to keep it all bottled up. He's seemed a little more worn out this week, and a part of me believes the excitement—the mere possibility—of winning is all that keeps him well for now.

I don't want to talk about this with him on quali day, so I try to play it cool. "Racer, they're requesting an interview after practice ..."

His eyes slide to mine as he pulls off his T-shirt and slips into his undershirt, and I feel a little breathless at the glimpse of bare chest. "Where?" he asks.

"I ... well right here at the tent is fine."

He nods, his lips curving a little as he seems to notice me get flustered. I see those blue eyes sort of scan over me— making me acutely conscious of my clothes, my half ponytail, and down to which underwear I decided to wear today. I've never been one for frilly underwear. I'm practical, cotton ones do just fine. But a part of me sometimes wants to own something sexier, something a guy like him would go for.

"Did you eat something?" I ask as he heads to the room in the back to change fully into his black racing suit.

He nods as he disappears, and comes back suited up with his Nomex. All gorgeous and ready to race. From the duffel, he pulls out his gloves, boots, socks, then sets them aside and comes over, cupping my face. "Been thinking of you."

"Huh," I breathe, sort of panicking because the touch makes me feel so hot, so warm, so wanton. I haven't felt like this for a guy in years. Not since David. And maybe not even then. David was my best friend. This guy ... I don't know even half of the things I wish I knew about him. I know he's physical, that he races, that he's reckless, that his dad was a famous fighter, that he has a mom and a sister, and the sexiest dimple, and the most toe-curling stare. But I want to know more … I feel like I *should* know more if he's to be working with us.

If he's to be doing … these things to me.

He's got an arrogant, sort of harshly handsome face. The eyes with a gleam that makes you feel as if he wants to eat you up alive. And when his lone dimple pops out, I want to take a thousand and one mental pictures—as if for some reason a part of me needs to memorize everything about this man. This boy. This sexy, twenty-two-year-old blue-eyed boy that makes my pulse race and my heart whack crazily in my breast.

I feel naked as he drinks me in, slowly, at first. As if there's no rush, and he has all the time he wants to look at me.

His hands are at his side, and I watch his fingers slowly, one by one, start to curl into his palms as he pulls in a deep, ragged breath.

"How about we pick up where we left off in St. Pete if I get P1 in qualifying." He smiles a little at that.

I remember his kisses and shake inside. "How about you stop flirting and get to work," I breathe.

He laughs softly, his eyes twinkling. "Stop crashing my car, Lana," he growls playfully, tugging my cap down over my head. "You look cute in this," he adds.

"You look hideous in your racing suit," I call as he heads out.

I realize my nipples are up at attention and frown down as I run my palms over them to calm them as I head to the side of the track, flustered because I'm not used to fielding advances. Usually my brothers are enough to help the drivers and mechanics stay away, and it's true that it makes me uncomfortable to feel the way Racer looks at me. But at the same time, I've never liked a feeling so much in my life.

It's as if everything I do, I want him to see me do it … while at the same time, every time I do it, I want to hide from his probing eyes.

It's such a confusing feeling that I don't know how to act around him.

I'm trying my best to pretend he's one of my brothers. Just a guy. I'm used to the testosterone. But the testosterone of this guy affects me differently. Well, it *affects* me. Period.

I sit and stand and move here pretending he's one of my brothers, but he doesn't smell like my brothers. He smells really male, really clean and warm and nice. He doesn't feel like my brothers. He's a little taller than the other drivers, a little bigger than them and my brothers, and a little more athletic and muscular. Well, he's actually pretty ripped. He could be a boxer, that kind of body with great upper arms and every part of his body cut.

I have always preferred sex when I know the guy, or at least am dating him. I've thought it seems more meaningful but at the end of the day, I've only slept with one guy my whole life. So who am I kidding to think that knowing each other makes sex better? Maybe it doesn't. Maybe hot sexy sex with the most delicious guy you've ever met is just the ticket.

Except he won't be a stranger for long.

He's on my *team*.

But I can't help wonder that it might make me forget how much I miss David. I know it's been long and I need to put myself out there, and maybe I have it all wrong. Maybe instead of trying to find a replacement of a relationship that meant so much to me, I should look for the opposite. I should not look for a replacement, simply embrace single Lana and sleep with whoever I want, live the single life proudly, knowing I'm the girl that has already found love and will always cherish it.

I don't think anyone can ever compete with what I had with David. We knew each other since we were kids. He protected me, cared for me, he loved me. Sometimes I miss him so much my chest hurts, and I press my hand to it to try to quell the pain.

I try to forget it as I suck on a bottle of water and tip my cap down to shield me from the sun. I've already got too many freckles and I don't want anymore.

"The Clarks are really strong this year," Dad mutters as I come stand next to him, a warning.

"Are they not any year?" I roll my eyes.

"Is Clark himself still after your bones?" Drake asks from behind us.

"No!" I cry, glaring at him past my shoulder. "He just wants info. I'm not going to give it to him." I frown, then I turn around and wade my way to pits as I watch the drivers head to their cars.

Racer and I make eye contact as he polishes his visor and as my brothers and the team get the car ready.

I keep bringing drinks to everyone, even offer one to Racer, which he declines with a look into my eyes and a shake of his head.

It makes me blush, for some reason, but I keep trying to help in any way I can. I suppose I need the activity to help calm my own nerves.

Once he's got his helmet on, and his visor lowered and is settled and strapped down in the car, I leave pits as the motors turn on.

Brrrmmmm!!!!!

I can't bear to watch. First time in the track for qualifying. First time in a Formula One car. This could be painful. I can't watch.

I head over to take a seat next to my dad. My dad pats my hand. "Trust your gut."

"My gut is knotted right now."

He laughs.

I see the laughter reach all the way into his eyes and I ease.

"Clayton's on the radio with him?"

"Yep."

"Tell me when it's over."

I hear the wheels spinning—the car roars out of pits, and I am not sure I've ever heard Kelsey sound so angry and so fired-up.

I inhale, and then hear my dad inhale too. Before he says, looking at his chronometer, "Decent as fuck time."

I open my eyes and look at Dad. I'm seeing something I recognize as hope in his eyes, and it makes my stomach knot up even more—this time with something similar to excitement.

I turn my head and watch as Kelsey speeds like a demon on Red Bull down the track.

"He's a natural, Lainie baby," Dad whispers, looking at me with pride.

"He's so good, Dad," I admit, something in my heart swelling in ways that it doesn't even swell when I get complimented myself. "On my way to the US I kept praying for me to find someone like Seth. I didn't—I found someone better. He was too rare to leave alone."

People really have no idea how difficult it is to drive at 225 mph with a shit ton of G force pushing back at you. You need to be extremely fit to endure that for hours.

After the cars circle around and their times are adjusted and their cars are adjusted, qualifying is wrapped up with Clark in first, the Clark's second driver in second,

"AND RACER TATE IS THIRD," the announcers are saying. "QUALIFYING FOR P3, a great *great* comeback for HW Racing this year."

When Racer pulls into pits and hops on the scale, I take note of his weight and notice he's lost 10 lbs of body water in sweat. I hurry to bring him a bottle of Gatorade, coconut water, lemonade, or plain water, tucking them all in my arms so that he gets to pick.

"P3. Not fucking bad!!" I hear my brothers cheer, slapping each other. I hurry over as he climbs out of the car for his interview.

He grabs the first drink I offer, a Gatorade, and is attacked by the press before we even reach the motorhome.

"Racer Tate, you're the year's only rookie and are taking no prisoners, already you've set the internet ablaze with your talent. What's the difference between racing out on the streets versus a track like this one?" the attractive reporter asks as she puts the microphone up to his lips.

"I get to hear whispers in my ear," he grins, and Clayton laughs behind us.

"Is the horsepower too much ..."

"Not too much. I like the power. It's the walls I need to watch out for—not a lot of those off the track. Usually trees."

Laughter.

"So when we asked for this interview and how on earth the team at HW Racing found you, Lana told us she found you ... by accident, *literally* ..."

I groan inside as the reporter continues,

"... Is she a good driver?"

"We'll work on that," Racer says gruffly, his dimple appearing as he winks at me and he takes my elbow with a little crackle in my skin as he leads me away.

"That's Racer Tate," the TV lady says to the camera as we walk away, "live from the F1 track in Australia."

"I can't believe I told them that," I groan, brushing my fingers over the spot he touched.

He's eyeing me speculatively, his blue eyes shining so bright under the sunlight, I can't look away. "Lucky for you, you now have the best driver in the world at your disposal," he growls.

He sounds dehydrated. And mischievous.

"Ha! I'll be the judge of that. Plus I'm not sure what you're implying I do with him." I shoot him a scowl.

He laughs, and shakes his head. "Anything you want. Free of charge. Driving lessons. Petting sessions."

"Really?" I frown. "I don't believe you."

"Believe me, Alana." He stops me, his eyes twinkling as he frowns down at my mouth as if he wants to take a bite out of it and is annoyed that he can't. His voice lowers. "I'll stop by tonight for a kiss, for P3."

My lungs suddenly feel like rocks in my chest, but I try to sound stern as I say, "You can knock, but that doesn't mean that door is going to open." I see his dimple deepen as he watches me walk away, my whole stomach buzzing in a way it has

never
in my whole damned *life*
buzzed before.

hyped

Racer

'm hyped and wired, not one bit tired after the day. P fucking 3.

I'll take it.

Not bad for a first timer. I'm planning to work myself up from there, get to know the car better. The wheels. The turns.

I'm freshly showered after hitting the hotel gym for an hour, and rather than strip and hit the bed, I'm pulling on a pair of jeans and a fresh T-shirt.

Some Clark guy is after her.

I don't want anyone touching her. Looking at her. Kissing her.

I want to kiss her again, deep this time, figure out what she tastes like in every hot spot of hers, draw out more and more of that taste, and add a little moan or two. I'm working myself to a lather over the idea of it, my cock already taking to the idea—fast and hard like I like it—and immediately I clench my jaw because I'm being a selfish prick. No girl should need to live with my bullshit. Hell I even try to spare my mom; she's got enough with my dad.

But I head over—needing a look at her.

I knock on her door.

She opens in a little pajama that makes my cock thick.

She blinks.

"Hey."

She exhales, looking at me, and I look at her and see her nipples, want to touch them, suck them, and I can't snap out of it for a long time. I know she's worried we work together and I shouldn't kiss her, but I don't have any qualms about that.

I want to take it easy on her, though, so I just stand there and get a whiff of her scent. What is that?

She's talking to me.

My eyes feel heavy as I pull them up from watching her lips speak to looking into her eyes. She's saying—

"Racer, please."

I open my mouth to correct her, to tell her to call me just Tate. That's my preference. I snap it shut. Frown down at her.

Well shit I kind of like my name coming from her mouth. I kind of like the idea of her saying it when she's coming.

I'm fast in all things but not in this. Hell I don't even know what this is. I reach out. There's a slight widening of her eyes, and I can see it. Interest. Lust. Whatnot. Whatever you want to call it.

This girl's hot for me; her eyes say it so much. And I'm burning like fuel at full speed.

"You want to try saying it again." I feel my lips curve into a smile.

"What? Racer?" she asks, confused.

"All of it."

"Racer ... please."

"Please what."

"I ..."

"Please what."

"Please make me look good. No more of this." She starts shaking her head, and I lean down to peck her lips.

Like I knew, she knew, I would do.

"Tell you what, Alana," I rasp, cupping her face and teasing her with her bullshit name. "Tell me you're fixing my car because you know I'm the best driver in the world, and I'll go back to my room."

"Tell you what, Racer," she says, pushing me at arm's length. "Go get some rest. Keep trying to achieve your dreams. And maybe when you get there, I'll be close to admitting that." She grins, and as she starts to close the door, she kisses the tip of two fingers and places them on my jaw.

I laugh, and scrape a hand down my jaw where she just set the sweetest fucking kiss on me.

race

Racer

I'm fired up. I hit the gym at midnight, worked on my stamina, upper body, killed my legs, worked my arms.

I snatch up a coffee early morning, get one for Lana, and head out to the track.

I spot her with her brothers. Her eyes widen when I give her a cup of coffee, and she has a shit ton of coffees on the table beside her. "Oh. I brought you one too."

I nod, and eye her as I watch her take mine and drink it in silence before I head to the drivers' meeting.

The race director briefs us all on the basics. *"This is the situation with the safety car ..."* he's saying.

He indicates which turns have safe havens (in case a car breaks down). *"The safe havens are indicated with orange cones or turn marks."*

The Clarks snicker and whisper among themselves.

What jackasses.

It'll be a goddamned pleasure to beat their asses this year.

After the drivers' briefing, I head back to the tent to talk strategy with Adrian, Lana's youngest brother. Aside from the mechanics that make up HW Racing Team, Lana's family make up the most important roles. Adrian is the race engineer. Clayton's the driver's coach, the guy I usually discuss driving skills with and am on the headset with during the races. The eldest, Drake, is the team manager. Lana's dad is the team owner: a man who loves to live on the track and rarely leaves until the entire team does.

Adrian and I discuss how many pit stops we'll do, what tire compounds we'll be starting out with.

I feel eerily calm; I'm good at being calm under pressure. There's something about knowing your life is on the line that clears your head. Heightens your every sense.

I focus on the strategy and keep my body relaxed, my mind focused.

Soon, the drivers are called out to pits.

I approach number 38. Lana's "Kelsey."

It's an exotic machine, built for speed. Built for racing.

She's ready. And so am I.

I grab my gloves and zip up my racing suit, then ease on my helmet. Before I lower my visor, I let my eyes scan over Lana, who's been watching me from the side. I let the testosterone she stimulates run over me—and I give her a look that says *this one's for you.*

My dick fills up and stiffens under that adoring look in those expressive eyes of hers.

That flush on her is just the cherry on top of my Lana Sexy as Fuck Cake.

By the time I slide into the car, strap down, and ignite the engine, I've got a huge hard-on.

F1 cars are much rawer than normal cars. Louder, faster, with more grip, much harder to drive. It's harder to freaking *win*. It's not a one-on-one race here; I'm racing against sixteen other drivers, all of them hungry. As hungry to win as me.

We follow the car as we get into positions, and then, it's green flag—and I get a good solid launch.

It's all about easy clutch release.

I've got it nailed, and I'm speeding up, holding position as I head up to 230 mph on the straight. The seat shudders beneath me. The wheel fights back at me as I take a fast turn.

Guess this is where I thank my dad for teaching me to exercise.

My core is engaged, my every muscle engaged, my heart pumping, lungs working as I catch up with number 8.

I wait to pass—biding my time.

"Easy," I hear on the mic.

It's Clay.

"You're P3 holding steady, catching up on P2," the voice says.

I push the pedal, waiting for the chance to overtake him, then take a slow turn and head to the next.

The voice says, "Trailing .10 seconds after P2 and gaining."

We head into the straightaway, and I'm at full speed. I use his draft to get closer. You need to be careful when you get too close or you can understeer—the car gets jacked up with the other car's draft and doesn't want to turn.

We head to a fast turn and head into a heavy braking zone, and I don't brake when #8 starts braking.

I keep my foot on the accelerator—outbraking him at the last instant, braking harder and later. Within a second, I pass him.

He steers awkwardly into the curve, nipping the back of my car as he does. I'm off into the straightaway, hearing something clink.

"Second …!" I hear.

#8 is eating my dirty air as I shift gears.

The gears on an F1 are on the wheel. The wheel is for more than steering; it's the car's goddamned brain. I upshift with my right hand, downshift with my left, and even check the status of the track; any yellow or red flags appear as flashing lights on the wheel as I steer.

The track is clear, and I'm chasing after Clark. Number fucking 9 is on my radar and I'm catching up.

"You're P2. P3 coming up behind you fast," Clay says.

I feel his nose nip the back of my car. I hold her steady, outbraking him again, and leaving him behind.

The white flag appears, and I know the checkered one is coming.

I catch up to #9, but don't have enough time to overtake him.

I try anyway, my nose basically a hair away from his ass.

"Don't risk it, Tate," Clay says, as if he's reading my mind.

I grit my jaw and decide to listen—a P2 is better than getting pulled off the track at the last lap.

My body's so wired from the adrenaline, I'm high. When I get down, I want to fucking kiss her.

I've got about every brain cell honed in on the expression on her face she'll be wearing. Every brain cell is honed in on wanting to kiss her, long and hard, wanting her to tell me I'm the best fucking driver in the world.

She's reluctant to yield to me, to admit to wanting me, to me being exactly what she's been waiting for, but I'll be patient. Dad always said I was impatient as fuck, but that one day I'd find something that would make me realize just how much I wanted to be patient for.

Her name's Lana fucking future Tate.

breathless

Lana

I could barely watch. But I could hear every time 38 drove past how Racer was shifting, accelerating.

Brap, brap, brap, braaaaap, like hard, fast, wicked slaps on the motor as he effortlessly switched gears.

The adrenaline is so high in my body my legs are trembling.

"P2! Fucking shit me right now!" Clayton and Adrian are whooting.

"Kelsey's never gone this fast."

"Jesus," Drake curses in disbelief.

My dad is pulling me into a hug, and I pull free as Racer pulls in.

The car gets weighed, and then *he* gets weighed. I know we can get disqualified if the car and driver weigh less than expected.

When Racer hops on the scale, I take note of his weight and notice he's lost 8 lbs of body water in sweat (something we'd thankfully calculated when adding the proper weights to the car). I hurry to bring him a bottle of plain water, Gatorades in different flavors, and my favorite coconut water, tucking them all in my arms so that he gets to pick.

Once he's cleared, he leaps off the scale, seething with energy as he pulls off his helmet and marches away, tossing the helmet back into his car seat.

I don't know what's going on but he starts right for the motorhome, and I have to chase after him.

"Racer?"

I follow him up the motorhome steps, and I stop the door from slamming shut so I can enter behind him.

"Racer!"

The door shuts behind me.

He spins around and pulls me flat against his hard-as-fuck body. One second, I am standing inside the steps of the motorhome, and the next, I'm in the air, pressed against his warm, sweaty body as his lips crush down on mine.

I hear a splat as the bottle hits the ground. Our mouths are moving in synchrony, and I desperately hang onto my heart as his tongue flicks over mine—wet. Slow.

He's kissing me.

Hard.

And he kisses so good that I can only struggle to breathe right as his hand slides down to grab my butt and pull me a little closer to him, where he sets another kiss, this one a peck on the lips, on me.

He eases back, and all I know is my world is blue, the most electric gorgeous blue. There's no words to how I feel when he looks down at me like that, his gaze brilliant blue and fired up, his lips slightly curving to show his dimple. His whole body feels electric, and his eyes seem the most electric of all as he looks down at my lips, then at me with the most mischievous smile in the world.

"Why—why did you do that," I whisper, first breathless, then a little panicked and mad.

He moves his hand to cup my skull, pressing them a little harder before he eases back. It takes me seconds, maybe a minute, to register the feel of his warm lips, to calm down the fire that suddenly exploded inside of me at the touch of his lips.

I'm breathless, my chest rising and falling fast. "You know I have three brothers, and a father, who happens to be your boss. What the fuck."

"So."

"So you can't go around doing that."

"I couldn't help myself." He inhales me and growls, leaning close again. "I just want to fucking kiss you right now."

"Don't kiss me here," I protest. "Not on the track."

"Where," he grinds out impatiently.

"Somewhere else," I breathe, stepping away before my brothers can see.

Did I just say *somewhere else*?

Like I want it to happen, just not here?

Judging by the look in his eyes when I glance past my shoulders, I think we both know I did.

We head to dinner that night, to celebrate.

My brothers are looking at him and me all night, and it takes all my effort not to crawl under the tablecloth. I focus on my meal and am happy to see my dad's appetite is well and solid as they talk cars and strategy at the dinner table. Racer seems keen on hearing suggestions from the team, and I try to keep my attention on anything but him.

But I marvel over that internal radar of his, something that seems to make him aware of me because every time I lift my eyes to him, they meet his, and he's looking at me.

flowers

Racer

I'm all packed for the Shanghai Grand Prix next, and that evening, I call home. I know what Lana's brothers are concerned about. I've got a little sister. I know what I'd do if someone were thinking of her like that. I get that. I respect that. But I can't shut my mind. Merely sensing that Lana is near I get all worked up.

"So tell me. If you had to choose something about me you like, what would it be?"

"I need to think of one thing?"

I don't laugh.

"Who are you trying to impress here? That girl?" Iris asks.

"Just tell me what you'd like from a guy who's after you. You like chats, flowers, what?"

"I don't know. I don't plan to get married, I told you so. Nothing works with me."

I exhale in frustration. "Iris, focus here. It's about her."

She laughs, then sounds serious. "Wow. Am I seriously getting asked these questions by you? I thought you were going to be a successful car racer, live in a mansion like the one Iron Man has, have a butler, lots of cars, and no wife."

"Thanks for the help, little sis."

She laughs. "Racer, wait!" I put the phone back on my ear. "Just be real with her."

"I don't think girls want real, I don't think she can take the real me."

"Well you'll never know until you try. Wait—hang on. Dad says fucking roses. A shit ton. Or just one."

"Thanks."

Dad's old times are not our new times. But I might as well try.

At midnight, I'm knocking on Lana's door.

She opens dressed in that blue nightie again, her nipples poking out.

The fingers of my free hand itch, while I extend out the ones holding the twelve roses in my grip.

"I got you some flowers."

"What for?" She blinks at me and I look down at her, smiling.

"For your room. Hell, I don't know. Throw them away if you want."

"No! I'm …" She blushes and takes them from my hand, quickly setting them aside.

I drag my hand across my face. "Sex I'm used to. This is kind of a first."

"What's this."

I shrug. Lean against the door.

"I think about you, Lana. The way you walk, and talk, the way you look at me, the way you stand there, the way you smell, even the way you dress."

"It's nothing special."

"Doesn't look unspecial from here."

"Um Racer ..."

She exhales, looking at me, and I look at her and see her nipples, want to touch them, suck them, and I can't snap out of it for a long time. I know she's worried we work together and I shouldn't kiss her, but I don't have any qualms about that. I reach out. "You going to stand there and look gorgeous in that nightie or are you going to let me run my tongue over what's beneath?" I rasp.

I touch her lips in a way I want to touch my mouth to hers, and she flushes wild.

"I ... someone can see you here. Come in."

She's blushing beet red, and I walk in, scanning her room, and then her lovely ass and legs as she walks to her room. I shift and move my cock, look down at my palms, rub them together before I rub them down my jeans.

"You can't keep coming over here to tell me anything. Here, write down my text."

She leans over me to get her phone, and I smell her, her skin inches away. I reach out, put my hands on her waist, and draw her down to my lap. My mouth searches, finds, and fucking seizes her, and I fucking kiss her like I wanted to from the moment I saw her standing there last night.

"What are you doing?"

"This," I murmur, licking into her mouth. I brush her hair back, looking into her pretty eyes, round with shock. If nobody's ever gone after her like this, I'm fucking glad, but I'm not backing off. I grab the back of her head, press her closer. I need a deeper taste, fucking explore that mouth, warm wet and minty.

Fill my hands with her ass, shift her so my cock is right up against her opening. She feels damn good and I'm getting worked up.

"I want this now."

She groans, but she's breathing heavily, her pupils dilated.

"I want this. You. Me, this. I want this now."

"Now now?" she gasps.

I laugh, let her go and run my hand through my hair, grinning. "Not now now, but now."

She shakes her head. "My dad ..." She shakes her head. "We can't. We don't even know each other."

"I want to know more. I want to know everything about you. Physical, mental, the shit that matters to you."

"Why?"

"I don't know. You tell me what it is about you." I run my thumb down her cheek, and to be honest I don't care what it is. I just know it's there and I just know it's her.

"Trust me, there's nothing special about me."

"There's so much special I don't know where to begin."

"Please get some sleep, Racer. We have qualifying tomorrow."

I lean back and smile. "I'm not tired."

"Well tire yourself out!"

I take her hand before she turns away. "One day soon I'm going to take you out on a drive with me and you'll never be the same."

"Is that why you rented some fancy car?" she says. She seems to realize I never told her this detail, and she blushes. "I overheard you and Clay talking about which one you should rent. Something fast."

"For such little ears, they sure seem to work right."

She laughs.

Damn, I want her in my car, the wind in her hair, I want to play some tunes and hear her laugh about them. Reach out to shift gears, and put my hands in her thighs instead.

"Maybe. If you let me drive." She smirks.

"Fat chance. I'm the driver here," I growl, laughing.

I fall sober after a moment.

"I want this now, crasher," I repeat.

So, yeah you could say I'm relentless. You could say I'm the sort of guy who knows what he wants and isn't afraid of anything, not the law, or the rules. I'm my father's son. I like to go for what I want. Chase my ambitions.

I want this girl beneath me and that's that.

I'm Racer Tate and this girl is mine.

fall

Lana

I tried to ignore him as we traveled to Shanghai. My brothers are keeping a watchful eye, and my dad, whose stamina I worry about, is better off concentrating on our goal at hand.

We traveled for nearly a full day, nonstop, then crashed in our rooms, recovering before setting up our tent at the Shanghai race track.

Now we're looking to be in top shape after our best practice session to date.

"This guy's fucking insane."

Drake laughs, while Racer eases out of the car and pulls off his helmet. His hair is a little wet and rumpled, and as he unzips the top of his Nomex suit and pulls it down to his waist, the white undershirt he's wearing plasters to his muscular chest like second skin.

I'm scrambling to bring him something to drink, an assortment of bottles in my hand, when I fall splat on my face. Fuck! Oh my god. The water bottles roll around.

"Jesus, Lainie," Clay rants, kicking a bottle back in my direction so that it gently rolls closer to where I lie.

I'm praying he didn't see it when I feel him come close and hunch down before me.

I start to reach out for the drinks.

Racer takes my face and forces me to look at him, and the center of my universe is suddenly immersed in blue.

"I can get my own drinks," he gruffs.

He's soaked, his sweat smelling of soap and salt and guy, and something in my chest moves when he then grips me by the elbow and gently rises to his feet, pulling me up with him.

I am used to being bullied by my brothers, to us fighting a little more than to them being, well, tender to me. Racer's unexpected concern for me makes me feel vulnerable and weak, and I don't like it. I pull my arm free and snatch up the water bottles.

"Okay then, I won't," I say, shoving the Gatorade and the coconut water, the ones closest to me, into each of his hands before starting to storm away.

My brothers are hauling the car up from pits to bring it to our tents, but I know that they didn't miss a beat of what went down. The three are scowling deeply, a fact that Racer ignores as he just comes to his feet, cracks open a coconut water, and chugs it down, his keen blue eyes watching me—laser into the back of my head, actually—as I head into the motorhome.

I'm panting when I walk into the motorhome and then just sort of sit there, horribly embarrassed.

I rub my face and sigh, warm all over. Then I head into the bathroom, splash water onto my face, and look at myself in the mirror.

"Just because he seems to do it all right doesn't mean that he doesn't fuck up sometimes. You're human, you fell, you're fine."

I feel a little recovered from my humiliation when I step out of the bathroom and nearly crash into his chest.

I squeak in surprise, and his arm flies out, his hand grabbing my wrist to catch me from stumbling again.

"God. Stop doing this to me," I grumble, snatching my wrist away as I glare.

He chuckles, sounding puzzled. "Doing the fuck what."

"What you're doing. Unnerving me. I've never fallen like that in the track before. Plus for your information, bringing drinks to the team is part of my job!" I part yell. "If I worry a little overmuch it's because I want this year to be perfect. I want this team to be perfect."

I stop myself from saying more, but something about the way he looks at me—as if he can already tell there's more—prods me on. "My dad is not quite well. And I want him to be unstressed, for everything to be right for *once* in our racing career."

His eyes linger thoughtfully on mine for a moment, and I feel like stuffing something into my face to shut myself up.

"I mean, he's doing fine, but … I like to take care of my loved ones," I ramble, sitting in one of the couches as I start to pick up invisible lint on my T-shirt.

He takes the opposite seat from mine and he shifts forward. "Your dad's sick?"

"I … that's what they say," I say.

He keeps watching me, starting to frown.

"Who says that?"

"The doctors," I admit. "He's sick." I drop my gaze at my admission, my throat suddenly very tight. I try to make my voice sound level, but it breaks. "There's nothing they can do about it. He doesn't want to spend his last days in a hospital. So …" I bite down on my lip and look away.

Silence.

"I'm sorry."

It sounds so truthful that I look back at him, his face a little blurry through the tears in my eyes.

There's something about the way he looks at me that unnerves me, as if he knows how much it hurts, as if he knows more about me than even I know or maybe anyone on this planet knows.

"He's my dad, you know." I blink the moisture back and I swallow the bile in my throat, rubbing my lower lip with my thumb. "My mother calls once a year. She's emotionally unavailable, I guess. She was never satisfied with what he did, always wanted more, never showed even an ounce of gratitude for everything he tried to do to please her. I guess I resent her for that. For hurting my dad."

"And you."

"Mm?"

"For hurting you," he says, staring deeply into me.

"Oh, yeah, maybe." I shrug, surprised that he thinks this immediately. That his immediate concern was me. "I don't know why I always think that her hurting my brothers and dad hurts worse. Me? I can take it." I shake my head. I glance out the window. "My dad's my everything."

Silence.

I lift my head. "Maybe you think it's childish but …"

"I don't think it's childish."

"Oh." I stare at him.

"You care about your family," he says, smoothing his thumb along my brow.

"I'm sorry, it's just … I'm sometimes too much a pleaser. And with you it's worse." My eyes go round when I realize what I said. "It's just that I care, for some reason, what you think of me."

He smiles in bemusement, and I smile and duck my face to hide my blush, then I scowl at him because he is driving me crazy.

He chuckles, then softly, admiringly, "Come here, crash-er."

I go to his seat and Racer slides his arms around me.

"I get hugged all the time, I've been a very loved girl," I inform him, but even then, for some reason, I'm still letting him envelop me in his.

And oh god.

It feels like heaven.

I'm enveloped by him all of a sudden. It's probably the best hug of my life.

I can smell his soap on his shirt and skin.

"How am I doing?" he gruffs in my ear.

"Poorly. A little tighter," I say greedily.

He tightens his hold and pushes my hair back and stares into my face. "This tight? Hmm?" There is a way that he holds me, a little tighter than my dad and brother, more possessively. I meet his gaze and close my eyes and inhale his neck, and we just hug then, his chin in my hair and his hand wrapped around my hair.

Drake walks in, and I jerk back in surprise, so fast Racer slowly lowers his arms in puzzlement.

"Hey," Drake says, eyeing me.

Racer looks at him levelly. "Hey," he answers, looking at him directly. Almost challengingly. I remain mute.

Drake just stares, and I stand up.

"It's past lunchtime. The food should be here soon," I tell them both, as if I hadn't just been caught snuggling up with our driver.

I hurry outside and absently trail my fingers along my arms across the places that tingle after Racer's arms were possessively around me.

on

Racer

"So your dad, Remington Tate? Is he glad you're racing?" Lana's father asks me as we sit in a set of tables around the tents, lunching on chicken-and-spinach wraps that Lana ordered from a Shanghai food delivery service.

I sip on my Gatorade, having finished two wraps already while the rest of them seem to still be working on their first.

"My mom doesn't like the risk I take. My dad always wanted me to be a fighter like he was," I explain. I don't tell them that my dad doesn't trust me behind the wheel of a car knowing I'm BP1. That he's concerned I might lose control, or not make the wisest choices.

He doesn't get that cars make me feel better. Keep my brain sharp.

"I used to race little go-karts when I was young," Mr. Heyworth says with a reminiscent look on his face. "I stopped when I married. My wife …" he smiles a regretful smile, "let's just say she didn't want my attention on anything that could detract from my attention to her. I set my dreams aside. She left, and I decided it was time to chase my dreams before it was really too late." He lifts his water bottle in a toast. "You've got what it takes, kid."

I lift my Gatorade. "Thanks, sir."

His phone rings, and he tosses his wrap away, and I watch Lana follow him to the chair with a heavy sensation in my chest, a frown on my face. She didn't say what he had, but she looked completely wrecked about it.

"Tate. You stare at my sister far, far longer than I'm comfortable with," Drake drawls.

"Look away." I shoot him a look and smirk.

"Hands off. You hear?"

I meet his determined gaze, then I realize this is going to have to get settled the old way. I stand. "I'll fight you for her." I start to roll up the sleeves of my white undershirt.

"Huh?"

"You heard me. I'll fight you for her."

"Jesus, you're insane. Hands off, Lana, buddy."

"Not that easy, Drake. Can't."

"Why the fuck can't you, Tate."

"I'm going to marry your sister." I give him a meaningful look, and he narrows his eyes.

"You're insane." He laughs, then narrows his eyes. "She's been hurt before. She doesn't want to go through that again."

"Guys! We have a sponsor!" Lana comes over, flushed and excited, her whole body trembling.

"That's great, Lainie baby," Clay says, amused as he glances at both me and Drake.

She looks at me then, and her smile falters, and her cheeks flush even more.

"They love you," she tells me, and I see her dad walk up behind her, beaming as she explains, "We'll have more budget now. Better tires."

I nod at that, my chest doing shit at the sight of her so happy. "What do you want me to do?" I ask.

"Keep it going. And wear this—they sent a package!"

She slides a cap with a logo of a sports company on my head, and I grab her hips and tilt my head down to her as she examines the way it looks on my head.

"Yep. You'll have to do," she says. "The dimple makes it look even better."

She laughs, and I feel my dimple deepen even more as our eyes lock.

Her smile falters as her eyes lock on mine, and I force myself to release her hips when I actually want to grab her ass and pull her closer. She turns me the hell on, and I don't think she'll ever know how much. Seeing her happy drives me insane. I want to urge her closer, want to open her mouth with mine, tasting her smile, soft and slow.

I can't.

I force my arms down at my sides, tightening my jaw as I try to suppress the testosterone in my body. Goes ape-shit when she's near.

"Only reason I'll wear one is if you wear one too," I say, to be difficult.

"What, why?" She scowls as I take off my cap and try it on her face.

"You look cute with it."

She flushes, pulling out another cap from a bag and setting it back on me.

"Okay. But it's *you* they want, champ. Wear that on our next podium, okay?"

"Our first-place podium," I gruff out.

Her smile widens even more, and her eyes gleam with hope. "Yep."

I shift the cap and make as if I'm going to kiss her, but instead I whisper, "Come to my room tonight."

Her eyes widen, and before she can even seem to think about it, she smiles a little wider and licks her lips in nervousness and gives me a nod of consent. My dick jerks, and I can barely keep it in my pants.

That afternoon, as we're heading out of the track, her brothers slap my back.

"Boy, that was some great performance out there. I nearly had a heart attack," her father says.

"No!" Lana says, her eyes wide. "Daddy. *No*."

She seems to realize her reaction and looks at me, then lowers her face and just smiles, breathing fast from the excitement.

I curl my hands at my sides, heading down the walkway by the track.

"An illegal street racer. Really, Lainie?" I hear Clark yell as he steps out of his tent.

I pass him and bump my shoulder hard against his.

"Hey," he calls.

"Motherfucker," I growl at him.

I shoot him an eat-shit grin and keep walking, feeling his fury behind me.

It's on.

his room

Lana

I'm going to his room.

It's a big deal, but I'm telling myself it's not.

I'm downplaying it.

Because I don't dare admit to myself that I want what I want.

I'm not in Florida anymore.

My family is in this hotel, just like his was.

We could bump into them.

But Daddy is asleep after dinner. And my brothers just stepped off on their floor. They're too high on the win to think of anything else.

So am I.

Higher than high.

I think Racer Tate is higher than high from it too.

The air around us crackles and burns as we step off on our floor. I tell myself I'll just kiss him for five minutes. One goodnight kiss just because I'm on cloud nine and I need to get down from there. But being with him doesn't get me down.

Quite the opposite.

And yet here I am, a little bit like a junkie who cannot save herself, no matter what. All because he said he wanted to be alone with me tonight … and because I want that too.

Have wanted that since St. Petersburg—

A shiver of anticipation runs through me as he slides the key into the slot and holds the door open, and I know I really shouldn't be here, but at the same time I cannot turn back. Something happened, something is happening—every second we look at each other, every breath he and I take.

I walk inside.

He narrows his eyes and looks at me. He towers over me, his hair a little rumpled from the breeze out on the track, and he runs his hand over it as I look at him questioningly.

"I want you. I'm not going to lie. I want you in that bed with me tonight."

I swallow thickly, laughing and shaking my head.

He laughs too and reaches out, pulling me closer. "You're not going to spend the night with me, Lana?"

"No," I breathe as I lean on the shut door. "I just wanted to spend some time with you."

His eyes darken, and he exhales a sound of frustration. "Go out on a drive with me."

"Where?"

He touches my cheek, and my reaction is so visceral, so strong, that I arch and moan softly, pressing closer as I whisper his name.

And in that name is the real reason that I'm here.

And in that name is all the pent-up feelings I've tried to lock away ever since that night in St. Petersburg where I brought him with me to my hotel.

And then Racer is scraping his thumb along my lip as if he means to destroy it. He scrapes his thumb along my mouth, side to side. And Racer is leaning his dark head. And Racer is pressing his lips to mine as if I'm the petal of a rose and any brush of wind would break it off.

I lose all semblance of control and rationale. I don't know what's going on, all I know is suddenly my hands are curving along the back of his neck, and my whole body is trembling beneath the sensual, seductive, barely there graze of his lips.

He eases back to look at me with blue, blue eyes fringed with dark lashes, half-mast over his sleepy-looking eyes.

And then he ducks his dark head again, and his tongue flicks out. He touches the tip against mine, rubbing, back and forth, and his taste swarms me. Cinnamon bubble gum and guy.

Kissing me slow and deep. Lips moving. Tongues stroking, tasting. His fingers bite into my waist as he murmurs that he wants me.

His voice thick as he strokes his hand down my sides, working open my buttons as he sets his forehead on mine and watches my reactions.

"My whole life I've guarded against addictions. Driving was my one addiction. Never smoked, don't drink except socially, eat right, but you, Lana. You're an addiction I can't say no to. Don't want to say no to. If I don't have you beneath me now I'm going implode on myself."

I pull his T-shirt up to his neck, and my fingers run along the velvety muscles of his chest, hard and smooth; my lips follow to suck on his nipple. A sound very much like a growl runs up his throat, rumbling against my hair.

The air burns between us. His hands push my racing-team T-shirt off and over my head, leaving me in my bra and jeans. My nails rake along his back as his hungry mouth runs all over my body. My breasts, my stomach, my neck, my mouth. I undulate and press him closer, needing more but afraid to voice it.

He circles his tongue along the tip of my breast, suckling gently. Oh wow. My nipples are always so sensitive when he's around, but the feel of his warm mouth on them debilitates me. The pull of his mouth causes me to gasp and my whole body to squeeze pleasurably. I'm so wet I can smell myself, and when I see his nostrils flare, I feel myself blush because I know Racer can probably smell me too.

He holds me by the waist, he unzips my jeans and shoves his hand into my panties, then he plays with my wet flesh and I jerk and thrust my hips out—begging for it, begging for him.

He eases one finger inside me.

He moves it *slowly* in, and *slowly* out, repeating the motion, watching as I arch up, fighting not to go off too soon, the pleasure too intense. His eyes are like blue lightning pinning me down, his finger-thrusts filling me so much with desire that I cannot take any second more. I start to convulse.

My nails sink into his scalp, a cry leaves me, and he smothers it with his mouth, pumping his finger deeper and harder to keep me there—at the pinnacle of pleasure. His hand moves faster, harder, my own hips recklessly, haphazardly trying to meet his hand-thrusts and keep him touching me forever. Every atom and cell in my body shivering for him, craving him, wanting him, needing him.

My breath sounds raspy when I ask him, "Do you sleep with women after you and she, well after—"

"No. Usually I call them an Uber and send them home."

"I don't need an Uber so I'll head to my room …"

He snatches my wrist. "Stay," he rasps, his gaze hungry and possessive.

I exhale and ease back to his side. "If I stay I may lose control again."

"Why is that wrong?"

"Because …" I flush. My eyes run over him and I can barely keep my hands at my sides. Because I really want to touch him, taste him. I want to run my fingers over that gorgeous chest, look at him without a stitch of clothing on in ways that I didn't dare look at him when he stripped at the pool.

"I'm about hanging on by a thread myself," he husks, gaze heavy-lidded as he keeps staring down at me.

"Really?" I breathe. Surprised that he seemed to read my mind.

He nods somberly, his eyes twinkling before they become engulfed in some dark lustfulness.

"Do you want to touch me. Huh," he prods, reaching out to tug me closer.

My heart turns over in my chest while the rest of my body clutches wantonly as he guides me to the bed. "I … yes."

At the edge of the bed, I see him tug his shirt over his head in one easy jerk of his hand, then he unzips and strips his jeans.

I'm staring—wide-eyed—and salivating as he pulls the sheets off the bed, then pulls me down on the bed with him, and something is growing and growing under the sheets, and before I know it the whole damn bed sheet is tented.

Racer grins, his eyes predatory as he wraps one arm around me, locking my chest to his chest.

He sets his forehead on mine and guides my hand to his cock. "Here." He groans as he drags the tip of his nose along my temple with a rumbling sound as he guides my hand under the sheets, to the very warmest hardest part of his being. "It wants your touch."

Oh god. He's so big.

So smooth.

So HARD.

My hand runs over him tremulously, and he exhales roughly through his nostrils as he watches my expression of awe. "God, baby, those little fingers feel good on me."

He smiles down at me, and my throat is tight with desire as I bite down on my lips and I start to flutter my fingers more greedily over his thick length.

He's huge, so thick he pulsates under my touch. I can feel the thick veins on his cock and the way the crown is fully stretched and swollen. I couldn't wrap my fist around him if I tried, he's too thick, so I just envelop what I can and skim my hand up his hard length, up and down, up and down, my body tightening with wanting when little drops of arousal start to seep out of the tip of his cock.

His face is raw with need, his forehead still on mine as he scans my face and brushes my hair back. "You're driving me crazy," he rasps, rocking his hips up to my hand, the pre-cum wetting my fingertips as I brush them over the top of his cock.

I'm breathing hard, and he's breathing harder, grabbing my face to hold me still as he begins to kiss me like crazy, tongue thrusting into my mouth, swerving side to side to taste every nook and cranny, rubbing to arouse my own to fierce and thirsty action.

I move my fingers faster, addicted to the way he's kissing me—the hunger there, the way his hips roll up commandingly to my hand, the way his tongue mates with mine, and the way his cock keeps pulsing in my hand and obviously wanting more of my touch.

He reaches down to grab my hand, squeezing it around his cock, and murmurs, "Do you want to taste me too, huh. You want to taste me?"

As I start to breathe out yes he picks up a drop of cum from the tip of his cock and slides his thumb into my mouth, where I taste him.

I've never tasted a guy, and there is something about his taste that makes my pussy water.

"You like that," he rasps, slipping his hands back into my hair to kiss me deep, with his taste in my mouth, as I keep moving my fingers over his cock.

"I want to feel you when you come," I admit, breathless as I keep moving my hand, craving to see him—see that he has a reaction to me, that he loves me touching him the way I go crazy when he touches me.

He goes off almost instantly, shooting off so hard I feel a splat of cum fall on my chin and jaw, more coming out as I keep trying to squeeze and work my fingers, his cock jerking powerfully as he shoots off another eight times.

I gasp, and he groans and licks my mouth, cleaning my jaw of his cum with his thumb and then pressing it on my mouth. I groan, starting to move my hips, needing to come again too.

And that's when I feel him reach out to my partly open jeans and shove his hand gently into my underwear and rub his fingertips, still with some cum on them, along my opening and my pussy folds. Surprised by my lightning-fast reaction, I cry out as a thousand and one shudders wrack me, making me cry out.

I lie in a daze as Racer goes clean up—dazed at the sight of that RT tattoo on his firm buttocks. When he returns and slips his strong arms around me, I slip my arms around him too.

My eyes drift shut, and I feel him look at me.

He's completely naked in bed.

And I'm completely hormone-filled.

And my ovaries hurt looking at how gorgeous and masculine he is.

Boyish and yet at the same time, so male.

He presses his thumb into my palm, smiling. My heart speeds up with a mix of longing and dread to what I feel. I am falling. It feels as if my ribs have just collapsed in my chest, crushing my lungs. "You okay?"

"Can't sleep." He stares at me.

"Racer … I'm not ready for anything."

He smiles, stroking his hand down my cheek. "I know. I was there where you are."

"What happened?"

"You crashed my car." He grins. I feel my stomach tingle from the inside out, and I open my lips and raise my head to kiss him, and he doesn't need to be asked twice, he crushes my head back down as he starts to kiss me in ways I never knew a human being on this earth could be kissed, a kiss that touches every part of me, my lips and body, my mind, my heart, my very soul.

"I'll take it easy with you."

"Please," I say, and he shifts to lie down beside me, the most hot, handsome man I could have ever imagined in bed; kissing me like I'm the only girl he's ever wanted in his.

restless

Racer

’m restless as fuck. I glance at Lana across the track of the Bahrain Grand Prix.

We just arrived, and today she came to the track freshly showered, her face scrubbed of anything other than those cute freckles and that soft pink shade from too much sun exposure.

I like her without makeup. She's wearing a little sweater, crossing her arms over her puckered nipples, and I can barely keep my hands to myself. When she's cold, I want to be the one that warms her. I feel like she owns me, and I want to own her. But I still look at her and wonder how the fuck I'll be able to deserve this girl.

The curse of being me, one I inherited from my father. He found someone to like that about him, at least to get him. I wonder if she'll be the one to love and get every part of me.

Just thinking about it makes my pulse race. I'm masturbating several times a day now, can't seem to be under control when I'm close to her. I want inside her. And I want it slowly. Breathe in her neck. Whisper in her ear. Make her remember the feel of me inside her when she's not with me. I want her to move beneath me, scream my name, let me taste her mouth, taste and see the color of each damned moan.

Devour her slowly with kisses. Rock against her slowly, letting her absorb my length. Run my nose along her neck so my breath leaves a path on her skin that my tongue will soon trace. I want to memorize every scent, the one on her hair, her neck, her ear, her skin, her abdomen, her sweat, her sweet wet pussy.

Fuck.

I want her to teach my mouth what to do with her, what she likes, trace her goddamned shape.

But I promised her I'd take it slow, so here I am, in the back of the motorhome, shutting the door to the bedroom, stripping down my racing suit to my waist and shoving my hand into my boxers.

I pull out my hard cock, moving my fist over it, harder and harder. The door outside slams. Fuck. I let go as a spurt of cum shoots out. There's a knock on the door.

I pull up my racing suit to my waist and stand as the door opens, and I look at her. "Everything all right?"

"Yeah."

She moves inside and stops.

She glances down at me. I clench my fists at my sides, wanting to give it to her hard.

She notices the front of my pants and the large cum stain.

"Prepping before the race?" Her lips quirk.

"De-stressing some."

Her eyes look heavy, as heavy as mine feel.

She approaches me slowly and feathers her hand over my dick. I just came some, but it goes from semi-hard to hard the moment she touches it.

"Look at you having fun all by yourself," she breathes, looking up at me with lusty, gorgeous green eyes.

I shove my thumb into her mouth and make her eat the cum I have on my fingers from my blast, and she cups part of my cock, making me lean down to take her mouth and kiss her fiercely.

"I want you alone tonight for a while after the race," I rasp, cupping her face.

"Okay," she breathes, and my heart shudders in my chest as she suddenly kneels at my feet and sets a warm, soft kiss right on my dick before she rises back up.

"Okay," she says again, her smile wide, her eyes so lusty for me I'm a dead man and I'd never been happier about it.

"I'm getting first place," I gruff out, pecking her lips and stealing a taste with my tongue as she murmurs, *yes*.

trophy

Lana

O ut by pits, Racer's eyes meet mine before he lowers his visor and climbs into the car. Once the cars are heading into the track, Clayton hands me the headset. "He wants you."

I don't know what it is about the words that make something *do* something in me. It's confusing, and irritating, and it makes me march up to grab the headset. I put it over my head.

"You're pushing it, Tate."

Silence.

I press my lips together and focus as the cars gear up to start.

And then … they're off. Instead of holding position at fourth—his starting position—Racer immediately eats one spot with an impressively fast start. "You're P3 now, and gaining on P2," I say. "Clark is 0.2 seconds ahead of you."

"Got it," he replies.

I feel chills hearing his voice on the headset, and I try to isolate my reaction and stay focused on the game.

"Louis Day, Clark's second driver, is creeping in behind you."

"How close."

"Too damn close." I check the stats. "0.07 seconds."

"He'll eat shit in a bit," he growls.

I hold my breath at the determination in his voice as he overtakes second place, and suddenly he's gaining on first.

"You're P2 gaining on P1," I say, trying to keep my voice level even as the excitement threatens to overtake me.

Two laps later, I watch Racer Tate overtake the first place in the most killer maneuver on the riskiest turn on the track.

I hear my brothers yell like crazy behind me, the crowd yelling, and the announcer yelling even louder, *"AND THE NEW RACE LEADER IS U.S. ROOKIE RACER TATE! In a pass that is almost impossible to manage! What a surprise this year has been with this young, talented driver ..."*

I exhale in disbelief and whisper into the headset, "P1."

Racer doesn't respond.

"P1!" I yell excitedly, just to hear myself say it. "P1 ... Clark is ... he's trailing two car lengths behind."

I check how many laps remain.

"Hold steady for fifteen laps, champ, and you'll be the tallest man on the podium tonight."

I remain on the headset, watching him draw a clean line.

"You're currently holding the fastest track lap," I say, still disbelieving as Racer hangs tight and leads Kelsey to another perfect lap—and then, straight and at full speed past the waving checkered flag.

The first checkered flag HW Racing Team has ever seen in Formula One Grand Prix.

"What a stellar pass from rookie U.S. driver Racer Tate! Racer Tate, who jumped from starting point four to lead nearly the entire race ... " the announcer is saying.

"Holy shit," I breathe, my eyes wide as I take off the headset and turn to see my dad.

I feel my dad squeeze my hand, and his smile? It could brighten a whole sky; it's like the sun.

We're both silent, smiling at each other, before I launch myself at him and he catches me, laughing gregariously.

"P1!!!" Drake yells, coming over to lift my dad in the air.

"Careful, Drake!" I call worriedly, but my dad couldn't care less. His whole face is pink with excitement.

Oh god.

Is this really the same team that was scrambling to make it just a little while ago?

And as the car pulls into pits, it feels as if I hold my breath for an eternity, because my lungs ache the moment Racer leaps out of the car, onto his feet, his fist pumping the air in pure devil's pride.

I take a ton of pictures as he goes up to the podium to get recognized for this achievement. *"And this year's surprise, U.S. rookie Racer Tate, with his first first-place trophy here at the Grand Prix ... "*

The crowd cheers, and his dimple is on full display, and I can't get enough pictures as I snap, snap, snap my phone and wish I had a professional camera—but I know professional photographers are taking these shots and I'll be hounding for them online; our team will get tagged with them for sure.

"Hope you enjoy P1—that's going to be my place from now on," I hear Clark say as he comes up beside him.

Racer scoffs. "Not if I nudge you towards a wall." A razor-sharp smile touches his lips.

I feel chills rise up my arms because Racer sounds quietly determined, and I don't think I've ever heard anyone stand up to the Clarks before. They're legends around here, and usually everyone kisses their ass, hoping one day to enjoy even half of the support the Clarks do. Well. Racer Tate doesn't seem to know whom to treat nicely here, or maybe he just doesn't care.

"Sir," he says as he brings up his huge silver trophy.

Dad is grinning ear to ear as Racer hands him the trophy.

"I can't believe we have two podiums and already a first place," Adrian says, congratulating him.

They make a great team, Racer and Adrian. Racer seems to know exactly what he wants the car to do and Adrian is good at giving it to him.

I also step up to congratulate him, and I shake. Just completely shake with anticipation. And when his strong, lean-muscled arms embrace me as my arms go around his wide frame, the shakes increase tenfold. "Congratulations," I tremulously say, feeling as if the whole contents of a volcano have been poured into my veins and muscles.

He stares down at me with those magnetic, male, satisfied blue eyes, his dimple so close I could rise up on tiptoes, lean forward a few inches, and lick it.

As soon as we're able to pack up, we head to the hotel.

In the elevator, Racer and I stand close to each other, while my dad hugs his trophy and my brothers keep making plans for subsequent races. Racer's breath is warm on the top of my head as he stands behind me, all of us sort of crammed in here. My heart pounds as someone else steps in, and I take a step back, nearly tripping on his feet.

"Sorry," I breathe, turning my head a bit to meet his gaze.

He looks at me with the most intense expression on his face.

I suck in a breath and turn forward again, aware of his hand curling around my hip. I want to close my eyes, and I want to turn and draw his arm closer and tighter around me. I want my lips on his and I want to share everything that I know and am with him, and I want him to share all of himself with me too.

It's crazy, I don't even know this guy—but he looks at me as if he's known me for a long time. Maybe, even, as if he's waited for me for a long, long time.

My family steps out. "Lainie, you getting off?" Clayton asks.

"I'm just making sure this guy eats," I call back, because we all ended up with rooms on the same floor except Racer.

They all nod—Drake looking a little suspicious—and the elevator doors shut, and we're alone.

He smiles a little as I turn to him and give him a smile too.

"You're going to stay out of trouble. Aren't you?" I ask.

"Depends." His dimple appears.

"On what?" We step out and walk toward his room.

"On whether trouble wants to step into my room with me."

He opens the door, then pushes it wide open, looking down at me.

I gulp because I'd never seen such a hot, inviting look in anyone's eyes before.

I said I'd see him tonight, but I can't help evading for a moment.

"You won," I say.

"Aha."

"And you think you get laid if you win. This isn't street racing."

"I won't touch you if you don't want me to."

He waits, watching me with this gorgeous smile on his lips, and then I step inside and let him draw me up to the bed. We lie down side by side, and I let him move me so that I'm spooning his side, one of my legs draped over the length of his as I look up at him, my heart racing so hard I think I'll go deaf from the racket it's making.

He shoots me a lazy smile. "Comfortable?"

"Yes."

"Come closer then." He drags me a little closer, his eyes never missing a beat of my expression.

His smile is cocky and boyish, but his eyes are never playful, ever. They're always intense, always gleaming, and

I'm shocked to realize that almost every time I look, I find them resting on *me*.

He runs his fingertip along the bridge of my nose. "You always had these freckles?"

"No. Not always. They've become more numerous since we started racing."

I look at his face. "Do you have any birth marks?"

"Not on skin-surface," he says.

"Were you a quiet baby?"

"Restless one. You?"

"Me too. My dad says you either work it out when you're young, or when you're older."

"I definitely am still in the process of working it out." He smirks.

I laugh, and then whisper, "My boyfriend. His name was David. He passed."

His eyes drop to my body as I tremble at the memory. He looks like he wants to reach out and grab me even closer, but he doesn't. He keeps his hold loose, giving me a chance to move away.

"I'm sorry," he says.

"He was my best friend since we were little. He died. It was … at a high school rally. He fell off the back of a pickup truck and broke his head."

He's quiet.

"Have you ever loved someone?" I ask.

He doesn't answer; he just looks at me intently.

"I loved him very much," I continue. "I've been focused on racing because I just don't believe lightning can strike in the same place twice. My family is my world. My brothers and my dad—" My voice cracks. "I should go to my room."

He eases off the bed when I step away from him and head to the door. "I wanted you in St. Petersburg because it seemed like I needed a good bout of casual sex. But there's nothing casual about you and me, Racer. Or about this."

"No. There's nothing casual about it," he gruffs out.

I smile wanly before retracing my steps, cupping his jaw and pressing my lips to his dimple, even though it's hiding now. "Thank you for giving your trophy to my dad. I haven't seen him this happy."

I open the door to leave.

"Lana," his growl reaches me.

I turn, and his eyes gleam dark and sharp.

"David's not here anymore. But I am."

Racer

Watching her leave was never part of the plan. Hell neither was the look in her eyes; the look of someone who's lost somebody she cared about.

She's been gone for an hour. I'm still battling the urge to go to her room, knock on her door, and pull her into my arms.

I'm caving into the impulse and dressing to do just that when I get a text from a fighter friend of my dad, saying he's visiting my parents with his wife and wants to Skype. I turn on my iPad and take the call. I can see him on camera with my dad behind him, both of them peering into the screen.

"Racer. Hey, buddy, congratulations," he says. "I thought I'd check in with the champ and advise you one thing: don't fuck before a race. Keeps your testosterone up. I do that before fights and works like a charm."

My dad laughs behind him. "That's total bullshit," he growls. "I fuck before fighting all the time. When I fought."

"TMI, Dad." I laugh and shoot him a scowl.

He gives me the finger. I give him two. Mom walks in and peers at the screen, and I fold back my fingers.

"Wow. So much love in this household," she says sarcastically. We laugh, and she says, "I miss your face, baby boy."

"I miss yours, Mom."

She blows me a kiss and tells me to call them soon, that they're watching every race and are proud of me, and then it's back to my dad and Maverick.

"Seriously, Maverick, you can fuck whenever you want, but stop telling me when you fuck Reese," I tell the guy.

"Why, you jealous?"

"Yeah, she's my girl," I say, yanking his chain. I've always suspected he's jealous Reese changed my diapers and cleaned my dick before his. Reese is the first girl I loved aside from my mother. She was my babysitter when I was three, and was a little too sweet to put up with a little devil like me.

"Too bad she married me. And is too old for you," Maverick says, that usual possessive look on his face when he talks about his wife.

Reese's laughter reaches me, and she peers from behind Maverick as my dad gives her space. "Racer, Iris told us that a girl caught your eye," she says.

"Yeah. More than my eye, actually."

"Wow. You like this girl," Reese says.

"I'm going to marry her."

"Wow." She seems genuinely stunned. "One day, she was going about her life as usual, and next thing she knows, she's met one of the most amazing men I have ever known." She smiles and taps the screen where I suppose my forehead is. "Show her the kind of good trouble you can stir, sir."

"Reese …" I begin, and she stops before leaving.

"I should tell her. Right?"

She hesitates.

"I'm lying to her. The whole team."

"Don't tell her until you feel she's ready. Sometimes it's a lot."

I'm silent, restless.

"It's recent for you," Reese says. "You'll learn to manage it, figure out what triggers you, you will cope like your father.

You'll come to terms with it, and if she's even half as worthy as she sounds, she'll be ready at some point."

"I want her to be ready now," I growl, and she just laughs and we hang up.

I pace my room, glancing at the time and realizing it's way past her bedtime. I picture her sleeping in bed all sweet and warm, and I want her to get used to sleeping with me by her side.

Exhaling restlessly, I grab my tennis shoes, my phone, and my earbuds and head out for a run, wanting to give her space even when every atom and cell in my body screams for me to make her mine once and for all.

Patience, I hear my father say. Rome wasn't built in a day … and nobody said it was easy to fall in love with a Tate.

traveling

Lana

We travel for the next two days, organizing the transport of the team and the cars before we fly to Spain. I sit between Dad and Racer. They're talking cars.

I'm trying not to notice the way he smells and how many times his elbow and mine bump on the armrest. He seems to know I'm on edge because I jump every time they connect.

He smiles at me, and the smile melts me. I see him pull out his earbuds and connect them to his phone, then unlock it and hand it over.

I don't know why, but I feel as if I'm peering into his soul as I scroll through his playlist, seeing songs like *Walk* by Kwabs and *True Hardstyler* by DJ Zealot.

It feels intimate, especially when I see him keep chatting with my dad but turning his phone around to peer in and see what I'm listening to: *Battle Scars* by Lupe Fiasco and Guy Sebastian.

At the hotel we check into our rooms. I tell myself I can act grown up about what happened. He's the hottest guy I've ever beheld and girls are panting over him left and right, so he must do this all the time. No need to worry.

Either way, as soon as my brothers dump their pile of clothes to get cleaned in my room, I bathe and change and decide to go and knock on Racer's door, and I ask him if he has any clothes or requisites.

"No," he says, frowning at me thoughtfully.

He also bathed and changed, and is wearing comfortable torn jeans and a soft-looking grey T-shirt that licks his body just right.

"Someone should take care of you for a change," he gruffs out all of a sudden.

I start. "No, it's ... it's my job."

"Someone should take care of you for a change."

No one's ever said that to me. I exhale, and try to focus on my job and wait there to see if he needs anything.

Racer just frowns.

"Where are you going in that?"

I run my hands down my dress.

"Nowhere. Here." Shit. Was it too much to change into a dress before coming over here?

"No. Not here," he says, lips curving as his gaze scans over me. He pushes himself off the doorframe and into his room. "Let's take you somewhere."

"Why."

He stops in the middle of the room to shoot me a get-serious look. "Because you look gorgeous and I want to look at you."

I melt a little but then jerk at that. "No, I told you, I'm supposed to be sure you behave."

He gets his keys and wallet and returns in the sexiest walk I've ever seen, confident, sleek and lithe. "I can behave at a club."

"I don't think so."

He takes my hand and shuts his door and drags me down the hall.

"Racer," I groan. "You said you'd behave."

"I said I could, not that I would. Can you?" He chucks my chin, a devilish sparkle in his eye.

"I don't know," I say.

He laughs, then says, pressing the elevator down arrow, "Come on. I'll drive."

I tug my hand free but remain standing by his side, crossing my arms over my chest to hide my suddenly very erect and tingling nipples. "Bummer. I really wanted the wheel."

"Be a good girl, and I might give you a lesson," he says with a wink that lifts my toes up from the ground.

My nipples are overreacting even more. "I don't need a lesson, I can drive just fine."

He shoots me a look, and I shoot him one back as we board and head down to his rental.

I should've known it would be a very cool sports car.

The guy rented a blue Porsche, with cream seats, and convertible, to boot. I know the salary we've offered him isn't much and it leaves me wondering just how much money this guy made speed racing.

My brothers rarely will take me out to explore, but it turns out Racer doesn't have such qualms. We end up in one of the city's hottest clubs, a two-floor nightclub with pop music on one floor, and rap music on the next—and a gorgeous terrace upstairs that we have yet to discover.

We snag a booth at the far end, where we can listen to music, drink, and talk, and though the booth accommodates about five, Racer is sitting pretty close to me—his arm stretched out along the back of my seat as he sips on a prepared tomato juice (a glass of whiskey the waiter brought by mistake sitting untouched beside it), and I'm too engrossed talking to him to remember I've got a shot of tequila waiting on the table too.

"So your dad's a fighter?"

He nods, smiling a little as he looks at me. The flashing strobe lights above dance across his features, and is it really fair for any man in the world to be this hot and perfect?

No.

I don't think so.

Plus his dimple is out in full bloom. It's difficult not to be rendered helplessly enchanted by it.

"Why do you smile like that?" I scowl as if he's having no effect on me.

He runs his thumb along the bridge of my nose. "Because you're cute."

"Don't patronize me." I laugh, squirming as he lowers his hand back to the armrest. "Why didn't you become a fighter?"

"I don't like it enough. Not like he does." He shakes his head, eyeing me. "It's just a hobby to me. A way to blow off steam."

"Are your parents together?"

"Almost thirty years together. My dad's in his early fifties. Never looked at another woman after he met my mom."

I can tell he cares about his family, and it makes me yearn for my parents to still be together, for me to still have a home—with a mother in it, a father, and love to go around.

"And you, Lana?" He lowers his arm and shifts forward, his expression focused.

"My mom left us about … five years ago. It was the worst year of my life. A few months after she left, David …" I exhale, shaking my head. "My dad was very sad for some time. When he decided to move to Europe and start a Formula One team, I don't think either my brothers or I blinked twice. To me it felt like I had nothing left in Ohio."

"I'm sorry," he says.

"Me too." I glance at my drink, and suddenly feel the need to toss it back.

"Do you think it will be like that for you?" I ask as I set it down. "A marriage like your parents have?"

"I didn't used to believe that was possible." A waiter brings me a new glass of tequila, and Racer waits until he leaves before he continues—running his knuckles down my jaw. "Now I just wonder if it'll be the same for her like it was for my mom."

"What do you mean?"

"My mom loves my dad. She's crazy about him actually. She gets every part of him. Even the shit no one else would get or love about him. That's pretty rare."

"You don't think that someone could feel like this for you?"

"I used to think there was no way that would happen for me, so why try?" He smirks and lifts his drink as if toasting to that, then takes a long gulp, looks at me, and sets his glass back down. "Now I know when it feels this right for you, you better be sure you make her see it's just as right for her."

"Why do you think no one could feel like that for you!" I'm nearly affronted by the mere idea.

"Because loving me is a curse?"

"What? Why would loving you be a curse?"

He's silent, looking at me with that mischievous smile dancing on his lips. "You're the one who should be most concerned, crasher. Trust me, I'm better from afar." He shakes his head, that mischievous gleam still in his eyes. "No one can break your heart as hard as I'll be able to break it. No one could possibly ruin your life the way I can." His voice is a warning, but there is tenderness there, almost amusement—as if even when he's issuing a warning, he knows that I won't listen.

"No, you're not. You're better from up close," I contradict, and his eyes flash when he hears the conviction in my voice, then he grabs my face and leans down, his eyes blazing into me.

"You're so fucking adorable. I want you in my pocket, so you go everywhere with me and nothing can harm you." He curls his hand around my nape, smiling into me as he presses his forehead to mine.

"That would be so very wrong," I part groan, part laugh.

"I'm never wrong, Lana. Ever." He shakes his head playfully. "Not about anything. And not about you."

I laugh, feeling giddy and maybe like one shot of tequila plus a little bit of Racer is already enough to take me to the stratosphere, but I reach for my drink and I push it back.

I want to tip my face up and kiss him. I want him to kiss me. I don't want anything else in the world but this right now. But he seems incredibly agitated. Fiercely intense.

Something about his protectiveness, his blatant possessiveness, turns me on.

He takes a strand of my hair, pushes it behind my ear, and leans forward. He offers me his glass of whiskey, and I take it, downing a long gulp. He laughs when I do that, then scowls and takes it away. "Be careful," he warns.

I lick my lips as he draws his glass away, then I lean over, pressing my lips to him. "Racer," I groan.

I hold my breath as I ease back, and his gaze holds mine in a deadlock.

His nose is flaring, his eyes brilliant as he watches me.

He slides an arm around me and reels me in a little closer. He reaches out, and electricity runs down my spine so hard that I almost arch up against him. He smiles, setting his hands on my waist. They're so wide and big that I feel a little bit smaller, a little bit like the whole world just reduced to one person. Him.

I lick my lips, unable to take my eyes off him as he starts moving me—moving with me. He lowers his head and I feel his nose sort of nuzzling the top part of my ear. A tremor begins from that sensitive place where his lips are, down my neck, my spine, my legs, to my very toes.

He draws back with this wicked smile, and in his eyes, I can see the blatant heat. It's as if he wants me to know it. That he's a man and he's hungry and he's not one bit concerned about the fact that he might just be hungry for ... me.

Might have been talking ... about me.

Everything inside me throbs.

I sort of swallow back any protest because I'm sort of going willingly, my eyes holding his as I crash into him, my lips sort of falling on his dimple.

He groans, turning his head to press a peck to my lips, his tongue sliding out to lick the seam of my lips.

I shiver, licking him back.

"You don't drink at all?" I breathe.

"I've got other vices. Like cars. And you."

I start to pant a little harder, something I thought would be impossible. He looks at my face, then he sees something there. Lust? Desire? Need? Desperation?

Eyes darkening on me as if he's marking his territory with a look alone, he's suddenly pressing me back against the wall as he reaches between my legs and cups me over my flowy skirt. I rock my hips, gasping when he squeezes me a little.

Something flickers in his eyes as if he realizes what's going on with me.

He cages me in with one arm and leans his shoulder forward, easing his erection between my thighs as he cups me between my legs.

I can't formulate a single thought or pull in a single decent breath. It's just Racer all over me—his face and his eyes so close I feel like I'm drowning in a sea somewhere in Tahiti. His arm sliding between our bodies, his fingertip feathering over my wet sex, under the little dress I wore just for him to see me in something other than jeans and a T-shirt, and my whole body shaking in wanting.

I pull in a breath and slide my arm up his hand and along the back of his neck, while Racer watches me through those thick lashes, murmuring as he shakes his head, like he can't believe what he's seeing, "You're so damned gorgeous, Lana."

I quiver so hard that I want to raise my walls, know that it's best if I probably headed back to the hotel and just went to bed. But instead I sit here, sick and tired of being wary and on defense against men all the time. So that they don't hurt me. So that my brothers and father don't feel disappointed in me. So that I can keep my head on racing and that's it.

Suddenly I just want to feel. Only that. Just feel.

Feel him.

He lowers his other arm from the backrest and places it on my hips, drawing me a little closer as his lips curve like a devil's promise.

A fire churns inside me.

I'm aware of others glancing in our direction, Racer tugging me a little closer to him. And there, in his gaze is a fire churning, too, like the fire churning inside of me.

I lean my head and smell him, nuzzling my nose to his shirt.

He uses his nose to nudge my head up, and then his mouth.

His.

Mouth.

It's covering mine. Pressing and opening mine. And every inch of me awakens when he slips his tongue in my mouth, grabbing me by the back of the thighs and drawing me over his lap as he kisses me, slow and lazy and yet with such hunger and fever that I feel already taken and we're not even naked yet.

I groan.

He eases back in concern, as if concerned he kissed me too hard.

I can barely open my eyes, I'm so in lust with this guy.

He takes me in. And his expression slips, and instead of indifference or arrogance, his expression reveals the rawness of his need as he caresses me over my panties again.

It does something to me, seeing that he wants me like this.

He slides his hand along the edge of my panties, then eases his fingers through, touching my folds—easing his finger inside me until I feel myself grip him so hard that the pleasure nearly wrecks me.

"Tell me you want my tongue right here," he rasps against my cheek as he strokes his fingers along my opening.

I picture him naked, moving over me, and cup the back of his head as I press a kiss to his jaw, telling him without words.

He strokes his knuckles down my jaw, his voice thick with emotion. "You're right to be afraid of me."

He slides his hand from my hip to my face and holds my face within it, his thumb on one cheek, the finger of his other hand inside me as he's forcing me to meet his stormy blue gaze.

"I can be a lot to handle sometimes, but do you know how much I want you, Lana? How good I want to make you feel? How often I think of you?"

His eyes, bright and blue, watch my face as he eases one finger inside me and dips his thumb into my mouth. I can't remember ever feeling this hot, ever feeling as if I'm on a track going 1000 mph and about to burst through a finish line marked with a wall of flames.

I feel myself blush at my own thoughts and how fast this has been escalating.

He leans his head, and kisses me hard now, one of his hands so big it's framing my face with his thumb on one side, and his four fingers on the other, as he tongues me, quite hard and so erotically that as he strokes me under my panties, I come like a rocket, gasping against his mouth. Shuddering between him in the booth, completely undone by his touch.

He growls softly as he eases back, and he tugs my panties back into place and helps me straighten, all the while watching me.

"I …" I brush a sweaty tendril of hair back, feeling awkward now that it's over. "I got carried away again …"

His eyes gleam raw. "Don't make excuses. Tell me you want this. That you feel this."

He's looking intense—his blue gaze really piercing. I swallow and don't know that I have the courage to admit it, because what will it gain me? Really?

"I needed that, so thank you," I say with a little grateful smile, as far as I could let myself admit.

He smiles too, then reaches out to tug my dress back down. "Spend the night with me, Lana," he rasps, nuzzling my face.

"I'm not sure either of us would rest, and you need to rest."

"That's not what I need." He smirks as he eases back.

How I want to kiss him again, kiss the smile on his gorgeous face, grab his face and kiss him all night. In his bed, feel his arms around me, no clothes between us. Feel his hardness against me—no jeans, no underwear, nothing but his sex and mine.

I feel myself blush and think of what it would be like to spend the whole night with him, in his arms, having my way with him … letting *him* have his dirty, sexy way with *me*.

"We'd better go," I breathe, jumping to my feet and watching him slowly come to his and set a couple bills on the table.

He opens the door of the car for me, and as he's strapping the seatbelt around me, our eyes are holding, his intent and glimmering as if he knows what I really want and am not voicing.

"I want this, but … the team. My brothers and my dad, and …" I don't even know how to explain it.

"You always sacrifice yourself for the team?" he asks, he sounds patient, but intent as he comes around the car, gets behind the wheel, and ignites the engine.

"Huh?"

He pulls into the streets and reaches around and tugs me close to him, over the sideboard, and I realize that he's holding me to his chest, and that his hand has slid down my back and his fingers are dangerously close to my bum. My heart starts to pound and I can't seem to think straight because his eyes are so so close, so so blue, and so so hypnotizing even as he stares angrily ahead.

"I … I don't succumb to my every whim, if that's what you're asking," I defend myself.

He just stares at me, then at the road, driving with one hand, the other on me.

"Right now I could be thinking of doing things I want to do, I feel compelled to do, but because I know I'm going to regret them, I don't do them."

"What things," he wants to know, pointedly surveying my mouth.

"Well … I, uh."

He's breathing hard still, his nostrils flaring as he visually dissects my features. And I'm partly straddling and partway lying on his chest, his lap beneath me—his erection so prominent it hurts to look at because my whole body is jealous of my eyes.

I pry free of his embrace, meeting his expression.

"I want to make love to you and I want you to make love to me," I admit, sitting back in my seat, and he just looks at me hotly.

I cover my mouth. "Oh my god. I'm ... I think I'm buzzed."

He smiles, laughing, but his eyes are still so hot. "I'm taking you up on that," he rasps, a low promise as he reaches out, looking at me fiercely and stroking his thumb along my jaw. "I need to go out for a run, chill myself out, because you just set me on fire, girl. But I'm *definitely* taking you up on that when you're sober, and you look at me the way you're looking at me now."

I close my eyes and shudder, nodding. We say nothing else until we arrive at the hotel; he walks me to my room, and then, when I open my door, he walks in with me.

He starts to undress me, kissing the back of my neck as he unzips my dress from behind, and I'm shocked to feel how expertly he does it, pull off my dress, unhook my bra, leave me in just my panties as he scoops me up and sets me down on the bed.

He seems agitated and a little hyper as he removes my shoes, kissing every part of me that's near; my thigh, the inside of my ankle, he pulls off my strappy heels and strokes his hand up my leg, the inside of my knee, growling softly, squeezing my thigh in one big, callused hand as he then leans forward and kisses my pussy over my panties.

"I want you so bad," he says, licking the wet spot there, before he exchanges his tongue with his thumb and looks up at me. "I'm never going to get enough of you," he promises me, leaning over and kissing my lips—and they taste of me, of my pussy—before he pulls the sheet to my chest.

His forehead is against mine, his eyes holding my gaze hostage.

"When I get my hands on you, you'll be made love to like you've never been made love to before." He grabs my face, squeezes it and pecks my lips in the fiercest way he's ever done. "I'm going to fuck all those moans out of you until the whole hotel and city hears you."

With that the guy is gone, leaving me the horniest I've ever been in my whole damn life, ready to scream from the unfairness of it. I don't hear him go into his room; and the whole night I wonder where he went.

I toss and turn. Naked or almost naked in my bed (I never sleep like this!) with nothing but a pair of panties that are wet from my own arousal and his delicious kiss.

I can't seem to sleep at all. I'm worried about my dad, my brothers' relationship with Racer, I'm worried about Racer and his attitude and his recklessness—and his panty-twisting, soul-searing kisses and the way he looks at me. I don't know why this is happening to me right now. When we uprooted, I never once thought about complaining, about what I would miss. My friends back home, going to a normal college instead of an online one while doing it in some hotel room. I never once thought about me, because my dad and my brothers' dreams became my own. Because David was gone, Mom didn't love me, and as far as I was concerned, I didn't have anything left that I couldn't afford to lose. Then comes this guy, the one guy who has the talent and guts enough to help us achieve what we've been working so hard for. And I'm feeling selfish, because I want him for myself as much as I want to win this championship. I'm tempted to throw all caution to the wind, and let myself fall for him even when I am afraid I am not getting much of a choice.

fuck-up

Lana

We're in Russia, having breakfast at the hotel, when the Clark drivers come in. Clark does a double take when they see us. "What? She your girlfriend?"

"She will be." Racer smiles cockily and winks at me, and I frown at him and stiffen my spine as I keep eating my omelet.

"Lainie ... seriously, you can do much better."

Racer kicks his chair back and stands, looking at him. "Take a hike, Clark."

A self-absorbed smile appears on his face and he shoots me a smile. "You'll come around. Nobody wants to date a loser. Especially when she can have a champ."

One second everything is fine, the next Clark is getting shoved back—HARD. "I said, take a hike." Clark stumbles for balance as Racer gives him a look that could peel off the skin from his bones.

Racer sits back down, looking at me as Clark exits the shop with his brother without buying a single thing. "Let's get dessert," Racer says as he calls the waiter, calm and confident, as if nothing happened.

I blink, still stunned by what happened. "I don't like guys that are violent," I whisper, flushing because no man has ever fought for me before. "Too much testosterone if you ask me."

"I'm not violent." He grins, but his eyes look a little dark and angry. A little lusty, too, as he watches me finish my ome-let. "If I were, I'd have cracked that motherfucker's skull," he gruffs out.

We do well in practice, but during qualifying, Clark gets in the way, and we don't seem to be able to catch up with his fastest lap.

"Tate said she didn't have enough torque," Drake is fill-ing me in. "Doesn't seem comfortable in the car. He seems off these past few days."

I watch Kelsey get too close to the car in front. Suddenly Kelsey's nose grazes the car in front, and she flips. He's in the air.

In

The

Fucking

AIR.

I'm on my feet, screaming "NO!!" and covering my mouth as the car flips three times before he lands with a crash against the wall. Debris is landing everywhere; and the car parts are scattered all across the track. The nose. Two wheels. Broken parts from the tail. I can only see the cockpit, and the cloud of dark steam coming off the engine against the wall.

My whole body collapses and I feel my dad catch me.

"Lainie baby," my dad says worriedly.

I start to hyperventilate, and they bring me a little bag to breathe in. "Is he okay?!" I'm begging my brothers to know as I breathe into the bag and frantically try to see some movement from inside the cockpit.

One hand comes out to flip his visor back—and I almost faint from the relief washing over my ice-cold bones.

"He's signaling from the car, I think he's okay," Clayton assures me.

It takes forever for the car to be brought back, in shambles.

And Racer has to walk the way home from the track. He storms into pits like a devil on a vengeance spree. He sends me a heated look when his helmet comes off, his hair standing this way and that, his eyes blue like laser beams. He grits his jaw and heads over to our tent and slam his helmet down. "What the fuck," Clayton tells him.

"I wasn't concentrating." He drags his hand along the back of his neck and makes a fist at his side.

"You—"

"I wasn't concentrating."

"This is our best car," Clayton says.

"Was," Drake says.

Racer storms away, more furious than my three brothers combined.

There's dead silence as we ride back to the hotel in my family's rented van.

Finally, Drake breaks it. "Look, I don't know what goes on in your personal life, but you can't fuck up like this. Get it?"

"I got it," Racer growls, frustrated as he stares out the window, frowning.

We're almost at the hotel, and the tension after Racer crashed hasn't gone down.

I'm wringing my hands. Remembering what it felt like to feel him touch me intimately, how hard I came, how he watched me with a look of total lust in his eyes.

Oh *god*.

Drake shoots him a scowling look. "We can't afford this shit again."

"I'll cover it," he growls.

Drake laughs softly and shakes his head. "You won't have anything left from what we're paying you."

He clenches his hand around the back of his neck, his teeth gritted. "I made a mistake. Won't happen again."

He looks at me. And my stomach flips inside my body.

"He made a mistake, Drake, drop it okay?" I hiss.

There's silence. My dad just looks at Racer, and reaches out and pats him on the back.

"You're human, it's all right. Won't happen again," he tells Racer as we climb out of the car.

My throat constricts when I see the tiredness in my father's eyes, and when they all descend and head to their rooms, I feel Racer curl his hand around my arm.

"Hey."

I turn at the roughly spoken word, meeting his gaze.

He clenches his jaw, then releases my elbow and plunges his hands into his pockets.

I don't know if he just didn't want me to leave or if he wanted to say something, but we stay like this, wordless, for a moment . . .

He turns away and I turn away too, both of us too frustrated to talk.

Racer

The disappointment in her eyes … yeah, that kills me most of all.

I miss her smile, I want it back.

You fucked up and it's gone, Tate.

I lost my head. I was distracted. Badly slept, and too damned crazed over her to think straight today.

I head to my room, but I'm too restless and angry at myself for fucking up, and I need to take the edge off. So I do what I never do and I head to the bar because it's either a glass of something hard, or my lithium pills. And I really don't want to pass down any of that unless I want to fucking *lose* the Grand Prix.

Lithium makes me slow as shit and if HW Racing had wanted slow, they could've fixed up #38 with a grandpa.

frustrations

Lana

I try to calm down for a few minutes, alone in my room, trying to gather my thoughts, but my heart still won't stop feeling heavy and crazy in my chest. My hands are shaking, and even my legs are quivering from the fright. I pull out my phone and I send Racer a text.

I just want to know he's okay. That he's aware of his mistake and will be more careful.

But what I REALLY want is maybe for him to promise me that I will never in my life have to see him flip like that again.

Can you talk?

R.T.: Downstairs at the bar

You don't drink ... I text, frowning.

He sends me an image of an empty tequila shot.

My frown deepens, and I head back downstairs, trying to calm my racing heart, but I think I might need a little sugar for the scare. My brain keeps replaying as Kelsey flipped in the air, and all I could think of was Racer.

His dimple.

His playful blue eyes.

And wanting to die.

I spot him at the bar, nursing his drink, and my stomach shudders uncontrollably. I don't think I've ever been so scared at the track. It's always frightening to see an accident … but today, the guy in the accident was …

HIM.

My knees quake as I take the seat next to his.

His body heat envelops me. He looks about as sturdy as stone, like nobody can hurt him. And suddenly I can't bear to think of what I'd do if he got hurt.

His hand runs across his jaw as he shakes his head in frustration and eyes me. "I am not feeling quite right, right now, Lana. And I don't want to say shit to hurt you, and I'm mad at myself." His eyes are a stormy dark blue that take my breath away. "I don't want you to hate me. You fucking get that?" That restless little muscle tics in the back of his jaw again. "So leave. Now."

"I don't want to," I croak. "What's wrong?"

I don't reach out to touch him; I can sense the energy simmering, just beneath the surface of his clothes. But I sit here, beside him, feeling my own body sort of feel unsettled because his is. Because *he* is.

"What is it that you're hiding?" I ask him. "Your physical came out great. You're in top shape. You're a serious athlete.

You eat right, you pay attention to what goes into your body, you're disciplined. I've never had a driver with your dedication to health."

"Not everything can be measured in tests … not everything is static. Situations change. In the blink of an eye, they change."

"What's changed?"

He clenches his jaw, shakes his head. "Nothing. But I don't want it to. I fucked up. I'm fucking sorry." He squeezes his jaw really tight. "I don't know why I … I wanted to slam Clark into the wall. I've never been jealous before."

"Jealous over what?"

"You."

I'm still trembling from the scare he gave me. "Clark is an asshole."

"He wants what's mine!" he growls.

"I'm not … Racer. Goddammit! What the fuck. Were you concentrating at all? You flipped and could have fucking died. What were you thinking?!"

"Your pussy." His eyes flash darkly. "Your sweet wet pussy craving me and only me, taking me and only me." He looks a little wild as he grabs my elbow, tugging me close until our foreheads touch and our eyes are locked. "Tell me you want me, all of me."

My throat closes as he lifts his eyes from my mouth to mine, and they look dark and tortured.

"I was scared, you *jerk*." I punch his arm, a little harder than I expected, not that it has any effect at all. "Don't do that again. I was fucking scared!"

His eyes widen in shock, and I realize my voice sounds uneven and that I'm not really stable myself. He's right, I should leave, so I whip up to my feet and start walking away toward the elevator.

He comes up behind me, following me into the elevator like a black storm.

"What the fuck?! You think I *wanted* to screw up?" he demands, grabbing my shoulders and forcing me to turn.

I clench my lips together, my eyes watering.

"I don't want to care about you! I'm already losing my dad, day by day, I already lost the only boy I ever loved, and I don't want to lose *you. You fucking asshole!*" I punch him, and he grabs my wrist to stop me.

"I'm not going anywhere," he rasps, his eyes vivid with emotion.

I swallow the lump in my throat and when the doors open, I wiggle my wrist free and hurry towards my room, afraid I'm going to cry.

He plants an arm around me and cages me against my door, breathing in the back of my ear, "Turn around and look at me. I'm not going anywhere. I'm the best driver in the world, remember."

"No you're not." I swallow and open the door, walk inside and avoid turning to look at him, but he walks in behind me, kicking the door shut behind him.

"Yes I am. Best kisser, too." He grabs me up in his arms, turns me around, and lifts me, and suddenly everything I feel is unleashed in the kiss he gives me and that I give him back. He fucks my tongue almost as if our lives depend on it, and he squeezes my ass as my mouth attacks his in return, my nails in his scalp as we devour each other.

He thrusts me against the door.

I claw my nails down his arms and tug at his shirt, suddenly not wanting this shirt, not wanting anything between us, nothing to keep me from tasting him, *feeling* him.

I've got his shirt halfway over his dark head when he helps me by yanking it up with one fist. His hair stands up on end as he tosses it aside and dives back for my mouth, stealing his hands under my top. I shudder when his fingers make contact with my skin, and I make a soft sound against his mouth, like a moan.

"You like that?" he rasps against my mouth, easing back to look down at me. He's shirtless, his hair chaotic, and his one dimple appears as I nod vigorously. So vigorously my head almost snaps.

"What else do you like, huh?" he rasps, pulling me closer, sliding his warm hands around my waist and then sliding them up my back to unfasten my bra as his mouth brushes across my jaw, teasing my lips. "What else do you like, Lana?"

"I like when you call me Lana."

"You do, do you?"

"Yes. It makes me feel like a woman, and I like feeling like a woman when I'm with you."

"What other ways do you like to feel, huh?" he husks as he pulls my top over my head and drinks me in, in my bra and jeans.

"You know what?" His eyes scan me, head to toe, and he slips his hand under my jeans to grab and massage my butt. "I want to lick you up head to toe until I've tasted every inch of you, and then I want to do it again."

He ducks his head, pressing his mouth to my ear, licking my earlobe and then behind my ear. The tickles are everywhere, in my wet spot especially, and the tips of my breasts and my chest.

"Racer ..." I slip my arms around him and trail my fingers up the muscles of his back, my body arching against his, moving in this aching, cutting need to get closer to him. To feel his warmth, feel that he wants me.

He presses his hard—bulging—jeans against me and there's not even a doubt about that. I feel his hardness biting into my abdomen as he grabs me by the underarms and lifts me up to turn me around and sit me on top of the couch rest.

"I'm not going anywhere, sweetheart," he reassures me as he curls his palm around my cheek and scrapes his thumb along my lower lip, his eyes bright and fiery. "I want to make you feel so good you'll scream from it—you'll think you're floating tomorrow. But right now I'm going to thrust into you so hard you'll think you're breaking. 'Cause I swear to god every time you look at me with desire in your eyes, you're breaking *me*."

He tugs my jeans down, and then my panties. I feel completely exposed as he nudges my legs apart and runs his greedy gaze along my pussy. "Fucking perfect," he rasps, his gaze bright blue as he feathers his finger over my folds.

He frees his cock and teases my folds with the tip of his thick length, and I almost *come* by this.

"Take me," he growls.

I'm practically breaking from the pleasure.

He cups my breast. My nipple is puckered and sensitive and every time he rubs the pad of his thumb across the peak I nearly spasm from how good it feels. And as he drives inside me, I have never in my life felt so full.

"Take me," he says again, driving into me.

I take him with a groan, arching up, nails in his scalp, teeth in his jaw.

"Fuck! FUCK!" he growls, pulling out.

I watch him struggle to find something in his jeans, then he pulls out the condom and slides it on.

I almost tell him to forget it.

I think he notices my desperation when he looks down at me. Because something in him seems to snap. Something in me seems to snap. We're suddenly tearing at each other's very skin as he lifts me up in his arms.

He carries me to the bed and falls down on top of me.

"Oh god," I plead, clutching his jaw as our mouths twirl and fight around.

He grabs my face and presses his mouth down harder on mine, groaning when I open without a fight.

"God, I've been hungering for this sweet mouth, this sweet bod of yours." He holds me still as he twists his head this way and that, doing things to my mouth that should be outlawed, accessing from one side and then the other, his tongue tasting and taking everything while his hands simply hold me here—breathless, toe-curling, tingling in every pore— as Racer's tongue moves and takes. And takes. And takes.

And I let him take because my whole body is a live flame, because every time he takes from me I want to give him more, because every time he takes from me he fills me with the most delicious sensations, the most wicked sensations, the most pleasurable feelings I've ever had in my life. His kisses are driving my heart to near heart attack and my lungs to work like crazy, and my skin to pull taut, and my muscles to constrict with waiting.

"You okay with this, huh?" he growls, easing back to look at me, panting hard.

He's spread out his body over mine, the muscles of his shoulders rippling as he curls his arms at my sides and frames my face with his hands as I nod.

I nod and nod frantically, looking into his eyes, seeing something very deep and raw inside those dark baby blues.

"Fuck me, girl," he hisses to himself as he smothers my mouth with his, his mouth wet and passionate as he strokes his right hand down my front, squeezing my breast like he just needed to be unleashed.

His cock drifts along my folds, to and fro, teasingly.

My eyes drift shut and I hear myself groan softly. I swear I'd never before in my life heard myself make this kind of noise.

Racer is breathing hard, in the dark.

His own breaths mingle with my own and with the sound of his hands, stroking across my skin.

It feels so good, I am shivering uncontrollably, his body hot as he looms above me, one of his thighs jammed between mine, his chest close to my own, so that every simultaneous breath of ours makes my nipples nearly touch his own.

He's got really tough palms—the palms of a guy that's holding a steering wheel for hours straight, fighting against it even when it wants to pull back. Feeling his strong, large hands cup my breasts makes me feel about as physically fragile as I am feeling emotionally fragile right now.

Right now as his wet mouth seeks the tip of my other nipple. Finds it. Laves it. Suckles it. His breath hot and coming out in fast blasts, his tongue snaking out to taste and torture the peak to a full stand.

"You're gorgeous, Lana. I can't get over how wet and tight your pussy felt around my dick with no condom on," he rasps as he keeps kissing me wetly, one nipple, then the other, and then my mouth again. He grinds himself gently but firmly against me.

Shivers race down my body as I nod, sliding my hands over the back of his head as I impulsively kiss his jaw, never in my life so hungry for anything. For a guy. For *this* guy.

"Good?" He rocks against me, ducking his head to taste and suck on my nipple as his hand squeezes my flesh, pushing out the tip for his suckling, hot, ravenous mouth.

"So good," I rasp. My fingers trace up the back of his arms and over his hair, memorizing his skull.

"How much do you want this? How much do you want this, do you want it like this?" His voice is thick and raspy as he speaks, and he moves harder against me, grabbing his cock and pressing it to my entrance once more.

I'd been aching for it.

Dying for it.

"Yes," I bubble out.

"Don't stop looking at me, huh. I want to drown in those fucking eyes."

I can't believe he's pressing his dick into my opening. I can't believe I'm feeling the head of his cock part me open and then … start driving in. I cannot believe all of this as I stare back into his blue eyes. "I'm drowning in yours and in you," I breathe.

He keeps grabbing his cock by the base as he gives it to me, inch by inch, never once taking his eyes off my face as he goes in—opening me completely. My breath snags in my throat—the feel of him stretching me taking all of my oxygen from my lungs.

"Oh god." I claw him closer, hips tilting upward as I press my mouth to his jaw.

"Racer," I plead against his hard jaw, my eyes closed as I blindly search his mouth. He turns his head and gives it to me, soft but firm, driving the last inches inside me.

We moan at the same time, his arms clenching around me before he releases one to brace himself up on his arms as if to keep from crushing me. He starts to move, the shadows playing across his handsome face, his features etched in pleasure, both of us watching each other even as our bodies strain to get closer, to take more of and from the other, our hips sort of working in unison.

"Look at me, Lana." His thrusts become faster and deeper. "Let my eyes see it. Let my dick feel it, every ripple, every squeeze."

It could break me, that tenderness on his face. The gleam in his blue eyes, the way he stares down at me like I'm so right, so right he couldn't have imagined anything better.

But to see his face undone like this? Nothing prepared me for how hot it would make me, how turned on. I sink my nails on his butt, squeeze the RT tattoo on his ass and get all of RT in me, deeper and harder and faster.

"Racer ..."

He grabs my hair in a fist and starts to kiss me voraciously. He smothers my mouth, thrusting me with fast, nearly too-fast jerks of his hips and tongue.

"Fuuuck," he groans.

He comes really hard. I feel his cock jerk inside me before he pulls out and, keeping a fist on his cock and yanking off the condom, he works the length of his cock as streams of semen explode into the air. Still jerking on himself, he spreads his semen all over my abdomen, his eyes the most brilliant I've ever seen them, his face etched in pleasure and heat and possessiveness as he bathes me with him.

"Oh god," I groan as he uses his other hand to stroke a finger over my sensitive spot, one hand on his cock, the other on my pussy. *His* pussy.

I come.

We pant as we recover.

"You felt too good," I breathe.

He's up on his knees between my legs, and I'm lying on the bed, panting as his chest heaves with his harsh breaths too.

I hold his gaze, reach down with my hand to his semen on my stomach, and I rub my fingertip against the wetness and bring it up to my mouth. I lick it up, and his eyebrows raise, then his lips curve at the corner.

"You like that?" he asks.

I nod quietly, and he reaches out to rub his finger over the wetness, bringing more cum to my mouth. I lick it, and the completely wild look in his gorgeous eyes is getting excited again, wanting me again.

"You like that?" I ask, noticing the way it seems to turn him on.

He grins. "You have no idea," he says, before he shows me just how much it turns him on.

headset

Lana

He's driving Dolly this weekend while Kelsey gets fixed up, and he asks for me on the headset again. He's racing from the very back, because when he flipped during qualifying, his position suffered.

He's been advancing every damn turn—going from P16, to P14, to P13.

"He wants you," Clay says again.

I hesitate, noticing Clay doesn't seem irritated anymore.

"He focuses better. Haven't you noticed? His best times come when you're on the radio with him."

My eyes widen; and I feel my hand tremble slightly as I step forward, take the headset, and slip it on.

"You're coming up behind P10. Your lap timing is close to P1, so if you keep this up …"

I watch him pass.

"P10!" I say. "Coming up behind P9 …" I check his time then. "You just broke the track record for fastest lap."

"Dinner, Lana," I suddenly hear his low, slightly dehydrated, sexy-as-fuck voice rumbling just like the motor in the background.

"What."

"Go out to dinner with me."

"Is this why you wanted me on? Are you inviting me out during a race?"

"Yeah, and I'm going to win again."

I smile.

"Lana," he prods.

Silence.

"Crasher …" He warns, sounding a little cocky. "You go out with me and you'll never look back. I swear, baby."

"Yes," I breathe. "Yes, I'll go to dinner with you," I say.

real

Racer

She stayed in my room. Hell if I got any sleep at all. I counted her damn freckles.

Stroked my hand down her back feeling every bump of her spine. Savored her smell like nobody's business. Fucking ready for the next round when she shifts against me.

She stirs awake, the sheets tangled at our feet, both of us bare fuck naked and my cock is quick to remind me. She starts upright and seems to panic, glancing around the room. "What time is it?"

"It's an off day," I rasp out, taking in her tangled hair and her kiss-swollen lips with pure male pride.

"I probably need to get my dad some breakfast," she says, rolling to the edge of the bed to dial his room.

"Daddy!" she says when he picks up. "Good morning. Have you had breakfast?"

I head over to the bathroom to pee and brush my teeth while I listen to her telling her dad she's going to rest for a bit.

As I brush my teeth, I take in her reflection in the mirror while she sits on the bed, the sheets at her waist with her tits poking out, her eyes trailing over my ass and admiring the tattoo of my initials with pure feminine lust because she thinks I'm not looking.

Her eyes widen when our eyes connect in the mirror, and I feel my lips pull up as I wash off my toothbrush, spit out the rest of my toothpaste, and head back into the room feeling very, very hungry and damn possessive of her.

She is, after all, the girl I want to spend the rest of my life with.

Also, and this must be said: she's the loveliest thing I've ever seen.

She shudders on the bed as if she can feel the heat inside me already, pulling the sheet up to her tits.

Her eyes drift down my chest, along my pecs, my ab muscles, down to my very hard cock.

She licks her lips. "Do we have more condoms?" She sounds breathless as she speaks, flushing head to toe as if my mouth hadn't sucked on those pretty little nipples of hers all night long.

"Nightstand. Or maybe my duffel." I lean over to check the nightstand while Lana wraps the sheets around her and leaps off the bed to search my duffel. "What are these for?" I hear her ask a moment later.

Glancing past my shoulder as I shut the drawer, I raise my brows and stare at the orange bottle in her hand.

My goddamned lithium pills.

For a moment, I just stare at her, my voice gruff and low. "Emergencies."

"What kind of emergencies?"

Silence.

I grab them and toss them back into the duffel.

"Come on. Tell me. What are they for? Nothing came out in your physical," she says.

She frowns at me as she comes back to bed, clutching the sheets to her chest.

I sit down on the side of the bed and drag a hand over the back of my neck, shifting to look at her.

"Racer!" she says.

Yeah, this isn't how I planned to break it to her.

"I'm manic-depressive," I husk out.

For a fraction of a second, she doesn't move.

It feels like it takes a moment for her to piece it together. She stares in puzzlement, and for a second, I dread the look in her eyes changing.

It doesn't.

They shine in concern. I'm used to lust, but concern from a girl other than my mother and sister? No.

"Manic depressive is …"

"Bipolar," I say, softly.

"But your physical …"

"It's not active right now." I shake my head, clenching my hands at my sides in frustration. This is definitely not how I planned to do this. Fuck me.

"When is it active?"

"I don't know. Randomly. I haven't figured out my triggers yet." I watch her look at me, those gorgeous eyes showing every emotion on her face. Concern, puzzlement, worry.

"So, what is it like? How do you feel when …" She trails off, staring at me.

"Sometimes on top of the world. Sometimes at the bottom, scraping to get up," I admit.

Those eyes of hers?

Fuck, they're killing me.

The concern there, the genuine shock and emotion there. I stroke a hand down the back of her head. "I'm okay," I husk.

"Are you?"

"Fuck yes." I grin.

But those eyes start to water now. She drops her face and swallows.

I curse softly and reach out to pull her closer to me.

"Why didn't you tell me?" she asks. The hurt in her voice nearly cuts me open.

I rake my hands through my hair, shaking my head as a shit-ton of frustration hits me where it damn hurts. "Come on, Lana. Why do you think?"

She looks away, and I can't fucking have that. I curse under my breath and seize her shoulders.

"Lana," I say, low but firm. "Look at me."

She squeezes her eyes shut and presses her cheek to my hand as if she needs my touch for balance. But it fucking unbalances me. Never felt pity for me. Too many good things in my life. I leave that for an episode when it all comes flooding me. But seeing her pain for me cuts me deep, and for a second, I wonder if I'm fucking selfish to want her.

If she wouldn't be better off without me.

No, she wouldn't, because I would walk on water, part oceans, and fucking turn green and three times my size for this girl.

I kiss her eyelids.

"I'm fucking okay. All right?"

She raises her eyes, and bites down on her lip, her eyebrows still joined in a frown of bewildered confusion.

"When were you going to tell me?"

I drink in her features and run my thumb gently down her jawline. "After we won the Grand Prix." I hold her gaze and will her to know how damn much she means to me. "This isn't how I wanted to tell you."

"How were you going to do it?"

I smile and almost fucking laugh, 'cause that's how fucked up this is. "Hell, I don't know. Wine you, dine you, ease you into it. Make you wet for it." I smirk at my own words, but she doesn't, and my smile fades.

"I told you about David, Racer," she says, still disappointed and fuck, I know she opened up. I know she wants me to trust her but this isn't something you just tell a girl like that. Not the one you want to fall for you.

"This is different, Lana."

"Why?"

"This is my fucking life," I growl, seizing her face in one hand and drinking in those bewildered green eyes. "And I want you to be a part of it."

Those eyes seem to flicker at my words.

"I didn't want to scare you away," I tell her, resting my head on hers as I inhale and grit out the rest. "Yes, I have it. I can hurt you, Lana. But I've never wanted anything so much in my life." I fist her hair in my hand and urge her to keep her eyes on mine. "I want you for real, and I know you want me too. It's all there, Lana. In your eyes. It's all there for me to see. I'm going to be okay. I'm going to *fight* to be okay. I'm the son of one of the world's greatest fighters, I know how to put up a fight, and I'll never stop putting it up against this."

A shudder wracks her body, and when she exhales a deep breath, I do too.

She bites down on her lip and looks at me.

"Tell me about it."

Hell, I don't like getting into details. This is my Achilles heel after all. I don't like remembering it's there and live my life like it's not.

But she wants to know. And I want to tell her. Be as real as possible with her.

"Some switch goes off in my head—and I'm either feeling immortal or like I want to die that day."

"Racer," she breathes, and I want to punch myself for admitting it so blatantly.

I stop her from turning her face away. "Hey," I command, looking into her eyes. "Yes, I have it, and it can't be easy to be with me when I do, but I've never wanted anything so much in my life the way I want you, crasher." I fist my hand in her hair and force her to look up at me. "I want you like nothing in my whole goddamned life, and I'd kill myself before I ever deliberately hurt you. Do you understand?"

She nods, her eyes still shining with emotion. "How did you find out?" she asks, lying down on her side on the bed.

I stretch out on my side and look at her, stroking a hand down her bare arm.

We stroke each other for a couple of minutes, and there's something about feeling her touch me that relaxes me. That calms the worry of her not taking this well.

"My whole life my parents were concerned about me or Iris having it because of my dad. But I was okay; 19 years, and nothing. Then at 20, something happened. I couldn't sleep. I couldn't focus or listen. I felt wired, like I was pounding Red

Bulls. The next week, I didn't come out of my room for days; nothing mattered. Nothing seemed important. Even shit I loved. Even music or food. Hate it most when I feel like that. At 21, I was diagnosed, put on Lithium."

She's still stroking my shoulder with the same arm I'm caressing, drinking in my every word.

I clench my jaw and stare up at the ceiling as I roll to my back and force myself to continue. "My dad … it was hard for me to deal. Looking at him."

"Why? Your dad loves you," she says, confused as she sits up to look into my eyes.

"Yeah, but it wasn't what he wanted for me. He has it too." I sit up and twist my mouth, remembering the day my father learned about me. Worst day of my fucking life and I'm only too happy to never remember it again. "It triggered him. I couldn't fucking deal with the fact that I was a huge disappointment to my father. That his perfect son turned out to have the one thing he didn't want him to have."

She swallows, and I push the memory away.

"It's hard to live up to your dad's worst fear. It took me some time on meds to stabilize. To look him in the eye and say I don't want to be this, but I'll take it." I smile at her and tweak her nose, gruffly say, "I'll make it my bitch."

She laughs. "Racer!"

I chuckle too, grab her skull and pull her closer. "Hey. Don't ever worry about me. This bitch is mine."

"And when it's not?"

"And when it's not … I've got it. That's what my meds are for," I tell her, stroking her cheek.

"Is there any way I can know when you've been … triggered?"

"I'll tell you," I assure her.

"Promise me?"

I look at her, into her eyes, and see my own worst fear reflected back at me. That one day, someone I love won't understand this, won't be able to live with this, bear with me through this, and leave. "It's not going to be pretty," I rasp.

She shakes her head, a twinkle in her eye. "I'm used to you not being pretty—have you seen your ugly face, Mr. Tate?"

I smile. Then clench my jaw and cover her cheek with my palm, staring down at her. "If I say or do anything to hurt you, Lana ..." I rasp, my eyes narrowed.

"You won't."

I hope so. Fucking pray so. No, I'll *make* it so. "Don't ever feel sorry for me."

"Never."

I peck her lips, rewarding her with my tongue. "Come here," I quietly summon.

She drops the sheets and slides beneath them, her bare skin flush against mine, getting me all riled up and then some.

"How did your mom take it when she found out about your dad?" she asks.

"She was already too in love with him to care," he says.

"I can relate," she mutters. She absently kisses my nipple as she speaks, looking up at me innocently as if she doesn't realize what she just did or fucking said.

Damn me, it does shit to me.

Makes my balls hurt, my cock swell even more, and my chest feel like it's doubled in width.

I take in her features as she waits for my reply, and she'll never fucking know how much I want that. How I'd never thought I'd want that until she crashed my goddamned cherry mustang.

I thought I'd best be a loner, race my heart out, live the single life, not make loving me become anyone's curse.

Then *she* happened, and all I can think of is this one girl and how much I want to take care of her.

Fuck, this girl, my girl, takes care of everybody—and I want to be the one taking care of her for a change.

I press my mouth to hers and open her lips with mine, smoothing my hands down her body, my cock continuing to stir hungrily as she moans softly under my kiss.

I'm kissing her raw and fierce because I feel all damn bare, bared my soul right here.

I've never been so fucking real with a girl in my life.

For the first time in my life. Bare as fuck before the girl I want. Wanting her to want me back. Letting her glimpse every facet of what makes me up.

And this girl presses her lips back to mine, her body closer against mine, pressing a hot kiss to my dimple. Of all things.

"You're wonderful, Racer Tate," she says as she slides her hands around my neck and presses me closer like she needs me like air.

Like she needs me like I fucking need her and need to be inside her right now.

"I know," I rasp, just to tease her, but maybe I'm lying because nothing has ever felt as wonderful—not even me at my goddamned best—as this green-eyed girl, taking me at my real value, and still wanting more.

not perfect

Lana

"We're changing this right now."

I watch Racer in our tent, his racing suit halfway down his body, his hair standing up after a practice session, and he's looming over Adrian as he points at the motor and gives him some specs.

"What the fuck do you want to take out? Why the fuck are you changing this shit an hour before qualifying?"

Racer laughs and slaps his back confidently. "Do it."

"Tate," he calls as Racer strides over to grab a water bottle from the cooler.

"I'm aiming for another track record," Racer says calmly, coming back after guzzling down half the bottle of water, peering into the engine as Adrian and the mechanics get to work on the changes he wants.

I feel a little thirsty myself.

But not for water.

I don't think that when my brothers commanded me to keep him out of trouble, the idea was to keep Racer Tate entertained with my body. But my body seems very entertained by feeling his.

Of feeling his hands run over me, let his eyes look at me in ways no guy has ever looked at me.

I grew up with four brothers, and my mother didn't even let me walk out to breakfast in my pajamas. I was always quite modest in that respect.

While they went around shirtless and in boxers, I've never really stood in my underwear in front of a guy. But this guy makes me greedy for those eyes of his, the way the blue turns a little more electric when he looks at me, and I'm both shy at the idea of those eyes seeing me, and at the same time, I'm excited about it.

What do I really know about BP? What do I know about mental illness except that it takes lives, that it's hard for everyone, the families, those suffering. It's scary, and it makes the scared girl in me, who's lost a loved one and fears of losing another every day, want to stay away—that is the truth. I'm only human and nobody wants to see the fire and fly straight in except the moths who don't know better. I'm not a moth, I'm a girl, and he's not only bipolar but a racer. And yet no matter how much I rationalize, the truth is that I don't get a choice, not when I'm already falling for him.

I'm trapped—helplessly and totally—in Racer Tate's irresistible fire.

I want more dates with him like the one we had the night before I found his pill bottle. Where we talked and ate in a small street café, stealing touches only because I was so worried that my brothers would walk past.

I want to find out his every secret, figure out what makes him up.

I want to make a bible out of his body, an encyclopedia out of his muscles and bones, every detail registered, examined, and stored away for me to enjoy and relive, over and over.

I want to do what we did last night again and again and again.

The problem is, my brothers seem to be noticing something's going on, and they're being … well. They're being my fucking brothers.

"Lana used to be a very fussy baby," Clayton tells Racer as we eat in one large table at the tent. "Even Mom said she was born with everything. Acid reflux, colic, she was born with it all, right Drake?" Clayton says.

"Yep. We never wanted to sleep near her 'cause she'd never let anyone shut an eye."

Racer just looks at me, one sleek eyebrow coming up questioningly, and I scowl at my three brothers, even Adrian who hasn't said a thing. Yet. "Stop telling Racer what's wrong with me," I whisper-hiss at Clayton, kicking Drake under the table too.

"Come on." Clayton laughs, not bothering to whisper. "Thank me we're not telling him how you are at the same time every month. Moody and crampy and chewing everyone's head off."

Racer grabs his drink, steps away, shooting my brothers a hard glare.

"Nice way to impress him." I glower, watching him head to the motorhome.

"That's the thing, Lane. Why are you not giving him the cold shoulder like you do all the other guys," Clayton says.

"He's on our team! And he's …" I stop myself from saying more.

My brothers are watching me. I think they suspect. They look pissy and protective. Are they trying to scare him off?

I start getting riled. "Shut up, Clay and Drake, and *you* shut up too," I tell Adrian.

Adrian raises his hands defensively. "I didn't say shit."

"You're trying to scare him off!" I grab my shoe and toss it at the table, spilling their food. "You're absolute dicks!" I throw the other one, and they laugh as I march to the motorhome.

Racer's grabbing his phone and his earbuds. He seems pissed.

"Hey," I say.

He clenches his jaw and tosses the earbuds and phone aside.

"Do me a favor," he growls, eyebrows slanted. He paces a little, cracks his knuckles, and wheels around. He curls his hand around my wrist and squeezes me, his gaze penetrating me all the way to the depths of my soul. "Don't ever let them treat you like that."

"They're my brothers, that's what they do."

"Don't ever let them talk about you like that."

I open my mouth, then shut it. "They were trying to scare you away," I breathe.

He stares at me, his eyes narrowed.

"Besides. Why do you care so much."

"Because you're mine."

"What?"

"That's right," he growls, still mad.

"Racer …" I start laughing, and he looks at my mouth, and I stop laughing because I want to kiss him so hard too that my lip gloss is going to be all over that sexy mouth of his.

"They're saying all that because they can obviously tell that you, that I … that I'm obsessed with everything about you. Your beautiful eyes and your hot bod, your personality and just … who you are."

He grins a little bit, studying me with those intense eyes. "Go out with me again. Let's go for a drive. Just you and me. Some music. The breeze. No cares in the world." His lips quirk mischievously, and so do mine. "Or will you have a cramp or colic?"

"No, no cramps or colic. I just had my period so I won't be ovulating until, well, another week or so …" I trail off.

"I have a sister, I know all about cycles. She and Mom talk about it over the dinner table."

I laugh and picture him and his father just bearing it. "Do you two get along?"

"I suppose. I feel protective of her. She's younger than me."

"Do you treat her like a baby like my brothers do?"

"Maybe. I don't mean to." He looks at me with intimate intensity. "You're very regular?"

I nod.

"Wh … why do you ask?"

His eyes are very dark.

"You're not thinking to have your way with me without any … um …"

"I want to come inside you."

I think my ovaries just shuddered.

"I want to put my stamp in your walls." He smirks, and I start to perspire.

"We'll ... we'll see."

I sit on his lap, and I start to realize that something very hard is growing beneath my bottom. And growing even more. I hear—I actually *hear*—the sound of me catching my breath, my eyes flying up to his.

He looks at me, his eyes a little hooded. "Can't help it." A smirk touches his eyes and I want to kiss the smirk on his lips and those eyes too.

I swallow nervously instead, reach out and place my hand on the squarish curve of his shoulder, holding his eyes.

His smile falters, and his eyes shadow like midnight.

I watch his Adam's apple work as he swallows too, his gaze dropping and fastening to my lips.

He tugs me close, his nose almost against mine. "I'm starting P2 today. P2's got to be more than kissing."

"You've just got to have the healthiest self-esteem of anyone I've ever known."

"I can be very stubborn too," he gruffs out, his eyes gleaming mischievously. He winks.

He lifts my hand and turns it around, gently kissing the center of my palm. I'm so surprised I hear my mouth open on a gasp, but my throat doesn't seem to release the gasp, it gets caught somewhere in the middle when his tongue flicks out to lick me.

Slowly, I look at his bent head, the head of messy black hair, his chiseled profile, his eyes drifting shut as he savors my palm like I'm the most delicious morsel on the planet.

"Racer ..." I begin.

He circles his tongue around the center, then sort of drags it into the sensitive skin on the inside of my wrist, where he presses both his lips and his hot wet tongue to my pulse point. I've never been seduced by a guy, or ever been wanted like this by a guy.

I can't move and am paralyzed from the pleasure as I simply watch him, grappling with the urge to duck my head and nuzzle the top of his head, nudge his face around so that his tongue—rather than lick my wrist, is licking inside me, inside my mouth.

I'm salivating for this guy and so wound-up that I'm suddenly doing just that, following the impulse to drop my head and nudge his face around, and as he turns, his hard jaw rasps against my cheek and then … then the softness of his mouth is pressing against mine and I'm pressing back just as hard.

I'm trembling so hard, my body is jerking a little, but my arms wind around his wide shoulders and I press closer, feeling as though he's the only thing that will center me right now, that will give me some semblance of balance now.

Our mouths move, simultaneously, his opening wider and going slower than mine.

His chest is a wall against my puckered nipples and his strength is like a cloak around him, around us both.

"Eight p.m. tonight, baby," he says, pecking my lips as a finale.

"Yes, baby," I whisper back, pecking him back.

His expression slips, and instead of indifference or arrogance, his expression reveals the rawness of his need.

It does something to me; seeing that he wants me like this.

He seems to lose control and pulls me closer, deeper into his arms. "You turn me on like nothing in my life, Lana," he rasps.

"Not even Kelsey."

He smirks, eyes dancing. "She's a close second. But yeah. Not even her. Or Dolly."

His contagious grin makes me smile and I wiggle free, perspiring head to toe, my toes curling as I step out of the motorhome, watching my brothers watch me walk away. I flip them the bird, seeing their smiles fade as my own appears. *Bullies.*

drive

Racer

We drive along the streets of London, the wind in her hair, before I park us at a cliff overlooking the Thames.

"All right, come here, Lana."

She hops out of the convertible and walks forward while I pull out some food and a cooler of drinks from the trunk.

I set them down and pull her down with me. She seems curious as she watches me open a bottle of wine, sized perfectly for one, and gifts me with a damn gorgeous smile when I hand it over to her.

"Time someone took care of you for a change," I gruff out, dropping a kiss on her lips.

I fiddle with my phone, setting it up to play music via Bluetooth. I scroll through my library looking for one of the ones I know she likes. I play *Favorite Record* and turn the car volume up.

Her eyes light up when it starts playing, and she seems impressed. "You remember."

"I pay attention."

She flushes pink.

"This is such a nice spot." She looks around at the river and at the city lights of London.

"I told you that you'd go out on a drive with me and never be the same again."

"Ha." She rolls her eyes, and I'm chuckling and reaching out to push her hair back.

"I'm into you, girl," I rasp, shifting to stare into her eyes.

"Yeah?" she breathes.

"You know it," I say, swooping down to kiss her, but before I do, I force myself to hold back and tease her. "And because I'm clearly sweeping you off your feet, I thought it fair to warn you of some of my more unsavory traits."

"Oh, wow, thank you, that's thoughtful."

I start counting with my fingers. "I'm a very light sleeper, and I like the room to be so damn cold a morgue couldn't compete. I'm also stubborn as fuck; I always get my way."

"Are you going to get your way with the championship?" she taunts.

"Watch me get my way." I grin.

She laughs, her eyes sparkling and flooded with happiness, her cheeks so pink I can notice her flush in the dark.

"We're doing well with the championship," she says, setting her bottle aside.

"Second place is not good enough," I say, staring out at the Thames. "It's first or it's nothing, as far as I'm concerned."

She eyes me in wonder, then out at the city as she draws her knees up to her chin and takes a sip of her wine. "Clark will play dirty."

I shrug, taking a long gulp of my bottle too as I lean back on my elbows. "I can play all kinds of ways."

"Did you always want to race?"

"Always." I wink at her. "Since I was a tiny thing, I grew obsessed with cars. The noise they make, fuck it turns me on," I growl, and she laughs, her eyes heavy.

"You broke the law for years just so you could get away with racing."

"I'm not ashamed of it."

She's quiet. "Does it help with the BP?"

"I think so, yes."

She nods and smiles sadly. "The year you were diagnosed, I think that was the year David died."

Our eyes meet. My girl. She's MY girl. And she's still hurting and I can't make it go away. "I'm sorry," I say, straightening.

Maybe he was meant to love her for a time, but I'm loving her forever.

I shift my arm and pull her close, and I raise the volume of my phone, and the car volume hikes up.

I pull her to my chest, and she sets her bottle aside and snuggles close to me, and I growl against her hair.

My senses heighten with the addictive scent of her, feel of her, look of her. I just want more. I know that when you're in a life-or-death situation, your senses clear, your mind is sharp as fuck—every detail stored in your mind because one of those details can mean the difference between life and death.

Happens when I'm racing.

Happens when she's around. Because every detail of her, every fucking word, every thing about her, is fucking *life*.

"I want to taste you," I gruff in her ear.

Her eyes widen.

"I want your pussy melting beneath my mouth and the rest of you, too. "

I tug her skirt up to her waist, revealing her violet-colored lace panties.

"Racer." She's trembling.

"Would you like that, Lana?"

"I think so."

"Then take my hand, baby. Go on. Take it and show me your favorite places, show my fingers." She does. Taking my fingers to her nipples. I growl, squeezing. "Now my mouth."

She takes my head and guides it to her belly button.

I set a kiss there, tracing her belly button with my tongue.

She gasps and guides my head even lower, parting her legs. I ease up and smile down at her, easing her panty aside with my thumb.

She's shaking as she watches me go back down to those soft, sweet curls.

I lick her.

One long lick.

She gasps and shifts beneath me, getting closer to me, and I kneel before her; I grab her by the hips and part her legs, sliding down to bury my mouth in her sweet-as-peach sex once more.

This time I don't come up for air; don't fucking want it.

I drag my tongue up and down, her taste addictive. Perfect. Fucking drugging. She smells like warm girl, *my* warm girl, and tastes better than fresh rain.

I dip my tongue inside, deeper and harder, my hunger growing with each taste.

Her hips start rocking upward, and Lana's kissing the top of my head, breathing faster and harder as my own breaths start to speed up.

She writhes and tries to snap her legs shut—gasping and rolling her head in the grass, out of control. I pry her legs wider open and move my head, licking and sucking her up, feeling her start to come when I lie over her, set my jean-clad cock above center, and kiss her as we grind each other on the ground, too damn hot for her to resist coming when she blows off beneath me.

I come with her.

Lana gasps as she recovers, catching her breath, and I tug her panties back into place and help her straighten, all the while watching her.

She's pink-cheeked and heavy-eyed, and I pluck the grass from her hair, grinning as she smiles shyly up at me.

"Wow," she says.

She sits up, her face soft after her orgasm, her lashes still heavy—her gaze wowed.

"God, those eyes," I say, cupping her face.

"They're just green," she says with a soft laugh, snuggling her cheek into my palm.

"They're everything. So fucking expressive you don't even need to say a word for me to know exactly how you feel."

"Really?"

"Yeah."

"How do I feel now?"

"You're having a good time."

"And?"

"And you're still hot for me. No matter how many times I make you come."

"Oh wow, he's so honest." She laughs and rolls her eyes.

"You're falling for me, Lana."

Her smile fades.

"I don't know if I should warn you again to stay away, but what's the point? I'd only chase you." I smile down at her, shaking my head in warning. "I'm not letting you go."

"What?" she scoffs. "Racer, seriously, your confidence knows no limits."

"I know what I know."

"You don't know shit." She scowls and shifts, lying down on the ground and scowling up at the sky. Despite the scowl, a smile starts tugging on her lips.

"I'm going to let you in on a secret, Lana."

Curiosity piqued, she looks at me and sits back up again, her eyes dancing no matter how she tries to hide it from me.

"I'm going to marry you," I say.

"Is that right?

"That is absolutely right," I croon, "and you're going to love every single second of being my wife."

"Is that right?"

"That is beyond right, baby."

She leans forward, her breath at my mouth. "I'm going to tell you something, Racer," she says, breathless when she looks at my mouth and at me. "Keep aiming for the moon, and maybe one day, you'll catch a star."

"Baby," I say, cupping the back of her head and leveling my eyes on hers, "I'm aiming to catch me the worst driver in the world."

"Racer!"

I chuckle, and she breathes, as she lies back down, "I'm still looking for the best driver in the world."

I raise my brows meaningfully—*tsk* and shake my head, a sign that she should know better. Then I brace my arms on each of her sides and lean over her, my nose level with hers.

"Look into my eyes and you'll find him," I husk out.

Her chest starts rising and falling.

"You've had him inside you already ..." I cup her where she's hottest. "You have him here." I give a little squeeze, then slide my hand upward, over her dress, and I put my hand on her left breast. "And *here*."

Her eyes are shining and they widen, a little scared. At this point, I've worked myself up to a fever, and my heart is beating like a crazed drum in my chest.

"You love me, Lana," I say.

Her eyes begin to glisten, and she starts to cry.

I'm confused. I sit back for a hot second, watching the tears start to stream as Lana tries to wipe them off.

"Hey, I love you." I reach out to take her wrist and keep her from drying her tears. Instead, I use my free hand to do it and peer into her face. "I've never loved anything this much in my life."

"I only ever said I love you to my family and David." Her tears keep falling onto my thumbs.

"You don't need to say it now. I *know*." I clench my jaw, keeping her face in my hands. "I know."

She drops her face and starts to gather the trash. "Take me back to the hotel."

I stop her. "I won't hurt you."

She raises her head. "Can you honestly promise me that?"

I look down at her, something in my chest on unsteady ground. My voice roughens defensively. "Are you afraid that I'd hurt you or that you'd get hurt because I'm bipolar? Lana."

She ignores my question and gets into the car.

"Take me to my room please."

I slam her car door shut, furious.

I climb into the driver's side, and Lana stares out the window on the drive back to the hotel, keeping those eyes from me.

After walking her to her room, I'm back in mine, a black spiral looming over me as I fight not to get sucked in.

I scrape my hand over my face, staring out the window, sleepless, my fucking heart down the hall and a few doors away, crying and in pain because she loves me.

track

Lana

I toss and turn all night.

I hate him.

I *love* him.

He's taken all my memories of David and replaced them with him. All my love and put his face on it, his stamp on it, now when I think of David … a dimple appears on his cheeks, his soft brown eyes turn bright blue and vivid, and his light brown hair becomes wild and spiky and black.

I sent him a text in the middle of the night—

I'm sorry I just need some space to think. Lana

And it hurt that he answered immediately with a curt **OK**, because it only confirmed the fact that he wasn't sleeping either.

I'm in a bit of a tired and highly wired state the next morning when I spot him at our tent at the side of the track, looking sharp as ever in his black racing suit, with the U.S. flag stitched at his belt, and his new sponsor logos plastered all across his muscular arms and chest—and he looks like everything I will ever possibly want, and like nothing I could have ever imagined myself having, and I don't know whether I want to pull him to the motorhome to tell him that he's right, that he's right and I'm a big ol' coward, or I don't know if I want to run away.

I don't run away though.

I sort of drink him in as he sits at a table with the mechanics and laughs at something Adrian says, and then I see him turn his head to spot me, fold his legs as he pulls them off the table, and come to his feet as he snatches up two coffees from nearby and brings them over.

My heart thuds a thousand and one times. "Good morning." His voice is husky.

"Good morning."

He hands me a cup of coffee, and I laugh and extend his too. "I brought you one too."

"We'll just keep bringing each other coffee until one of us gets it."

"You get it first."

"No. You do." He tweaks my nose and winks. "Couldn't sleep."

"Me neither," I say, breathless.

"I've been racing for quite a few Grand Prix, and I still haven't gotten you to admit I'm the best driver in the world. It won't do." He shakes his head. "My mustang is back in St. Pete, waiting to get fixed."

"*You* banged it up and I'm sure it's fixed already."

"We had a deal," he says. "Are you backing out on me?"

"No. Are you?"

"I never back out on anything," he says, giving me a look that says I'm his, that he'll be patient, that he'll wait.

I want to talk to him, but we're placing amazing in the championship points, fighting for second place with the Clark's second driver, and it's already going beyond my and my family's wildest dreams.

I don't want to bring my personal things here and dump them all in the track, so I hold back and try my best to keep everyone comfortable—and the team performing at their best.

So I just clear my throat and say, "You have six interviews after quali."

"I'm on it."

He looks at me for a second, a look that's secretive and frustrated and determined and melts my bones, and then I watch him with a pang of longing as he go gets ready to drive like the blue-eyed devil that he is.

He has a great qualifying session, coming in P3, so that's where he'll start the race.

I hurry to where he stands by the press, bringing his sponsors cap.

"You forgot this!" I say breathlessly as I reach out and put it on his head, and the cameras seem to love to notice the way he stared at me for an extra second.

"You and your team seem to get along pretty well, Racer, do you think that has anything to do with your marvelous performance so far this year?"

"Lana's my lucky charm," he says, and I'm turning the color of a chili pepper as I walk way, glancing back only to see him continue on with his next interviews—and that's when I notice he's tapping his fingers at his sides.

My stare lingers on those strong, long, restless fingers for a beat more before I chide myself for obsessing on him and everything about him and walk away.

Ever since Racer got P1 I've noticed all the other drivers (except Clark) are hounding him, asking him to hang out, to go out for drinks, etc. I swear it's like everyone is seeing Racer as their own ticket to the podium. As if befriending him will somehow get some of his luck to rub off on them.

Racing is a superstitious sport. Pre-race rituals and lucky charms are a norm. Because everyone knows that to win, you not only need a good car and an insane amount of talent, you need the universe to smile upon you.

So far, Racer has not only shown he has incredible talent, a lot of guts, and a strong car, but he's also shown to be the angels' golden boy.

It seems Racer finally caved in to their advances. I overheard him agree to hit up a party at Jay's, one of the drivers, place. Considering Jay races for one of the top three teams and enjoys a salary in the eight digits, he's got a penthouse in a prestigious London neighborhood, including a top-floor pool and terrace overlooking the city—and apparently there'll be DJs, a dance floor, and lots of girls and booze.

My stomach roiled thinking of Racer showing up there alone, looking absolutely edible with his bedroom eyes and dark head of hair. I can't stand the idea of having girls drape themselves over him, offering him the world and more between their legs.

No. That cannot fucking happen.

That evening, I see myself almost as if I were having an out-of-body experience: I see myself stand from the bed, grab my purse and storm out of my room like a mad woman—a bullet aimed straight at Racer Tate's door.

I'm just going to tell him that there is no way he is going there alone without me because I need to make sure he stays out of trouble and gets back home safe.

Complete bullshit, I know.

But I don't care. I need to go with him.

I knock on his door and he opens up with a towel draped across his hips and his hair spiky with water droplets hanging on to the end.

I swear my jaw drops an inch.

He is man mixed with animal, muscle mixed with danger, sex mixed with seduction.

"Hey you." He smirks at me. Taking his sweet time to look me up and down in my black running shorts and Team HW shirt.

"I … I just wanted to ask if you wanted me to send your racing suit to the dry cleaners."

Racer just frowns.

"Are you still working at this hour?"

"I …" I just look at him.

"I feel like I'm drowning in all this space. I can't breathe, I can't eat, I don't want us to fight anymore," I plead.

He's silent for a moment. "I don't want that either," he husks out. He props a muscled shoulder on the doorframe and looks at me in silence.

"So," I breathe.

"So," he repeats, his deep voice lowering an octave. "Are you going to stand there and make me come get you, or are you going to come here?" he asks.

I don't know why my heart jumps in excitement because I had been hoping we would make up, but the look in his eyes, as if he's still a little frustrated by what happened but is more eager to put that moment behind us, gets to me.

I start walking forward, and he watches me the whole time, making my heart leap more and more.

Before I reach him, his hands shoot out, and he reels me over to his hard body, nuzzles my ear and growls, "Are you going to stop putting up walls for me," he demands.

I nod, breathless.

He smiles a little, looking at my mouth as he steals his hand into my waistband, grabs my butt, and squeezes it as he draws me closer to set a kiss on me that sets my every toe and fingertip on fire—and everything in between.

"Are you mad that I didn't want to talk about it," I ask.

"You fucked me up, girl," he says, taking my chin between his thumb and forefinger and looking piercingly into my eyes.

"I'm sorry," I say. "You're just so much more than I ever bargained for."

There's the slightest upward tilt to his lips, and he almost smiles as he draws me closer. I curl my face to his chest.

"I was planning to come get you at nine. There's a party at Jay's place in the city. Why don't you go and slip into something sexy, I'll stop by in an hour."

He turns and leaves before I have time to come up with something smart to answer, and I'm left freaking out over what to wear.

I hurry back to my own hotel room, and I tear my suitcase apart looking for something to wear to this posh party. I know the girls the drivers hang out with are always models and gorgeous, and I don't want to wear anything short of spectacular.

I want something hot but elegant, and classy. I don't want any of the drivers getting any ideas and it always makes me uncomfortable to have them ogling me. It makes me feel like they don't take me seriously.

But I also want Racer to see me. I don't know why it makes me so high—to feel those blue eyes on me.

I stop at a nude silk dress and feel myself smirk. It's perfect. Backless with a high halter neckline tied with a bow at the back of my neck, leaving two long silk strands hanging down my exposed back. It's a little bit above the knee, but the material clings to me like a second skin.

Racer, baby, you're going to die.

I get my hair tools and curl my hair at the tips, then run my hands through them to give my hair a messy bedroom look to go with the silk dress. I don't travel with a lot of accessories but I add my usual pearl studs to my ears, and am grateful for my single pair of strappy sandals that I use for the important racing events.

I put on blush, mascara, and a bit of liner only on the top eyelid then run some dark rose lipstick over my lips. Just when I'm spraying a bit of perfume on my wrist I hear a knock on the door and I almost trip over my heels going to answer it.

I open and there stands Racer, in black slacks and a white button-down, cuffs rolled up, a small platinum chain I had never seen before glistening on his exposed collarbone. Ugh I can't take this man. Every time I see him I want to climb him like a tree and wrap my legs around him like vines. I don't know whether to cuddle him or let him fuck the shit out of me because the look he has on right now tells me he's thinking of just that.

His eyes look primal as he stares at my belly, then my breasts, then down to my legs, and up at my face again. I see his hands fist and unfist at his sides and his jaw tick.

"Fuck, are you trying to kill me," he growls.

I smile and do a little twirl, just to rile him up, and I don't know what happened to me but when I put on this dress and saw him looking so delectable I decided to throw all caution to the wind.

He's all I want.

Tonight's my night off. And so is his.

He comes toward me and wraps his hand around my neck, blue eyes staring intensely at me before dropping down to my chest. He places a kiss right at my cleavage and rubs his nose back and forth, before licking a small path from my cleavage up my neck, and jaw, to my lips.

"Let's go," he murmurs.

We get to Jay's London apartment and the drivers are already there, mingling and drinking with their dates of the night. Some of these women are over six feet tall and dressed in the latest European fashions. Some of the drivers came solo but most of them came with girls in tow.

The moment Jay opens the door, I hear the boys basically clamor to come greet the man I'm standing next to.

"Racer, man, looking good!" They slap him welcome, and Racer tugs me next to him with his hand on mine.

The drivers are trying to shake his hand all at the same time, so I pry my hand free, noticing him frown down at me as Jay leads him in, patting him on the back. "What's your poison, Tate? Vodka, tequila, whiskey? You look like a whiskey man, let me pour you some ..." He trails off and comes back carrying two glasses filled with an amber-colored liquid.

"Nah I don't drink."

"Oh, shit, seriously man? Well I mean we have other things to make this night special ..."

Oh, shit, really? What are they going to bring him? Girls?

Feeling out of place, because I've never really spent any time with the drivers—I suppose partying hard isn't my thing, and I've never been interested in one (until *now*)—I start making my way to the bathroom and turn back to see Racer caged in by some of the drivers introducing their dates and also pushing for him to have a little drink.

I turn away and get to the bathroom, closing the door behind me and putting my hands on the sink, ducking my head between.

I don't know why coming here tonight with Racer has me feeling like a charged ball of nerves.

I hear the door open next to me and I turn to tell whoever it is to get the fuck out but I see Racer come in. My mouth stops moving and then snaps shut.

"Racer, I would like a little privacy if that's okay with—"

I gasp as he shuts me up with his mouth crashing down on mine. He kisses me out of my mind, until all thoughts and nervousness go silent. He starts making out with me, lifting me by the ass to the edge of the sink and wrapping my legs around him so that he's nestled right between my legs. I can feel him, hard as steel, through his trousers and I moan into his mouth, bringing him closer to me, wrapping my arms around his neck and nestling my fingers into the hair at the back of his neck.

He kisses down my jaw and I thrum head to toe.

"Aren't we just the epitome of teenage lust right now," I murmur as my lungs struggle to work.

"We're not teenagers and this isn't lust, baby," he murmurs back, digging his hands into my ass to bring me closer to him as his mouth works along my jaw and neck.

I hear Redbone by Childish Gambino play in the background, the low pounding melody pulling all my control along with it, and the sultry vocals making me arch my back as I let myself be in the moment. Carried along with it.

His mouth comes back to mine and starts to open mine slowly.

He's enjoying every second of this, making every kiss feel like the best kiss I've ever received until the next one comes, even better than the last.

There's a knock on the door. "*Hey! I need to pee,*" I hear someone call from outside.

I struggle to catch my breath as Racer eases back and looks at me wolfishly.

He shakes his head no and starts to slide his hands up my dress, his thumbs caressing my inner thighs.

Fuck, he just made it so much harder for me to want to get out of this room …

I open my legs a little more for him and kiss him harder.

"We didn't finish last night. I was going to flood your insides with me," he smirks, his eyes brilliant.

"I ... that makes me a little nervous," And so *hot*. "But ..."

He strokes his thumb down my cheek, and I sense him more intense than usual, his eyes blue but a little darker shade of blue, his smile cocky, territorial, possessive, as he leans down to lick me.

"As much as I want to do that," he murmurs, seizing the back of my neck to kiss me deeply again and again. "I'm going to wait until you reciprocate before I do."

dad talk

Lana

The touches don't stop.

(Lucky meeee.)

Racer looks at me intensely, making me feel as if I'm his. We just reached Belgium. Racer has been relentless these past races—London, Hungary. We are seven races away from the final, in Abu Dhabi, and holding P2 in the points championship.

He sends me well kissed to my room every night. I'm a ball of wanting and lust and love—he's breaking me down and I know it.

"You look different, Lainie. Very … refreshed."

"Thank you, Daddy."

"There's that twinkle in your eye and glow to your cheeks."

He's staring at me with a smile.

"Daddy, come on," I say, taking a seat as I place our healthy yogurt and granola breakfasts before us.

I love Belgium. The track here—the Circuit de Spa-Francorchamps—is the most beautiful I've ever seen. Amidst rolling hills and a world of green trees, it's also the most challenging track because of its twisted curves and up/down inclines.

"You're in love," he says. He looks childlike. Laughing.

"Dad," I say, frowning as I open my yogurt. But my cheeks feel hot.

"You're in love, Lainie." He reaches out and pats my cheek. "Real love."

"Why do you say that?" I ask.

"I have a pair of eyes. And … a father's intuition."

I flush, scooping yogurt and eating granola as I scan the people around the hotel coffee shop to distract myself. My dad is looking at me all this time.

"See, from the moment that boy walked into my hotel room in Australia, I could feel the charge between you two."

"Dad!" I say, laughing and frowning as I open his yogurt. "Come on, eat."

"He feels the same," he says, as if he's assuring me as he takes a spoonful.

"Is that your dad intuition? Are you his father too?"

He chuckles and licks yogurt off his spoon, pointing at me with that boyish look on his face. "Male intuition. Quite powerful. Plus that boy doesn't even try to be subtle about it. Hell, he'll stare even when your brothers throw him a thousand dragons' fires with their eyes."

I laugh, then I just stare at my dad, craving for him to tell me more.

"He's a good kid. A bit of a handful, but you survived your dad and three brothers, so I think you can handle yourself," he says.

"I'm afraid," I whisper.

"Why?"

Silence. I just can't put into words the way it hurts to even be apart from him. The way I crave everything about him, adore everything about him.

"Of getting hurt?" he asks me, peering into my face.

I nod.

"Don't think that way. If I'd been afraid to open our team because we'd lose, I'd be on a couch somewhere, slowly dying."

"Daddy, don't talk like that."

"It's true. These past months, I've lived more than I had in years with your mom."

"But see, Daddy … You got hurt. You two thought you'd be together forever."

"We all get hurt. The question is: Who do you love enough, trust enough, and want enough to give the power to hurt you?"

He looks out at the streets and aims his gaze in the direction of the track.

"You race a car, you can die in an instant. And yet there they are. When you love it enough, it's worth it."

"We really had to talk about it in car terms, didn't we." I sigh.

He laughs, and I take his hand. "You look well."

"I'm doing okay." His eyes shutter as if he doesn't want to tell me something, and my stomach tightens a little. But he smiles next and starts eating his yogurt, and I relax and eat mine, marveling how well my father knows me …

Also marveling that I can feel this light, this happy, this blissful in my life. I cannot get enough of Racer, of being near him, talking to him, teasing him, looking at him, touching him, kissing him.

Racer appears, and the sight of him in a grey hoodie and comfortable track pants as he walks the line for coffee makes me drool. His hair looks a little spiky today, damp from a recent bath and black as midnight. My knees feel mushy as I hop to my feet and approach him, aware of a pair of girls seated at the far end ogling him from afar and frantically snapping pictures of him.

"Hey," I greet, a familiar warmth sweeping over me as his eyes flick down to me. "I'll get your coffee, you go sit with my dad."

He glances at my dad, then at me, and it feels as if there's something so hot inside of him that his eyes look like pools of tender heat. "Lana. I want to talk to your dad, formally date you."

My eyes go wide.

His eyes sparkle with devilish playfulness as I open my mouth, but I can't say a thing.

A wave of giddiness washes over me, but I wave it off as I wave off his comment.

"He'll likely say no anyway, so don't make any dinner reservations."

I say this mostly teasingly but Racer teases me right back, leaning forward enough that I quickly sense the girls in the restaurant shooting jealous glances my way.

"Get a sexy outfit ready, I mean to take you out—repeatedly." He allows me a glimpse of his dimple before he heads off to order his coffee, and I head back to my dad, feeling frustrated that he won't let me take care of him like all the men in my life do.

"G'morning, Mr. Heyworth," Racer greets minutes later in his low, deep voice as he joins us at the table. I shove a spoonful of yogurt into my mouth to try to hide the way I'm blushing.

"Well, no rain in the forecast ..." my dad begins, because the weather is always such a huge part of a racing weekend. "You glad for that?"

"Wet or dry, I can handle my ride," Racer answers.

Gosh, I must have sex on the brain because I choke a little and both men glance at me in concern—but then Racer's gaze seems to shift as he realizes what I must be thinking. And that damn dimpled smile appears as, beneath the table, he reaches out and gives my thigh one tight little squeeze.

I can barely keep my heart from stumbling on every damn beat as they keep talking race cars, and I keep waiting for that look, that stolen touch, that dimple, those eyes, this man.

Racer

"So you, Racer Tate, my number one, want to date my daughter?"

I watch Lana's father across the desk in his hotel room as he deliberates on what I just asked him. "Yes, sir."

"Seems to me you were already dating her?"

"I want to do it with your permission."

I drum my fingers on my thighs. This is fucking important. There's sweat on my damn neck and I don't think I ever expected to be right where I am—sitting here, asking for a father to let me date his daughter. He's my boss, a man I work with and fucking respect. Lana is also crazy about him. So I sit in this damn chair, because when I asked for a word with him this morning, and Lana's father told me to sit down if I wanted to chat, I parked my ass down and it's damned well staying here until I get what I want.

"You have my permission," her father agrees, watching me closely. "On the condition you vow that you won't lose focus, Tate. What you've been doing this year ..." He trails off, shaking his head in bewilderment as he motions to me with both hands. "I have never, in my *wildest* dreams, imagined HW Racing would come this far. I owe that to you—that drive of yours, something I've never seen in my lifetime. Even with past champions."

"Thank you, sir. I owe the opportunity to you and Lana." I nod, still drumming my fingers.

Heyworth glances at my hands. I stand up and brace my feet apart and cross my arms, trying to steady myself. I hold eye contact, my voice determined. "I care about your daughter as much as I do about the championship, and I won't fail you in either case."

"Good." He stands too and comes around the desk to look at me.

"My daughter …" His expression softens, and his voice changes. "If I ever thought that you'd hurt her, Tate, I would see to it that you never set eyes on her again. Even if I had to sacrifice my team in the process," he warns.

"I understand, sir."

"I've never seen her this happy. Never. Even before you came along," he adds, slapping me on the back.

My chest swells like he just blew all the air in the planet into my lungs.

Fuck me.

I make her happy.

"Thank you, sir." I nod and Heyworth grabs his room key and his sponsors cap. "Okay then. Now back to business. We have a race to catch. Let's get this show on the road."

He doesn't need to tell me twice.

We cross the hotel lobby. Lana waits for us by the car, speaking on the phone—maybe future hotel reservations, or plane tickets, or lunch.

My damn brain gets away from me.

She's standing in the middle of the parking lot. In the skimpiest little shorts I've ever seen on a girl. I can see her breasts under her T-shirt; her ass perfectly hugged by those shorts; her lovely toned legs exposed; her hair up in a ponytail.

She speaks on the phone and her lips are moving, but her eyes—yeah, those beauties are on me.

I keep walking. My damn heart kicks faster and harder into my ribs. My hands clench as my mind keeps running away from me.

And it really gets away from me.

I see her in my place at St. Pete. I see her with my kids, our kids. I see her in bed every morning. I see her sleeping in my arms, every damn night. I see her driving my car, laughing because I can't stop giving her instructions on how to shift gears right. I see her and cannot stop seeing her. I see her smiling, laughing, her lips shaping my name as I feed her everything in me and of me and about fucking me.

I exhale and shove my hands into my jeans as we reach her. Hell I'm trying to get a grip of my damn dick which responded to all that, which knows shit about manners considering her dad is next to me.

"Good morning, boys!" she greets us.

"Morning," her dad says with a smile, kissing her cheek.

She glances up at me next. Her smile even more fucking extraordinary than the last. Every muscle in my body engages. Every fiber of my body and synapse in my brain fires the hell up with her near.

I nod at her in a good morning and head up to open her car door, taking the keys her father extends out to me as he takes the passenger seat.

She slides in and brushes my hand with hers as she does, and my hands itch to touch her so much that I shut the door and clench them in fists as I come around to take the wheel and take us to the track.

Once we arrive the guys are working on the cars, and I watch Lana disappear into the motorhome, giving me a look. I follow after her.

Lana

"What did my dad say," I ask the man who's taken over my every thought as I hear him come in behind me.

"You're mine," he whispers, pressing in behind me, his hands all over me all of a sudden.

The vibrations coming from his low, manly groans are transferred over to me through his hot mouth. They make me tingle all over. His fingers start to play with the low hem of my shorts and I feel his erection through his racing suit. I almost laugh against his mouth because those suits are made of thick stuff. But apparently he's made of thicker stuff ...

I tilt my head back and feel my eyes roll towards the back of my skull as he lazily starts to suck the side of my neck.

"You better not give me a hickey," I breathe. As if he would ever listen.

"Hmm, really? That makes me more determined to give you one," he murmurs mischievously.

He's been so cocky. So territorial. So ... hot for me.

I feel his hand up my shorts, and his fingers start to rub my lips against my panties. My breath catches in my throat. I feel my panties getting soaked and his satisfied male groan tells me he likes my body's reaction to his touch. He reaches up to tear my tee over my head and my shorts off my body so that I'm standing naked in front of him except for my thong. Which he immediately takes care of, ripping the fabric and tossing it to the side as he pushes my legs apart.

"Racer," I breathe, burying my face in his neck, feeling exposed.

He kisses the top of my head and leans back a bit, boosting me up on his arms and carrying me to the small office in the back of the motorhome.

"Shh baby, let me see," he croons as he sets me down on the desk and shuts the door behind us.

I'm so wet I think I'm going to leave a wet mark on the desk. I tell Racer this and he curses, "Fuck that's hot, baby."

We're in the motorhome at the track.

And funny thing is, Racer seems to think this is his own personal home at the track.

He immediately pushes the team's laptop to the side of the desk, leaving the desktop empty except for a small lamp, and me.

He closes the blinds a half an inch more than they were already closed, the sunlight stealing through the slats, cutting lines of light across his handsome face.

"Racer, someone can come in and I'll be naked," I warn.

He clucks, and I know he locked the door, but still …

"Whoever does decide to come in here is a very, very stupid and unlucky man."

I laugh at his protectiveness and arch my back against his hand, which is now rubbing the inside of my thigh, dangerously close to my pussy. Yet so far away at the same time.

He looks sinfully hot in his tight black undershirt and racing suit with the sleeves tied at his hips. His blazing blue eyes pinning me down to the desk and his hot mouth begging me to kiss it.

He leans down towards me and kisses me deeply, stroking the inside of my mouth with his tongue, "You're so gorgeous," he tells me right before I feel a finger push inside me. I moan, pretty loudly, against his mouth and he just takes this as further invitation to keep doing what he's doing. He brings my legs up so that my feet are on the edge of the desk, with my knees spread apart framing him in between. His finger pumps in and out of me and I can feel him hitting the sweetest spot.

Hitting it every single time.

I can't control my noises at this point as I move my hips against his hand. His fingers leave me and I look up to see him take his glistening middle and index finger and put them in his mouth, sucking them and looking at me possessively.

I vaguely hear him say "yummy" before he sticks them back inside me, this time giving it to me faster and harder. Just when I'm about to come he stops and takes a step back.

"Racer, are you serious!" I half-heartedly protest.

He smirks and kisses the inside of my thigh. "Let me do what I want. I promise you'll love it."

He strips off until he's all naked except for his tight white boxers, which are basically ripping at the seams with his erection.

My heartbeat stalls as I take him in, all muscle, tanned golden skin, with a face so strikingly beautiful it would make any angel fall in love, and every devil fall in lust.

This time, when he comes back to me, he falls to his knees, wrapping his arms around my thighs.

My breath and my heart both stop when I realize what he's about to do and my only thought is holy fucking shit.

Something tells me this man can please a woman like none other and I don't even know if I'm ready for what he wants to give.

"I ... Racer, are you sure you want to ... right now, I mean we're ..."

He looks up at me with his beautiful, dangerous blue eyes. Which right now look like they are on fire with need, turning a deep dark hungry blue.

"I've wanted to do this ever since I saw you step into the elevator wearing your little pink skirt and wearing your little racing hat and I knew I wanted you spread out in front of me, just like this, with my head buried between your legs and you screaming out my name."

He stops and reaches out to squeeze my waist, planting a kiss by my bellybutton, rubbing his nose back and forth against my skin and then groaning, "Please let me do this to you."

If I was wet before, I am soaking now, and I have never wanted anything more than him to do just that.

I nod and spread my legs further and he gives me a little smile, flashing me his dimple, as he dips his head.

I expect him to go right to it but instead he turns his head and licks the point where my inner thigh joins my pelvis, right where my panty lines go.

My body joints at the feel of his hot wet tongue on the sensitive skin there. I moan a little and grip the edges of the desk.

He kisses and sucks there, and I hear him murmur devilishly, a gruff tone, "I think this is where I'll give you your hickey ..."

I can't even laugh at that because it feels so good I am nothing but sensations.

His tongue on my skin, his hands gripping my hips, his hair grazing my stomach, my back touching the mahogany wood below me, my hair dangling down the edge of the desk, my nipples hard against the cool air.

He switches to my other leg, and start to lick and suck along my hip and inner thigh. It's so close to my clit I want to scream with frustration but I also never want him to stop.

Just when I think I can't take another second he moves closer to where I want him to go and starts to lick my outer lips, stopping occasionally to suck a little bit when he finds a spot he likes.

I'm dying at this point and he hasn't even done anything to me directly.

He slips a finger inside and I do just what he wants me to. I say his name. Really loud.

His tongue starts to lick from where his finger is to my clit and I arch my back, losing all control at the feel of it.

I look down to see his manly hand wrapped around one of my legs, his dark head of hair bent down over me, nestled between my open legs, his lips wrapping around me, sucking, releasing, kissing, licking, and then repeating—I've never seen anything so hot in my life.

He looks like he's eating chocolate cake.

He spreads my legs out even more and keeps slowly fucking me with his finger, his mouth basically making out with my clit.

He's just as into this as I am and that makes me even hotter as I feel myself getting so close to the edge. My muscles clench and release against his fingers. I gasp and shake. I feel vulnerable and just as if he can read my mind, I feel his other hand gently pry my fingers off the edge of the desk so that he can hold my hand.

Meanwhile his face is buried between my legs, making me feel my blood pulse harder and my heart race.

I can't take it anymore and I arch my back as I come with a scream, my legs shaking and my muscles clenching.

He stays there and kisses me softly before standing up and looking at me with his deep blue eyes, his chin wet with my juices, and the sight makes me melt.

He is so damn sexy I don't even know who could create such a being.

I suddenly crave him closer. I need his kiss, so I wrap my legs around his hips and bring him to me, opening my arms up to him like a child, letting him know I need him here.

He bends down and embraces me completely, enveloping me in his warmth. He kisses my neck and showers kisses along my collarbones, my jawline, and then my mouth.

"Please fuck me," I beg.

I already came but I need him inside me. Now. More than ever.

He swiftly takes off his boxers and slowly pushes inside me, stretching me out and filling me up so much I feel like he's going to pop put of my stomach.

I gasp because he feels so good. He wraps his arms around me and holds me up at an angle before he starts to slide in and out of me. And it feels so good, hitting just the right spot, I basically come again. He pounds in and out of me and I tilt my head back, unable to control my moans.

He lays me back down on the desk, bringing my hips right to the edge and then wrapping my legs around his shoulders. Then he leans forward a bit, bringing my legs towards my chest, and thrusts deeper and I scream his name again because he is in so deep I don't even know if I can take it.

His jaw clenches as he keeps pounding into me, little beads of sweat glistening on his collarbones.

I gasp, "God, Racer, I'm there ..."

He starts to pound faster and I come, clenching around him, my body pulsating after my release. He scoops me up in his arms and sits down on a leather chair by the window, completely enveloping me in his warmth, his mouth whispering sweet things into my ear. That he's crazy about me, that nothing turns him the fuck on like me ...

It's then I realize his erection is still pulsing fiercely against my bottom and I look up at him, confused.

"Tate ... did you not? Why didn't you finish?" I ask, confused and breathless, and before I can have a complete freak-out thinking I had done something terribly wrong he just smirks, flashing me that sexy dimple of his and he says, "I'm denying myself until I finish the race. I want to be pumped up and full of adrenaline—and amped to take on the Clarks."

He then plants a warm kiss on my breast. "And nothing gets me riled up as much as you do." He winks.

Wow. My mouth hangs open. I simply cannot believe this man has the willpower to fuck me senseless, give me multiple orgasms, and then not let himself finish—all so that he can use all that pent-up energy on the race track.

"Are you for real?" I laugh.

"I'm fucking high on you. On how fucking amazing it is to be me." He pulls out of me—his dick so thick, long and hard that I can trace the bulging veins running up his throbbing length—and he maneuvers it into his boxers and zips up his racing suit, cracking his neck from side to side. "I'm never coming down from this high."

"Is that right?" I say, giggling as I watch him.

"That's right," he assures, giving me a wolfish grin.

I laugh, giddy.

Sighing, I ease up to a sit, fixing myself up too.

He starts coming over, grasping the back of my head and murmuring at the top of my ear. "You look good enough to eat," he rasps, sliding his hand over my cheek and pressing his smiling lips to my jaw. He nibbles on me.

"Racer ... Racer 2.0 ..." I giggle and moan. Lately he just seems like Racer Tate on steroids. A version of him in double the intensity (if that's even possible) ... Racer 2.0.

"Yeah," he croons, and he starts to kiss me, and I can tell he needs me, that he wants to come inside me so bad, because his kiss is crazy hot.

My lips swell, and it's a good swell. A great swell. And my heart follows. Something in my chest shudders and grows. I know deep in my gut that something isn't quite right. He's a little sexy and reckless and crazy right now, being more territorial, more demanding, tireless. I'm not supposed to like him like this, but the truth is that I do. I should be concerned, making sure he's okay, but he's so sexy and charming ... and happy. I love seeing him so happy, and it's impossible not to get caught up in it ... in him.

He makes me want him more, want to have him and protect him, and be there for him when he needs me because I always seem to need *him*.

I embrace him to me and kiss his dimple, whispering, "You're okay, Racer?" and peering into his gorgeous face.

And gosh, it's a gorgeous face. Wearing the most gorgeous dimpled grin.

He pecks my lips as he helps me to my feet, his eyes roaming over me, looking at me in a really sexy and territorial

way, and I run my fingers along my inside upper thigh, touching the hot little hickey he left me as he says, "Yeah," keeping
his glinting blue eyes on me for a long time.

I watch him finally charge out as if he's on steroids, and I
drop my hand from the mark. It's a small mark, really, compared to the chunks he keeps biting off my heart.

nose to gearbox

Racer

I'm simmering with energy, my dick hard as rock after stopping myself from blowing up inside my warm, wet Lana. I'm ready to prove myself to the Heyworths. To her. It's me against 22 assholes, all with fast as fuck cars.

It's hard to pass in this track—twists and turns like a rollercoaster, the moment we get green flag, the track's got my heart pumping and my lungs working like mad. Every one of my muscles is engaged as I twist and turn, accelerate and brake.

The Clark's #2 driver tries to push me off the track when I try to pass him, and I spin and take a few seconds to regain control. I pull back onto the track, losing position. My anger mounts, and suddenly I'm shifting gears and charging back after him.

"Car ok?" Clay asks.

"Yeah, I think so but it's fucked up in the straight."

"Shit. Use your talent."

"Hell I am."

I try to recover my place, and it takes me a full lap to get back behind P2.

I'm biding my time, upshifting as I get closer, aiming my nose cone at the gearbox behind Clark's #2 driver car.

No one fucks with me—and gets away with it.

I narrow my eyes, my heartbeat slow and steady.

My car rumbles down the straightaway, the wheel shuddering in my hands, the seat vibrating from the power. I stay on point. If the nose hits a moving part, like a wheel, it'll fly off and I'll get fucked. And yeah, that's not the point.

If our wheels lock, we'll spin and crash. Maybe even flip.

That's not the point either.

Eyes narrowed as I aim, I aim for the gearbox, outbrake him, and touch my nose to his gearbox and take him out—I watch as dust flies behind him and he spins off the track. *Arrivederci, fucker* ...

I upshift and push forward and watch, through my rearview mirror, as he tries to recover and pass me; his aim fails. His nose touches my wheels, and I flip him. The car flips and flies across the track.

"Holy shit," I hear on the radio. "You all right?"

"Dandy."

I smile and approach a heavy braking turn, after P1.

This car's got a lot of torque—torque is acceleration power, and horsepower is velocity. When you've got both of these working for you, you're flying.

"There's a yellow flag of caution. Debris on track."

"Got it."

A yellow light is flashing at the wheel. We all need to slow down—we cannot pass until we get green again.

We drive around for two laps and green flashes.

I jump the green flag, accelerating to full speed and jumping the start without being too obvious or I get a pit drive-through penalty.

I wait to see if I get away with it, I think I do. I upshift and hear myself growl and narrow my eyes at Clark up ahead.

Oh yeah, I'm coming for you.

moves

Lana

"**T**hat move, damn I get hard thinking about it," Clay laughs.

"Clayton," I chide.

Drake comes and smacks a kiss on my cheek. "Epic, Lainie baby. He took Clark the fuck out!"

"It was risky," I say, frowning at Racer.

He shrugs, sipping on a dark coffee after dining by our motorhome at the track.

"What's up with you and Clark," Clay asks.

"We're competitors," Drake says, "You know that."

I wait for a moment, and Racer finally speaks, in a growl, "He wants what's mine."

My brothers' brows rise simultaneously, and I expect them to say something but oddly enough, no one says a word. Not even Drake.

Right then, Clark enters the tent.

"Lainie, you got one of those for me?" He reaches out to obnoxiously steal the bottled water I was sipping from.

Before my brothers can blink and in shocking, fluid lightning-fast speed that I'd never seen on a guy before, Racer is on his feet, snatching back the water and stepping in before Clark and me.

"You touch her or anything of hers again, I'm breaking your hand," I hear him warn in a chillingly cold voice, reaching behind us to put it back on the table before me.

I peer past his body to notice how Clark sort of turns bright red all over as Racer stares him down.

"Try driving with a bad hand. Your career will be over. *You're* fucking over," Racer adds in a cold and menacing tone. I can tell that he means it—and it sends warning little frissons down my spine.

I notice that my brothers' eyes are wide with a mix of respect, shock, and admiration, but I, on the other hand, am weak in the knees. Something about the way Racer is standing, staring Clark down, the way the entire air seems to burn around him, makes me react.

Nobody's ever stepped up to me like he does—and while a part of me is thrumming to reach out and kiss him in thank you, another wants to calm down the volcano before it erupts.

I reach out and put my hand on his, and Racer's shoulders relax slightly, his nostrils flaring as he takes my hand firmly in his grip and leads me down the track.

"What are you doing? If it had been any earlier the TVs could've captured that …!" I cry, eyeing his handsome, frowning profile in disbelief. "What? You're going to get ready to beat everyone who's a jerk to me?"

"That's the plan."

"No, that's not the plan. The plan is you ignore them. We don't make a scene." I smile over the primitive possessive gleam in his eye, but my smile fades to worry. "Are you okay?"

He notices my concern, and his shoulders relax even more as he says, "Yeah," and he smiles and leans his head to me, and pecks my lips, and I want the kiss so much that I almost break when my body bends in an arch for more.

"Racer," I breathe. I want you, I need you, you turn me on.

I part my lips, and he steals his tongue inside as if knowing what I need.

"Are you wet, Lana?"

"Yes," I breathe.

"Wet for me." He drags his lips against mine, breathing harshly, his body coiled tight and hard against mine as he keeps seductively dragging his lips along mine, both parted, our breaths mingling, my whole body tittering on the edge of losing control.

"Yes," I breathe. "Touch me, please Racer."

"Get in my car."

He looks at me, and I open my mouth to keep ranting, but our eyes lock and I can see the wild jealousy in his eyes as he looks at me.

I climb in the passenger seat, and he climbs behind the wheel, and it's another convertible. He lowers the top, and the wind flaps on my hair, making me close my eyes as the wind hits me and he blasts the music—*Animal* by Def Leppard—on the stereo.

He sets his hand on my thigh, and it takes all my effort not to pull it up between my legs and ask him to touch me there. "You have my father to thank for my amazing music taste," he says.

"Oh. Thank you, Racer's dad." I grin.

He grins back.

He's still looking edgy and restless, and very, very hot.

He screeches down each turn, leaving skid marks behind us and making me feel like I'm on a roller coaster until he parks us at a lone spot where there are plenty of trees as cover, and he climbs out fast, then he comes to open my door and guides me to the clearing. I lie down on a flat spot on the grass and thrum inside when he lowers himself above me. I'm hungry, panting, and Racer grabs my face and presses his mouth down on mine, groaning when I open.

He kisses me and fondles my face with his fingers, his tongue tasting and taking everything while his hands simply hold my face in place—my body lax and breathless, toe-curling, tingling in every pore—as Racer's tongue moves and takes. And takes. And takes.

"One day soon, I'm going to fuck you bareback, and there won't ever need to be anything between us again," he rumbles, pulling off his tee and unbuttoning and unzipping his jeans. "Touch me, Lana." He plants my hands on his chest and I run my fingers over those rippling muscles.

"Racer."

"Under my jeans," he commands, shoving one of my hands under his boxers. Where he is hot as hell. Hard as steel. I slide my fingers up his hard cock, and he groans and nuzzles my nose with his, breathing hard. "Are you playing me, Alana?" he asks quietly, pulling back to look down at me—so gorgeous that the sight of him, messy hair and bare chest and blue eyes above me cause my saliva glands to flood.

"No," I breathlessly admit.

"I'm trying to be real with you. Level with me, Lana," he husks out as he grabs my arms and guides them around him, my fingers locking at his nape.

"I'm scared okay." I take his head and pull him down so that he kisses me, helping him shove his jeans and boxers down to his hips and then lower.

His erection pops out, and I'm burning and clutching everywhere for him.

"You think you can't ever care for me?" He watches me curiously, blue eyes male and intimate as he rolls on a condom.

"No! It's ..."

"Let me love you." He presses his forehead to mine, his rough whisper making my heart squeeze. "Love me back, baby." He cups my face in one hand and asks it reverently, as if he doesn't deserve to ask but is still asking, and then I curl my legs around him and Racer impales me without even a moment's hesitation.

He fills and stretches my walls so much I feel like exploding. I gasp and groan, letting him fill me even deeper as he drives in again.

Our mouths fuse and suddenly our hands cannot get enough of feeling each other, our tongues tasting each other. We move together on the grass, his thrusts sure and expert and also possessive. My body arches up like a bow, silently asking for more, my hands clawing at his back, my body wanting just to get closer, to get all of him.

I cannot get enough of him or his kisses, his hot tongue and warm hands.

Especially his eyes. That drink me in as if he cannot get enough of me.

I'm overcome by the passion, the lust, the way he moves in me as if he's known my body in another life. Oh god ...

And he moves, so RIGHT ...

so fast ... hard ... so raw ...

his mouth everywhere ... hands everywhere ... this fucking *boy* everywhere ...

Hands on my hips gripping me as we go off, coming together,

looking into each other's eyes as we do.

I'm left gaping up at him after. At this sex fiend.

Will it always be like this?

I'm dazed and smiling happily as I catch my breath, and Racer is smirking, looking down at my rumpled form with satisfaction as he treks his eyes along my features and presses a kiss to my nose.

"Why do you like me on the headset," I breathe as he remains inside me, looking at me as if he wants to do it again.

"I feel like you're there with me." He looks down at me, his eyes a little dark and vivid with intensity. "I like racing, because it's a very independent sport, there's only you and the car when it comes down to it. I like the feeling of being alone." His sharp blue gaze seems to dig right into me as his cock begins to thicken again. "Never wanted anyone to share that until I met you. I don't want to be alone anymore."

He grins at me, starting to move inside me, starting to kiss me and heat me back up, and he's irresistible, the grin, the boy, all of it.

pendulum

Racer

My dad once said I could feel it coming when I felt myself swing, like a pendulum, from one side to the other.

I'm the freaking embodiment of a pendulum right now.

We flew to Italy; during the flight I hunkered down with my music, trying to get my damn focus back.

Thoughts keep racing in my head nonstop now—preventing sleep. Preventing any peace of mind. It's been two hours since I dropped her off at her room, and I'm blue as fuck.

It's been building up, the mood swings, first, the high on my power and my strength, the high of fucking claiming her as *mine*.

And now the damn low is coming.

The monsters telling me, I'm an asshole. That she has enough worries with her dad, enough pain having lost the boy she loved, enough pain for me to bring mine on.

And yet I can't fucking keep away.

Those damn eyes call to me like a siren song, every piece of her magnetizes me.

I fucking crave her like air.

I've been piling up the championship points. I'm currently second place between the two Clark drivers, and I need another first to knock my prime competition out of P1. I can't fucking afford to go dark now.

Exhaling, I pull out my rope and jump on it, something my father does to calm himself down when he's "speedy," as my mom calls it.

Jumping rope doesn't help. From manic I'm swinging now to depression, replacing the former urge to go to her room and wake her up, steal her away into the damned sunset, take her to church and fucking marry her, to now wanting to disappear from her life and save her from me.

FUCK.

I rummage through my duffel, stare at my pills, wondering if I should take them. Makes me slower. Makes my thinking slower. Makes me feel dead.

And I know, sure as fuck, that it won't help to take my damn pills now. I'm immersed in this shit now—it'll have to be something jammed up my veins to balance me out.

Tell her you're having trouble ...

No. Fuck, that's not what I want.

Lana has been hurt before. And a part of me keeps niggling at me, telling me I'm a bastard for wanting her for me when I'm not good enough for her.

But deep down, I know I am.

I know she's mine.

I know she was meant for me; that she's the one for me.

I'm fucking good enough.

But when an episode looms it's hard to believe that I am.

I wanted freedom in my life, and now all I want is for this girl to love me.

I grab the stuff for my duffel and shove them in, then stop, clenching my hands.

I slam my fist into the table. "FUCK!"

I clench my jaw; my pride sore for having to ask, even my dad. I'm a guy who likes to need no one. I like doing my things, feeling good. Feeling this low and worthless isn't me. So I know after a whole night, I'm screwed.

I feel animal.

I stroke my hand across my hair and dial the only number I dial at times like this.

"Dad."

I can tell he knows it's on. There's a silence, and he says, "I'll get the pilots ready. Be there tonight. Italy. Right?"

"Right."

"Son?"

I pause on the line.

"Don't do anything stupid until I get there."

I just hang up, calculating how far the nearest body of water is, trying to stop thinking of how much I want to tie an anchor on my feet and throw myself in.

It's like a switch goes off, and death seems better, just less of a hassle, death is peace, life is misery.

I growl and grab my keys and head to my rental, drive to the hospital, my phone ringing off the hook.

It's the Heyworths.

I don't want to say the wrong thing, do the wrong thing. I power off my phone, driving and turning on the music. Fall

Out Boy has another good one, it's called Jet Pack Blues, where the lady on the road tempts him to come home.

black hole

Lana

Love me back ...

I shower early in the morning for practice for the Italian Grand Prix, then slip on my jeans and my team T-shirt. I want to do something pretty with my hair, so I blow-dry it and let it down, then I add some lipstick and look at myself again.

"Tell him," I tell myself. *Tell him how you feel,* I think, and I'm so determined to tell him that I even smile at myself in contentment as I head to the track.

"Where's Tate?" Drake asks when I arrive and anxiously scan our tent for the familiar sight of Racer in his Nomex suit.

"I don't know." I start in surprise. "He's not here?"

"Not here. Not in his room," Clay says in obvious worry and puzzlement.

"What?" I ask, and I grab my cell and dial ... only to go directly to voicemail.

"We've already left a dozen messages, don't even bother," Clay says, sighing and plopping down on a chair.

I still dial again. Get voicemail.

"Hey. It's Lana. Um, Alana," I try to make light of it. "Call me?"

An hour later, I'm with my heart in my throat. Three hours later, there's a black hole in my life where Racer used to be. All I know is that he's gone and that my stomach is in knots because I sense, deep down, that he needs me. That he's proud, that it'll cost him everything to tell me that he needs me. All I know is that I'm lost without him, and that the last time I remembered this feeling was the day they told me my dad had cancer and was refusing treatment.

italy

Racer

I hear him arrive sometime early morning.

I'm already checked in, getting shit up my veins. The doctor treating me called my doctor in St. Pete, and they're now giving me the same treatment they did last time to try level me out.

When I got diagnosed, worst thing was the frustration and guilt my dad battled with. I, on the other hand, battled with the shit-as-fuck feeling of living up to be a complete disappointment. My dad went black—that's what we call it when he gets triggered, because his eyes, blue like mine, change in color. Weird, I know, but possible. He's proof of it.

My mom was worried, but my dad recovered fast. He kept saying, "You don't have it. You fucking don't, all right?"

I didn't want to say, "Are you fucking deaf?! The doctors just confirmed it."

"He's in denial, he'll come around, Racer," Iris said when she came to visit.

I didn't reply to that.

"Do you think I'll get it someday too?" she asked me, worried.

"No," I immediately growled, pressing her to my chest and promising her, "I've got it for the both of us, okay? Never think that. You're perfect."

Now my dad steps into the room—quiet, like he always is.

Our eyes meet, and his jaw tightens.

We say nothing.

He pulls up a chair by the bed.

I lie here on this bed, battling a battle I'm going to probably face a hundred times in my lifetime.

"It's your phone. Do you want me to take it."

"No. I don't want her here."

My voice is low and rough, and my father digests that for a moment.

"I had a team to watch out for me when I was off meds. You're out here on your own, and you shouldn't be. You don't have to go this alone. That's what they're there for. Don't go off your meds, Racer." He regards me in frustration, his voice firm. "Don't let yourself climb that high and you'll hopefully prevent ever hitting this low again. You've got this, son. I know you do. You're too stubborn and too proud and too damn special. You have a lot to do—and I can't wait to fucking watch you do it."

I'm silent for a moment.

"Fuck you," I say. "Fuck you for giving me this shit."

Dad just stares at me as I say the words I've always wanted to say out loud.

He leans forward and levels his gaze on me.

"I gave you fucking life. It's up to you to get the rest of what you want. So, what do you want, Racer? Do you want this championship? Do you want the girl? Do you want to get fucking better? Do you want to beat this? John?"

"Stop calling me John."

"Stop wanting to be some other guy, Racer. A simple guy. Anyone but you. Own your name. Go fucking get it. Racer. Fucking. Tate. My son. Huh? Or is it John?"

He slaps my cheek part gently and part not. "Is it John?"

"Racer Fucking Tate, Dad."

"Good. OWN it. Get this thing."

He slams his fist into the chair, then stares at me and exhales when I give him nothing. "I don't know what else to say."

"Don't say anything."

"You're right, not good with words. But I'll help you get better. I know what you need."

note

Lana

He didn't show up at the track, and now it's evening and I'm at my hotel room, unable to eat or sleep or do anything at all.

I'm sitting next to my phone, waiting for a call, jumping every time it vibrates as my brothers keep asking "Any news?" on the family chat group.

I read a third message, from Adrian, and shake my head vehemently.

"No," I type, when there's a knock on the door.

I leap to my feet and head over, peering through the peephole and my heart leaps when I see a pair of familiar blue eyes.

I swing the door open, almost gasping Racer's name when I find myself staring up into his father's eyes rather than his.

"Lana."

Racer's dad is at my door. What is he doing in Italy?

Oh god.

The walls of my stomach collapse inside of me. "Is he okay?"

"He's okay. He's pulling through."

I'm trembling all over as we stare at each other. "I want to see him," I say.

"Good." He regards me for a moment. "He needs you."

I've never moved so fast. "Let me get my room key."

He drives in silence to the hospital, and I'm unnerved by how quiet his dad is until he speaks.

"He'll try to push you away. Fair warning." He shoots me a cautious look.

"I don't care. I want to see him," I say stubbornly. But I want more than that. I want to be there for him. He's my boy and he needs me, and if he's too proud to say that he needs me, I don't care. I'll be there for him anyway.

"Coping mechanism." His dad looks at me. "We've been through this before."

"He warned me about it," I admit quietly, staring out the window, only seeing Racer. Racer in his mustang, Racer in Kelsey, in Dolly, Racer in me. Racer everywhere. Racer in this world. Racer in my mind. Racer in my fucking heart.

"Oh, and he doesn't know you're here," his father adds as we head into the stark white hospital and take the elevator.

When we step out, I follow him down the hall, my heart beating like it's about to break out of my chest.

Or just break … inside my chest.

He opens the door, and he motions me forward. I peer through the door. The room is pitch black. A monitor is beeping. Racer is in bed, and for a moment I freeze at the sight of his dark mussed hair.

I hear the light switch, bathing the dark room in light.

He's lying face down, with his arm shoved under the pillow along with the IV cables. And still, he looks so masculine, making the bed seem small and stark white compared to that sexy dark hair of his. Those sexy muscles and tanned skin.

"Racer," his dad says bluntly.

Racer seems exasperated as he turns his head towards the door very slowly, as if he doesn't want to, and his eyes see me, and he freezes.

His eyes fix on his father, and his voice is craggy and dark. "I told you I didn't want her here."

"I don't give a fuck what you want."

I hear his dad step out, and I swallow.

Racer clenches his jaw and drops his face back down, and I see his chest expand on a deep inhale. The usual hum around him is down. I don't know why it affects me so much. I'm used to seeing him in charge, confident and strong, so determined—the most determined man I know.

I lift the sheets and climb in bed with him.

I can see him trying to be distant as he rolls to his back as if to make room for me, but his arm comes around me as if instinctively.

I hold my breath, expecting him to say something when I curl at his side.

He doesn't.

He won't look me in the eye.

I touch his face. He inhales deeply, still not looking at me. I reach my fingers up his forearms, and they're so hard, hard as the rest of him. Drivers have very well developed arms, necks, chests, and abs—but the forearms and necks are especially strong. Racer's are the strongest I've ever seen, more ripped than anyone I know.

I silently cry as I feel him stiff next to me. He doesn't belong here. This guy belongs at the top of the podium, behind the wheel of a car, in a woman's bed, in every fantasy, but not here.

"Don't shut me out," I beg.

I stroke his jaw quietly, and Racer shuts his eyes. He just shuts his eyes. His jaw so tight that a muscle works wildly in the back of it. I can't help but want to touch him more, crave to kiss him and tell him what I wanted to tell him since so long. What I've been so scared to admit.

But he looks like he's battling something in silence—as if he doesn't know if he wants me here or not.

"Let me take care of you," I whisper.

"I don't need you to take care of me."

He clenches his jaw and closes his eyes, and keeps his eyes closed.

The words sting, but he'd warned me that he'd say shit to hurt me, and even this—the worst moment I've had with him—is better than not being with him.

He remains with his jaw clenched, his arm around me. I set a kiss on his jaw. His hand tightens and he shuts his eyes tighter.

I run my fingers over his jaw.

Silent.

My phone is buzzing like crazy. I check the message and it's Drake.

We're gonna start looking for replacement drivers what the fuck is going on.

I look at him—and I realize he's more important than my dream, than my dad's dream and my brothers' dream. Than anything.

I text back, **Start looking for a replacement.**

And shut my phone off.

I see he opened his eyes and was eyeing my profile.

I look back at him "You'll be well soon and driving your car, heading off somewhere, you and I. I'll play some music on your stereo … we can play some now."

He just looks at me in silence as I search for one.

"Have you heard this one?" I show him *Favorite Record* and smile teasingly.

He drinks me in for a long, achingly wild heartbeat, and I smile at him wider, but my smile trembles on my face when he says nothing.

Nothing at all.

His eyes scan me quietly, his expression intense and fierce as I slide one earbud into his ear and play the music. I don't know why this song is the one I play, but I want him to remember the good times, I want to take him to a place away from here. Away where he's just … himself. So Fall Out Boy is singing and even with the upbeat song, the memories of being anywhere else with him but here make my chest hurt. I just desperately want my boy back.

Racer

I'm in fucking hell.

Trying to cheer me up, sweetly and innocently. Smiling at me, trying her damn best to get me out of the dark. She looks fucking incredible. Like a wet dream. The only thing worth looking at in this shitty room. The moonlight touches her skin and she looks like a damn angel, an angel sent for me.

A wave of despair punches me in the gut when I think of how she stood there, looking at me in this damn bed. Helpless and fucked up. *Fuck.*

I could hardly look her in the eye.

Too fucking afraid that what I saw there would finish breaking me.

She looked at me at the door and I almost glanced backward to see who she was staring at with all that concern in her eyes.

She was looking at me.

My girl was looking at *me*.

All fucked up as bad as I can be.

And Lana Heyworth the girl I love was staring straight at me with a look no woman has ever given me before.

Yeah because I just don't deserve her. I just don't think I deserve her at all.

Why does it feel like she was fucking made for me, if I was made wrong for her? I was made so fucking wrong I can't even keep my shit straight.

I want to rip my fucking heart out because I hurt her.

I said I didn't need her.

It gutted me to say it.

To know it cut her deep and that I did it because I'm too proud to admit that I do. Because I'm too proud to want her to see me like this.

I didn't say more, was afraid to say more.

I look at her now, in my arms, her eyes closed as the music playing stopped and the only sounds are her even breathing and the beeping of the IV monitor.

I loosen the hold of my arm; so she can leave. So she can get as far and fast away from me as possible.

She sighs in her sleep and snuggles closer to my chest, inhaling me and mumbling one word sleepily, with all the affection you can ever hear in a woman's voice. In your woman's voice. Like the word means something to her. She murmurs, *Racer*.

medicine

Lana

I wake up to feel him watching me. I stir awake and start when I realize where we are, sitting upright in the bed.

Racer's quiet as he looks at me. I'm startled to see the nurses come and go.

I stand and whisper, "I should go to the bathroom," and when he gives me the barest smile and opens the bed sheet for me to slide out, I smile nervously and hurry inside, despaired when I realize I look a mess. I try to fix my hair, use some of the toothpaste on the sink to wash my teeth with my finger, rub it all over my mouth and tongue, then I wash it off and wash my face. I pull my hair back—trying to look as least shitty as possible.

I exit the bathroom and Racer is standing by the window—a glimpse of his gorgeous ass peeking at me through the parting of his robe.

I see the RT tattoo on his butt and shiver inside as he turns—eyeing me quietly again.

I want to run into his arms and beg him to tell me it's going to be okay. Because if Racer says it, I will believe it. Because he's my hero and I admire him, trust him, aside from the fact that I also want and have fallen head-over-heels bat-shit crazy in love with him.

"You okay," he asks me as I stand there, trembling.

I bite down on my lip and nod. "Yes." The fact that he asks if I'm okay nearly wrecks me.

"I want you to eat something," he gruffs out.

"I'll grab something from outside," I assure.

I step out of the room and tell his dad I'm going to get something to eat. He's out there in the waiting room and simply nods and heads over to visit with him while I do.

When I come back, Racer is pacing the room.

"… she never comes back I'm going to rip this fucking roof off …"

He stops growling at his dad when he looks at me, his eyes widening.

His dad smiles as he drinks him in. "I'll go to the hotel, take a shower. Be back to check on you later," he says, smiling as he slaps Racer's back.

I meet Racer's blue, blue gaze, noticing his hair is standing up more crazily than before, as if he was raking his fingers through it. "What's up. Did you think I'd leave?" I ask, confused.

He curls his fingers into his hands and the muscle in his jaw starts working again.

"I'm spending the night here tonight," I say, then I flush when I realize how much I'm invading his space and already did last night. "But I want you to be comfortable. I'll take the chair," I explain as I head to the chair.

I cross the room, feeling his blue eyes watching me.

"Lana."

My stomach twists as the rough word reaches me and sort of wraps itself around my stomach and my heart, and I turn as I lift my head. His voice is raspy and textured.

"Come back here." He motions to the bed.

"I want you to be comfortable."

He grits his teeth in frustration, then pulls off his IV, and my eyes widen as he starts jamming his fingers into the beeping machine, trying to quiet it with a frown.

Finally the machine quiets, and he walks over and I'm on my feet, wide-eyed.

"What are you doing."

"You can come, or I can carry you," he says plainly.

He tugs me forward, and I can't breathe because I don't understand why this gesture undoes me so much. I don't understand why I want to cry but, afraid he's not going to lie here with me as he leads me with his warm, firm grip on my hand to the bed, I tug him down with me.

Racer doesn't seem to have been intent on leaving. He lifts the cover and slides his long, toned, muscular legs inside.

He slides his arm around me and I'm so desperate to touch him, to know that he is real, that I did not imagine a guy that has wanted me more than anything, that has taught me how to care for a guy again, that I press closer.

Suddenly Racer slides his hand under the covers and says, in my ear, "Take these off. I just want to feel you." His eyes are brilliant in the darkened room, and I don't need to be asked twice. I reach beneath the covers and flip open my jean button, and before I can take them off, Racer moves the sheet back and pulls them off me. He pulls them off me and then discards them, our bare legs touching under the covers.

I exhale a shuddering breath when he runs his hands along my skin.

"That shirt long enough to cover you when someone comes in?" His deep voice makes my skin pebble as he whispers the possessive question into my ear.

I'm melting and aching all over. "Yes."

He looks at me with those blue eyes and I buzz inside as he slides his hands over me, just looking at me in the dark with something fierce and intense in his eyes.

He sets his hand on my stomach and leans his head and smells me. I stroke his hair when he wraps his arm around me and just sets his face between my breasts, growling softly before he settles down. He shuts his eyes, kissing my stomach.

"Oh, goodness, that bed isn't made for two." I start at the voice of a middle-aged nurse.

"I think we need to give the patient his space," the nurse tells me chidingly.

I'm instantly making to move out of the bed when he grabs my wrist to halt me.

"I need her here."

The nurse was busy changing the med packets, but she pauses at that and looks at Racer after the raspy whisper.

Gruffly he repeats, "I need her here. She's my medicine."

She smiles. "Young love," she whispers as she fixes the machine and hooks him back up. "Enjoy it while it's young," she says laughingly.

We're both sitting on the bed now, and I turn to meet his intense gaze as he leans back on the bed and slowly reaches out and draws me to his chest.

Whereas yesterday when I came, he wouldn't look at me. Now it's like he cannot stop. His blue eyes drink me in in silence, and I drink him in while all my body clutches with yearning for this guy.

"You have no idea how hard it is for me for you to see me like this. I've never wanted anything less in my life," he gruffs out.

A muscle in his jaw twitches uncomfortably, his eyes dark and tormented when he looks at me.

"Don't hide from me. Both the good things and the bad," I plead.

His blue eyes seem sad, as if his whole life force is turned off. "I didn't want to give you the bad."

"I want it. I want all of you," I blurt out.

Those dark, sleek eyebrows of his shoot upward at that comment, and then his eyes begin to glow as if something about that lit up his fire.

"I'm not scared of this as much as I'm scared of what you make me feel, Racer," I whisper painfully. "I'm scared of the way it feels to be with you, everything so acute and alive and thinking I wouldn't bear to one day live without you. When David died it hurt too much and I never wanted that again, but I never thought I could feel it again a thousand times more intense until you. Guys didn't even draw my eye that much but you. Like I was meant for you, Racer."

I pause to get my breath.

"That day you told me that I … loved you … I was crying because I have never felt this intensely for anyone. And I don't know if I can be all you need." I catch my breath on a gush of emotion. "I want you, your whole being, your entire you. Even this."

He shuts his eyes and puts his forehead on mine, his arms like steel around me as he exhales.

He starts to growl as he clutches me tighter, whispering in my ear, "You have no idea what you're asking for," he warns.

"I do. I do, and I WANT it. I want you." I clutch his jaw and am so desperate for him to know how much I mean it, cuddle him. Smell him. Let my body say what I haven't said in words, that I love him, so much, so much I'd stay here with him forever if that were the only way I'd get to be with him.

I cup his strong jaw and look into his tortured blue eyes. "Are you okay. What are you thinking?"

"What I'm thinking stays in my head," he says, frowning determinedly. "I get sucked into this goddamned vortex, and I need to remind myself it's just perception. Just in my head. You're what's real. This."

He cradles my skull in his palms and presses me to his chest. I can hear his heartbeat. Strong and steady. His muscles feel lax, his blue eyes shadowed and his energy subdued, but his arms are still his arms. He is still him. And I'm even weaker against him, determined to be strong for him and at the same time, I'm completely vulnerable to him.

"I love you." I wipe my tear as I start to cry.

His strong, large body seems to jolt and tighten at that, and his embrace tightens around me as he drops his head and growls in my neck, "God. Don't say that. Don't tell me this now."

"Don't pretend you didn't want to hear it."

He releases me and drags a hand over his face, his fingers trembling. "You don't, crasher. You don't. You can do so much fucking better than me."

"You're it."

"I'm no good," he hisses. "I'm no fucking good for you. I'm as fucked up as it gets … look fucking around you, Lana. Is this really what you want?"

I stare at him squarely in the face. Never surer.

"I love *you*, Racer Tate. YOU."

His eyes flash, and his nostrils flare as if he's fighting to stay in control as he looks at my face like I'm not even real. Like he's imagining me.

He reaches out and drags his thumb along my jaw, his voice achingly tender and pained. He shakes his head warningly. "Don't say it because I can't take it if it's not true. If you leave me. If you get sick of me. Stop loving me. Don't give me hope only to take it away one day because it'll push me over the edge and make me insane."

"I won't ever take it away, it's yours. I'm yours."

He growls and yanks me to his chest, pressing my skull to his chest as he leans his head and kisses the top of my head. "Baby. My sweet girl," he whispers out on a hiss, shutting his eyes as he lovingly nuzzles my face.

"My strong, fast boy," I whisper as I feel him wipe another tear from the corner of my eye.

I wipe a small drop at the very edge of his and my whole being shudders.

He growls softly as he leans his head and pecks my lips. Just once. Easy first. I catch my breath. He eases back, looking at me again. He leans again. Pecks them again, this time on the side of my mouth. I thrum all over. He turns his head, his lips grazing another peck on the other side of my lips. I groan softly, and his eyelids lift, and his eyes are heavy and fixed on me as if nothing else exists but this. He shuts them up again as he parts my mouth, and when he teases his tongue into my mouth,

I feel like detonating from the feeling of love and hunger it brings. A feeling I'm only too familiar with now that Racer, this guy, my guy, has introduced me to it.

I start to kiss him with everything I have. Racer soon takes my kiss and makes it hotter, wilder, longer.

He jams his hands deeper into my hair, and my fingers slide around his shoulders to clutch the back of his neck. I feel his body start buzzing again, that relentless unyielding unbending force inside of Racer Tate coming back up.

He rolls me to my back, spreads me down on the bed and kisses my mouth as if he wants to fuck my body in the same way his tongue fucks my own, and I sense the way his strength and hunger keep returning, as if his fire is slowly blazing strong again. A fire that promises to soon be back to the Racer Tate inferno.

morning

Lana

"Hey. Crasher." I feel someone brush my hair back in such a delicious way that I smile in my sleep and shift in the bed. Damn. This bed is really uncomfortable. Where am I … mmm, it smells nice around here. It smells like Racer's smell under my pillow. "Let's go," I hear the sexy male voice speak again.

"Whaaa—" I shake my head and start to come fully awake as I glance around the hospital room—then spot him at the side of the bed.

"Let's go. We've got qualifying."

"No!" I gasp. "You're more important—"

"This is important to me. To us. Let's go."

I blink, and staring back at me fully dressed and shaved is …

Racer.

Racer Tate.

Not Racer 2.0, not Racer 3.0, not Racer—1. Just. Racer.

MY Racer.

Blue eyes sharp and clear, energy once again buzzing and buzzing around me.

I think my knees may, or may not, work as he helps me up to my feet. I stop by his hospital bathroom to clean up before exiting to see him winking goodbye to a middle-aged nurse as she mentions a follow-up call with his doctor from St. Pete as she hands him copies of his discharge papers and his prescription.

He stashes them in his back pocket and I follow him outside to say goodbye to his dad.

He slaps his dad's hand. "Thanks for coming," Racer tells his dad as they shake hands, and as they do, Racer drops his voice. "Dad, I'm—"

"Don't." His dad stops him. "I get it. You don't owe me anything."

Their gazes hold for a second—near identical, both men so similar I'm almost dizzy by the resemblance. "Thanks for coming," Racer finally says, sounding humbled and grateful.

His dad pulls him into his embrace. "I love you," he says. "Be well."

"I love you too. Be well, Dad."

I'm lingering back, giving them their moment, before I feel Racer reach behind him to seize my hand and draw me up to his side so I can say goodbye to his dad too. His dad is heading back to Seattle, and he promises to meet us in the U.S. for the U.S. leg of the Grand Prix tour soon.

I climb into Racer's car, and he turns on the motor and drives out of the parking lot, setting his hand on my thigh as we head back to the hotel for his gear. I exhale, close my eyes, the wind in my hair at dawn, squeezing his hand and rubbing my thumbs along his hard palm, caressing him. I open my eyes and he's drinking me in like a starved man.

"Thank you ..." His voice is raspy with emotion. "For being here," he specifies the last.

"I'll always be here," I whisper.

The sudden unexpected sight of his naughty, sexy-as-sin dimple makes my knees weak, and when he turns on the music, I feel like the happiest woman on the planet.

"Think they'll be okay with me coming back? Your family." He runs his eyes questioningly over me, a familiar gleam of determination sparking up in his eyes.

I smile hopefully. "We'll find out soon."

"I'm not sure how fast I can be, crasher, the meds slow me down." He shifts gears, clenching his jaw as he stares out at the road. "That's why I wasn't taking my pills in the first place."

"I'm sure the best driver in the world could figure it out, and last I heard, you were running for the title," I encourage.

And he grins, his whole face lighting up, as if my words just lit a fire in his hungry, driven, sexy soul and he just wants to prove to me that he's definitely got that in him and more.

I text my family and tell them that we're on our way, and I ask them for a meeting when we arrive on the track.

I'm relieved to see they didn't bring in any drivers.

I know that's not what they wanted.

I know that the driver they want—the driver they need, the only driver for us—

is walking right next to me.

I walk in with his hand in mine, and I don't pry it free.

"Where the fuck were you two?!" Drake rants. "I'm going to fucking kill you, you irresponsible motherfuck—"

"He was at the hospital," I cut in. "Now you three jerks are going to sit down and just listen to me for a second."

My brothers glare at me.

"*Now!*" I yell, planting my hands on my hips.

I see they're not happy about it, and they don't sit, but they calm down.

"I know that you guys have always been concerned about Racer's reckless reputation and were afraid that he would one day leave us for a better team. I know that you've been concerned that him and I … well, that's *none* of your concern now, because we're dating. And Dad is okay with that, so you three bozos have nothing to say about that. As for the other … Look. We've done things this year that we never even dreamed we would ever do. *We're* all in this together. Are we in agreement?"

"Yeah," Adrian says.

"Yeah." Clay.

Drake finally nods. "Yeah."

"Well then, now that we know we're a team … Family, Racer is—"

"I'm bipolar."

There's a moment as the words spoken in Racer's deep voice sink in.

Racer looks at my brothers in the eye, and then fixes his gaze on my dad. "I'm learning to handle my triggers. I'm also not kidding myself thinking this will never happen again—but I hope to god I can spot it in time and take care of it. I'm not perfect but you'll never find a driver as hungry as me. Or someone more devoted to this team."

My eyes wide, I think my heart just imploded. "What he said," I say as I watch my brothers and dad digest this. "I want you all to be there for him when he needs us."

Drake is the first to move.

"Hey, you're like family. We got you." He puts his hand out, and we pry our hands loose so that he can take it.

"Thanks. I'm okay," Racer growls, shaking everyone's hands and then letting my father silently pull him into an embrace.

"A man is made up of more than what he battles with," I hear my dad whisper privately to him.

"I'm sorry I disappeared for a while. It won't happen again, sir," he tells my father, and I know it takes a lot for proud Racer to ask for or accept help.

"Now let's get on that track and kick some ass," Clay says, handing Racer his duffel from the ground.

I look back at Racer. Pure vivid anticipation glimmers in his blue eyes, and I feel like I've never seen his jaw look that square or determined.

Can you love someone so hard that every part of your being feels it?

Yes, my heart whispers.

good

Racer

I slide into the seat and strap down, glancing around the car. "You're back too, Kelsey." I smirk and rap the dashboard. "Hell so am I. I hope you're ready."

I fire up the engine and pull out of pits, ready for qualifying.

Her taste is still in my mouth.

The taste of her soft tears, and her loving eyes.

My veins are chock-full of fucking meds, and I should feel slower.

I don't.

I feel more powerful than I ever have.

Because I let her see me—and she responded like I always prayed she would.

She fucking gets me.

And I've fucking got her.

"Okay girl," I say once I'm in the clear for qualifying. "Let's show the world who we are."

mine

Lana

"**F**UCKING SHIT, HE QUALIFIED FIRST!!"

"Un-fucking-believable—fresh out of the hospital, and he qualified first!"

I'm about to burst from the excitement, and while my brothers are yelling at each other in disbelief, Racer leaps out of the car.

Racer.

My Racer.

All mine, I think greedily. I want everything that he is, all for me.

There's euphoria bubbling up inside me as he reaches out for me and gives me a huge kiss and carries me, kissing me as I kiss him back.

When he sets me down, my brothers leap on him. My brothers' eyes are glistening, and their smiles are miles and miles wide as they lift him up from the ground.

My dad's eyes are misty.

Anybody who saw us would think we just won the championship.

They don't know that we had a moment there where we thought we'd lost him, our #1 driver, and that this is another kind of victory not in any books but ours.

The ride up the elevator to his floor feels like an eternity. It's just Racer and I riding upstairs. My dad and my brothers stayed with the rest of the team, making sure Kelsey remains in top-notch condition for the race and downloading the race data to review. I've never, ever, been the kind of girl to be obsessed with a guy. Guys had always been a second thing in my life, after David. Definitely not something I couldn't stop thinking about.

But this guy?

I never knew that one guy could melt me with a look or send me flying with a smile.

His body warmth seeping through my clothes. He's holding me by the waist and pinning me to his side as we ride upstairs.

I shift a little to get closer, and he tightens his hold on me, murmuring in my ear, "Are you happy with qualifying?"

I lift my eyes to his with a grin. "You tell me."

He smiles because he knows.

I shake my head in something beyond happiness, beyond any word. "I knew you could do it, but you were up against more than anyone out there," I say.

His eyes gleam mischievously as he looks into mine, sliding a hand down my side as if savoring this happiness of mine. "You're good medicine," he says with a husky smirk, pressing his mouth to the top of my head.

I groan as my whole body tightens for him.

He shifts me closer, and I hear the music playing in the elevator. The song, Maps by Maroon 5, before the elevator tings.

He presses his fingers to the small of my back when we reach his floor, and I step out, following him into his room.

"You were incredible," I breathe.

He smiles enough that his dimple shows, his eyes twinkling.

"I swear you were driving with everything you had. It's like you pulled out all your stored energy from the past few days," I continue.

Racer's eyes gleam devilishly as he opens his door and leads me inside.

"You didn't know if you could do this with your meds, and look what you did!" I say as he shuts the door behind us, leaning up and wrapping my arms around his hard shoulders. "You beat this, Racer Tate, and we can beat it again. As many times as we need to."

He chuckles softly, and he looks so boyish and so handsome as he eases back and looks into my face. "Felt good to be back in that car. Felt good to drive." He strokes his index finger along the freckles on the bridge of my nose, and my lungs begin to struggle for air. "Feels good for your brothers to know about us. And me." He runs his thumb down my throat and lower, to the start of my T-shirt. "And still nothing feels as good as you, Lana."

Racer's eyes smolder as my breath catches. He corners me against the wall, tugging my T-shirt from the waistband of my jeans.

My heart feels as if it can't fit in my chest—because discovering that you love a man this complex, this exciting, this demanding, this consuming ... well, it takes a bit from a girl. Not that I don't like what it takes; or how my heart thrums in my chest, my blood boils with his nearness, even my silly little nipples and how they stand shamelessly up to salute him when he's near.

I'm in his room, trembling and anxious to feel him. Racer watches me, those eyes eating me alive as he tugs the fabric of my top downward to reveal my bra. He then tugs my bra down, and pops out a nipple.

"You're so pretty. You know that right."

He keeps eye contact with me as he opens his mouth, and his tongue comes out to roll a little circle around my nipple.

I catch my breath, dying inside as I drown in those blue eyes and tremble under that hot tongue caressing my nipple.

I part swallow, part groan, "Don't torture me ..." I beg.

He smothers my nipple with his mouth, shutting his eyes as if he can't help it anymore, sliding his hand between my thighs. He cups me as he suckles me, groaning as he touches me over my panties.

"Give me all of this girl," he says, a soft commanding growl as he caresses me over my panties with his index finger.

I rock and roll my hips up to his fingers, realizing I'm out of control but ohmygod, ohmygod, I've never wanted anyone's touch so much, anyone's kiss so much, anyone so much.

His body vibrates as if he's holding himself back from doing other equally wicked and pleasurable things to me. I don't want him to hold back. I move against his hands and run my fingers along his arms, pressing my lips to his jaw. "Racer," I groan, a plea.

He groans back and eases his finger into my panties, licking into my ear. "God, baby, you want to come right here for me, don't you? You want to break apart for me, baby," he purrs.

I nod.

A possessive streak of lightning passes across his blue eyes.

"Tell me you're mine," he says, urging me down on the bed as he starts to flick open my buttons.

I'm trembling.

"Racer ..." I say.

"Say you're mine, Lana." His blue eyes look down at me and quietly demand for me to say it; eyes that are raw and true and so perceptive I know that he knows that it's true.

I swallow.

"Not anyone else's. Not David's anymore. Tell me you're all mine," he repeats, clenching his jaw in need and arousal. "You told me some stuff in the hospital, and I want you to tell me now that I'm okay, Lana."

He shifts, his eyes glimmering as he rubs the pad of his thumb over my lower lip in a caress that I feel down to my toes. He leans down and scents my neck, then pecks my lips, softly, like he does, before licking the seam and easing back to drink in my features once more. His voice rough, husky, male.

"Tell me who you want here. Who keeps you awake at night. Who you think of every second of the day."

He leans his forehead to mine, his eyes gripping my own, his voice deep and textured as he cups my face as a tear slips.

"It's me, baby," he croons tenderly, nuzzles my nose, and brushes the tear from my cheek as he presses a kiss there and then captures my gaze again, "Are you going to tell me my name?"

I tilt my head for his mouth, trying to stop shivering. "Racer, kiss me—"

He presses his thumb to my lips, silencing me. "Tell me," he says, looking down at me. "Tell me now," he says.

He slips his hand into the back of my neck and presses his lips to mine—firm but tender, giving me a minute before they stop feeling tender and begin to feel relentless.

"For me, it's you," he whispers in my ear. "The one keeping me awake at night. The one in my every thought." He slips his hand between my legs, sliding it under my skirt as he captures my mouth and kisses the living daylights out of me. The pain out of me. The fear of whatever is happening between us out of me. Until there is only one giant, tingling feeling—and it's all over my body. A fire shaking through me, under my skin, IN my skin, in my veins, my tummy, the tips of my breast, the warm spot between my legs that suddenly feels so swollen it's uncomfortable.

He nuzzles my curls.

I groan.

"Look at me. Look at me, crasher."

I do.

He kisses me. Wipes my tear. His face raw as he pushes his dick inside me. "You feel so right. I want to stay here. I want to pound a path all the way to your damn heart."

"Don't stop." I clutch him to me, whispering, "Racer, you had my heart from the moment you wrote on my page."

"Come again," he says, driving inside me.

"Racer Tate."

"Again, Lana. I fucking want you to look at me when you say it."

"You! You, RACER TATE!" I breathe, our eyes holding, and no one—ever—has ever looked at me with so much love, so much passion, has ever ignited me with those same emotions. I say, "I'm yours, Racer. I'm yours and you're mine."

freedom

Lana

We spend most of our free time together as we visit Malaysia, Singapore, and Japan.

Racer and I have hit every car museum in each of these cities for the past month and a half. He loves telling me the exact specifics of any car—and I always tease him that *this* is why he hasn't had a girlfriend before.

I don't think any girl would get turned on hearing about pipes and carburetors, but he's lucky that I happen to find it quite like dirty talk.

Not the words, really.

But the way this guy's voice sounds as he talks about it and the way he gets an emotional hard-on for cars and speed.

Not surprising, since he's a damn F1 pilot.

Also not surprising that driving around each city has become our thing.

We like taking drives and seeing the sights on our free days, listening to music we both like as we cruise around, thriving on the feeling of being free.

We stop at every place we feel like. And our rule is to always take a drive, at least once a week, with no destination in mind. Once, Racer stopped by a huge three-story mansion by the water, and we parked right across and just stared at it while we talked for hours about our upbringings.

I talked about my mom and never wanting to build a family only to leave it. Racer talked about hoping that, despite his career, he could set roots for his family like the ones his parents gave him when he was a kid.

I even got to drive a couple of times. He's giving me "lessons" though mostly he just frowns at me when I shift gears too soon and make the car squeal.

"Baby you're killing this vehicle," he said with a laugh and a frown.

"I'm trying!" I laughed.

I was surprised he'd even let me drive. He simply handed the keys over and said, "Drive."

"Where to?" I said excitedly.

"Wherever it takes us."

I grinned, loving to explore the world with him.

We stop for lunch at any place that calls to us. Racer eats a lot, but very clean, and I'm trying to join in for my wellbeing and to tell my father some health-food tips. I'm trying to exercise more too simply because dating a guy that is so fit that his skin is taut over his muscles to the point you can hardly pinch a tenth of an inch only makes you realize how soft your own body is.

Racer says he likes my softness, so I don't worry too much when he hits the gym and I end up staying at the hotel to organize the team's flights and future reservations.

I usually write down my reservation confirmations on a ton of Post-its and hotel pads, and I've noticed lately that he's writing his name on every one just to irk me.

We're negotiating the movie-watching at nights. He likes series, and I like movies with quick resolutions, so we usually alternate a series episode for a movie for me. I watch *Sense 8* with him; he watches *The Proposal*.

"I'm learning to appreciate the benefits of watching these movies with you, baby," he confided once after a movie ended and we were in a full-out make-out moment.

"Why," I asked, breathless.

"You acting all warm and romantic. Soft and eager for me." He grinned, and I groaned and smacked his chest.

"You're such a guy!"

"Good thing. Considering you're into guys."

"I'm into you," I whispered, unable to say more because his mouth proved too distracting.

I'm fully living again. Every moment feels meaningful with him, even the silly, meaningless ones of hurrying in the morning to get dressed.

Now I watch him climb the car, ready for the race in Japan, and I just wait for that look he always gives me before igniting—one glance, because his eyes are all I can see through his helmet. Just his eyes, connecting with mine, before that visor slips down, and then the hard rumble of the car igniting before it squeals onto the track.

u.s. grand prix

Lana

After kicking ass in Singapore, Malaysia, and Japan with two P2's and one P1, we arrive on U.S. soil.

I've always loved traveling from track to track, but I have a soft spot for the U.S. Grand Prix simply because it feels a little bit like home, even though we have been living abroad for several years now.

Now we're close to the end of the season, ready for the United States Grand Prix at the Circuit of the Americas in Austin, Texas.

I walk along the stands with Racer before the race, and he's pointing out his people to me while they wave at him or are too busy looking for their seats.

"So that's Melanie and Grey, a couple of my parents' friends."

He points to a beautiful blonde and a distinguished-looking dark-haired man in a black suit.

"And that's their other friends."

He points to a sable-haired woman with a guy wearing a diamond-stud earring.

"Pandora and Mackenna. And that's their daughter Eve."

He points to a late-twenties dark-haired girl, and then to a younger girl standing next to her.

"And their other daughter, Sophie."

He moves his finger down the aisle to another couple, him in about his forties, her a little younger with light honey hair.

"That's Maverick. He's a fighter, like my dad, he holds the record of most wins and is still at the top of his game. His wife is Reese. She was my babysitter."

"Really?" I laugh.

"Really."

"She's beautiful. Did you have a crush on her?" I ask, trying to keep the jealousy out of my voice.

"Nah. But she had a crush on me." He smirks and we watch them suddenly come over to say hello. Racer introduces us.

"Very nice to meet you, Lana," Reese says, and she won't stop staring at me with this knowing smile that makes me shift a little nervously.

"Tested your theory the other day," Racer tells Maverick, and Maverick's eyebrows rise in instant interest.

"And," Maverick prods.

"I fucking was ready to eat my competitors' heads off." Racer's lips twist into a wry smile as he shoots a meaningful look in my direction. "But I'm not sacrificing some time with my girl again."

"Only when it matters." Maverick steps beside him and lowers his voice so that maybe I don't overhear. "Besides, it's sweet to celebrate with your girl after."

"Yeah. But I intend to celebrate winning this champion-ship by walking her down the aisle in a fucking white dress."

"Wow! Look at him," Reese says in amazement, obvious-ly able to overhear like me. She confides to me in a whisper, "He never wanted to get married."

I'm surprised by that, but then realize Racer's intent blue gaze is fixed on me, as if he's curious as to my response to this, so I direct my question to him.

"Why didn't you?"

A naughty spark appears in his eyes. "I didn't want any-one to have to deal with my shit."

"Then what happened?"

"Then I met you, and I wanted to take care of you."

I bite my lip, and I see Reese take Maverick's hand and pull him away while Racer continues looking at me as if we're not in the track—as if there's no one but us here.

"And I knew myself enough to know that for the one time I'd need you to be patient with me, I would be a hundred times patient for you." He clenches his jaw as passion and lust and love glow in his eyes. "I've never loved anything in my life the way I love you. My crasher. You looked at me with these two eyes … and I haven't been able to see anything else. You little witch, you crashed my single party."

"Racer," I laugh, and he runs his thumb along the back of my arm as he starts leading me back to our tent.

I shiver head to toe, side to side; even inside of me there are tiny delicious shivers.

His mom is telling something to his dad close to our tent, and he's smiling, laughing at something she says. He's an old-er version of Racer, a little thicker, with blue eyes as dark as Racer's, two dimples, and a bit of silver at his temples. I feel my stomach clutch in yearning, and I never realized how much I want that. What his parents have.

"Your dad's a DILF."

Racer bursts out laughing, then shoots me a jealous look. "Thanks. I really didn't need to know that."

"Well, it's true."

He smiles and shakes his head, and I resist the urge to reach out and grab his fingers and tug him back to me and kiss him, tell him that I want that—the kind of relationship his parents have with each other—with him, and I'd never, ever, wanted it before in this way.

As we walk forward, his mom looks at me and pulls away from his dad.

She studies me as she approaches, and a part of me feels vulnerable—because I've never been studied this way by another woman. By a mother figure. It's been a long time since I've heard from my mom, and she never did really look into my eyes—my expressive eyes, as Racer calls them—and try to figure out what was up with me.

His mom looks at me. "Remy told me you were with Racer at the hospital. Thank you for taking care of him."

"Oh god, you don't need to thank me at all."

"Yeah, well"—her lips tilt a little—"I know it's frightening."

I nod, dropping my eyes.

"I could tell you that it's always worth it. But sometimes it's hard; it's hard for the both of you. He wants to be better, you want him to be better, and sometimes there's nothing either of you can do but hang on and ride the wave. And it *is* a wave. It passes. And then the water is calm again, and you can see the reflection of what you have, and that's when it's worth it. Every wave is worth it because one wave doesn't reflect the whole ocean."

A tear slips and I wipe it away.

I glance at Racer and see him sitting with his dad, his racing suit covering his thick thighs and the sleeves tied at his waist.

I want to go to him, I want to put my arm around him and tell him that I can't deny it, that he's my guy, that we don't get to choose the tests we will have in life, all we can hope for is to pass every one, and to hang on to those who matter, those who love and love you back. I want to tell him that maybe I don't deserve him, that I'm not as strong as his mom. But that I want to be. That I want to learn.

"You're a sweet girl. You're stronger than you think," his mom says.

"It's just that it all comes at you together. Like it's never a single wave; it's always two or three. My dad ..."

I swallow, and she comes to sit by me and puts her hand on mine. "You can talk to me, really."

"Thank you." Another tear slips, and I wipe it away.

We're silent for a moment as his dad and Racer walk up.

"Mr. Tate," I greet, on my feet.

"I think we can skip to the part where you call me Remington." He shakes my hand.

"Or Dad." Racer's gruff voice reaches me.

I feel my mouth part in surprise and maybe even a little excitement, and when he looks at me with a dark primal glimmer in his eyes, I feel myself blush.

His father slaps his back. "You're in trouble," he whispers to Racer, winking at him.

Racer suddenly is staring at me so possessively I feel a little bit impaled on the spot. A little bit … fucked. In the best ways. He moves up to me, and his body heat envelops me as we watch the other cars on the track as his parents head to their seats.

"I talked with your mom."

"I know."

"I embarrassed myself. I got super emotional."

"Lucky her." His voice is low and husky, tender.

I laugh.

"I've fallen for you, so hard, harder than ever. I'm obsessed with you, Racer. With everything about you. Your hot bod, and your gorgeous eyes, and your confidence and how fun and good you are," I say, breathless at my admission. "And I'm really scared."

He curses under his breath and laughs a bit, one hand running down that gorgeous face before he looks at me sideways, his blue eyes twinkling as he reaches out and embraces me, pulling me to his side. He peers down at my face. "I'd have given anything to hear you say that."

"Anything?" I ask with a frown.

"Anything."

"Not the championship," I tease.

"Not that or what will I impress my girl with?"

"You don't need to impress me."

He reaches out to rub his thumb along mine. I lift my index finger, and he takes it in his and draws me close, and then his big hand is engulfing mine.

His sister comes over, and Racer signals.

"And that's my sister Iris, as you know. Pain in the ass, this girl," he says as she comes over, and he rumples her hair and she scowls at him, but looks at him with love in her eyes.

"There's nothing as exciting as this, but this is absolutely nerve-wracking, I don't know how you do it," she says.

"I'm asking myself the same question and coming up blank," I admit, laughing.

"Racer!!" I hear his family yell from the stands, even to where my dad and I stand in our pit area, waiting for Racer to get weighed and the official results to be announced.

"U.S. rookie driver Racer Tate is drawing the crowds today at the F1 Grand Prix at the Circuit of Americas, and with his first-place finish, something formidable is happening, and that is that the top, record-holding team of most F1 championships has something to worry about ..." the announcers are saying, and I smile to myself, my chest swelling with pride as he finally steps off the scale, removes his helmet, and heads straight for me.

I'm already up on my toes, waiting for the quick peck on the lips he always gives me before he lets the rest of the team hug and congratulate him.

Except this time he reaches for my hand and draws me to his crowd, "Let's go out to dinner. All of us. On me."

The dinner with his family is fun, and delicious (we're at a famous U.S. steakhouse and eating protein and carbs like starved people), but it's also a little crazy. We occupy nearly half the restaurant, and between my brothers and father trying to get to know his parents and sister, I barely get to see Racer—we're both too concerned with our parents getting along to pay attention to anything else.

Racer ends up heading over to where my brothers are, and I get a chance to talk to Iris, who I instantly like because she not only looks like him, in girl version, but because she seems genuinely sweet and concerned for him.

"Dad told us you helped my brother when he was at the hospital. I think that's great of you," she says, still seeming to be wary around me.

"I'd have killed him if he didn't tell me," I admit, scowling at the mere thought as we have the best steak and potatoes I've had in ages.

"Really?" She laughs. "Most girls wouldn't want to bother with these things. I know twenty-two-year-old girls who are out just partying and having fun, not as driven as he is."

"I'm not most women. And I love him," I admit, saying the last with emphasis.

After that, she seems to warm up to me. "Is he a bully?" She glances at her big brother with love in her eyes but seems to want to have something to talk about with me. "He's such a bully with me, always scaring off any guy who wants anything with me," she complains. "I even promised him that one day, when he really liked a girl, *I'd* scare her away too. But I don't want to scare *you* away." She pauses, her voice softening. "You're good to him. I'd never seen him hooked on a girl. Never would be with the same one for more than a night out or two."

Her gaze turns wistful, and my heart is melting in my chest, then Iris goes on laughingly, "But for my pride's sake, because once he scared away a guy that I really liked—I need to say that I at least tried to scare you away. So please know that he's terribly bossy. And so confident it's irritating because I'm quite awkward and the opposite."

I burst out laughing. "You're not awkward, not in the slightest." I think she's charming and honest, and I'd have loved to have a sister like her to balance out my three brothers. Now *there's* a set of bullies for you. "Why did he scare the guy you like?" I ask, confused.

"Because he wasn't good enough for me. He said that if he'd cared he'd have been impossible to scare off in the first place."

"Hmm," I say, pursing my lips, terribly amused about my protective Racer. "Well I agree with you," I say, *and him,* I think to myself, trying to keep our interaction going. "He's a bully, over-confident, and completely bossy," I state, noticing Racer raising his eyebrows across the room, and I realize he heard every word I said because he winks—proudly—as if all of this were a *good* thing.

"He just heard and winked at me," I tell his sister.

She groans, glances past her shoulder, where he winks at her too, and she laughs and shifts back to me. "Yep. That's my brother. You could be saying the worst things about him, and he'll still puff his chest out like everything about him is golden."

I laugh, confiding in her, "He's wanted me to admit to him being the best driver in the world for so long, but I wouldn't budge an inch until recently."

"Good for you. Now prepare for him to get you to marry him. He's been announcing it since you met."

"Oh wow, seriously?"

"Yes!" she cries.

I think I look like a cherry because my cheeks and neck and whole face start to burn, like the rest of me, because the thought of marrying Racer Tate—of him truly making me his wife and telling everybody he plans to do this—gives me more butterflies than anything in my life has given me before.

If his sister thinks he'll be getting his way ...

Then I'll play it cool and classy, but secretly in my heart of hearts and right in my soul which is so deeply connected to his it's scary, I'll desperately hope that he *does*.

After a fun evening, we all head back to the hotel, and I notice that my father looks beat. "Daddy, do you feel well?"

"Yes, I'm enjoying every moment."

I shoot a pleading look at Drake.

"Let's get you to rest. So much excitement won't help your body stay strong," Drake tells him as we all step off the elevator on our floor.

"I think the excitement is helping," Dad jokes.

I laugh. And when we take him to his room, and say goodnight and head back, Racer takes my hand and gives me a squeeze. Noticing my worry and concern.

"How much time does he have?" he asks.

"I don't know. He didn't tell us and forbids the doctors to. It's cancer, but he doesn't want treatment." I shake my head. "He says he doesn't want to be feeling sick for the remainder of his life. But the doctors said he had a good chance if he got treated, he's just stubborn."

"I know someone like that," he says, tender.

"Really? Me too." I smile, because obviously I mean him, and Racer smiles too, his dimpled smile and his presence making me feel better.

Drake once told me that I had to respect my father's wishes, that people let go when they are ready, and I needed to learn to let go too. But feeling as if something you love with your whole heart is being taken from you, the truth is, human beings hang on tighter—and it only hurts more.

What I want doesn't matter.

Not really, not in these things. So I just tell myself that I, too, will enjoy every moment, because whenever my dad leaves, and I leave, and my brothers, and even my immortal Racer Tate leaves, we will always take these moments with us.

I follow him to his room; it just seems handier that we be where he has all his racing gear, etc. I also really like simply being in his space and feeling … well, safe and welcome there.

Racer rummages through his duffel and takes out his bottle and pops back his medicine, and downs a half glass of water.

"You're taking them every day now?" I ask as I watch him set that aside and give a hard yank to his T-shirt, his chiseled, perfect male chest in full view.

"I feel good. Feel fucking golden." He cracks his neck side to side, and stretches his arms, then drops them when he notices me ogling. His eyes gleam and he raises his brows. "Especially 'cause I've got you right here." His lips start to curve, and he reaches out, pulling me to his chest. I start to go up greedily on my toes and Racer just lifts me up higher, kissing me like only he knows.

prepping

Racer

We're in Mexico and have only Brazil to go, and then the final in Abu Dhabi. I'm geared up to put up a good fight for the championship and heading out early in the morning to the track with my girl at my side when a group of fans spot me at the hotel lobby.

"*Ay, Dios, es Racer Tate!*"

"Ohmigod, *Racer!*"

"Can I have your autograph?"

"Yeah, sure." I grab her pen and scribble down my name, then do the same for the other two.

"You're my favorite driver," one gushes.

Beside me, Lana prickles with jealousy.

"Nice girls," I say as we head out.

She presses her lips tight.

"They seem to think I'm a pretty good driver," I point out.

"Marry them, then."

I run my knuckles down her cheeks and cluck as I shake my head somberly. Yeah, I want her to know she's *it*; and there's nothing that will change that. "I can't do that. I've been promised since before I was born to the first girl to crash my cherry mustang."

Lana nibbles on her lip, and I can tell she's doing that to keep from smiling. I love this girl like crazy. I can't get enough of her scent. The feel of her. Taste of her. Teasing her. Making those green eyes widen with shock or delight, and especially with love and lust for her man. Her man, aka Racer fucking Tate.

I'm prepping for the upcoming races, exercising more. I'm trying to get some good sleep, eat right, keep my monsters at bay, have no more surprises.

The standings show me in second place.

Her brothers? Yeah, they seem to be more and more okay with me and Lana being together.

I've grown to admire them, appreciate her family. I don't want to disappoint them. Hell I don't want to disappoint my own family. Or me. Especially … I want my crasher to always have reason to be proud of me.

him

Lana

They say time flies when you're having fun, but I think it flies double when you're in love.

We're in fucking Abu Dhabi before we know it … and it's been a whirlwind few weeks of interviews, practices, qualifying, and races.

Evenings full of kisses and licks, days full of engine fuel and carburetors.

I told my dad I'd stopped booking rooms for me because I was staying with Racer … and Dad said that was all right.

Whenever we go out with my family and hold hands, I notice Racer trying to be respectful with my dad and not doing it in front of him.

But I also know that my dad watches us with a pleased look on his face, a look of peace almost as if … he's happy for me.

As if he wanted this for me and never knew it.

Maybe, I didn't know either.

Losing someone you love marks you in ways you've never known until you're left in the aftermath, struggling to heal that gaping hole.

I still remember that day David died, too young and too suddenly. I remember not even being able to cry for the first couple of minutes after my parents told me the news because I was screaming. I was sobbing, rocking my body on the floor, my own arms wrapped around me and I could not stop shaking but no tears were coming out. The sounds I was making were much more gut-wrenching, expressing much more than sadness. I felt my soul break; I felt my spirit break. I was in complete shock, my brain frantically searching for a way to prove nature wrong. Searching for a way to make this all go away, to make it all not be true. That day I lost that sense of hope and faith that we carry deep within us, that sense that everything will work out okay.

Some call this hope and faith childish—and the loss of it maturity. But I believe we all, even adults, carry this sense of hope and faith in life and in our safety with us. Death is one of those events that makes us question this hope. Makes us abandon this faith.

It took me a lot of time to regain this faith. It took passing through a few months of depression before realizing that acceptance of what is, what has been, and what will be is all that can bring us peace.

Although I regained faith in my life, I did not regain my faith in love. In ever being able to love like that again. A love unlike that given to friends and family—passionate, deep, consuming, erotic love, the deepest vulnerability anyone can have.

The reasons why love can bring us all incredible peace, satisfaction, fulfillment, and joy (these reasons being that love requires acceptance of oneself and another, creating harmony and balance through allowing oneself to be vulnerable) are the same reasons that make love so dangerous, and ultimately, so hurtful.

When we lose those we love, or those we love hurt us, or we hurt those we love—it is a pain deeper than any other. Because it hurts the expression of the purest, most innocent, powerful, human emotion: love.

I closed my heart up after that day. Because I needed to heal, and so did it. My trust in the universe, in life, in everything turning out okay was completely shattered. I was sure I'd never allow myself to be vulnerable again, to let myself love and be loved.

Almost.

Until I stared into the most striking blue eyes I have ever seen in my life. Until I met a man who touched me like I was made of glass. Who ran his fingers over my skin as if it were the finest silk. Who looked into my eyes without a shred of judgment, of doubt, of ANYTHING other than acceptance, joy, and love.

I didn't think I would ever find something like this ever again, much less that it could surpass it. I feel my heart almost burst open as I lie in bed cuddled up to this man who holds me to his chest now protecting me with his body against anything and everything. He lays over me as my shield.

I feel tenderness behind every look he gives me, every smile, every touch, and every kiss.

Even as he sleeps I can feel how fiercely he adores me. How he fights for me. How he cherishes me. And I want to cry.

And so I do.

I start to sob quietly under him because I didn't ever, ever think I would be looked at the way he looks at me.

I feel my body shake and my vision blur as I shut my eyes and continue to feel my body shake. I cry because I am so thankful. And so happy. He makes me so, so happy.

He wakes up then, his hair a mess, a beautiful rumpled mess, and his eyes a smooth warm shade of just-woke-up blue.

He looks at me and immediately cups my face in his hands and nuzzles my wet cheek with his nose.

His huge hands almost swallow my whole face, but they hold me with such tenderness it makes my heart ache even more.

"Hey, hey, I'm here baby …" he coos in my ear, wrapping his strong arms around me and bringing my face to his neck.

He rolls onto his back and holds me there, silently crying into his neck.

I don't know what is going on with me but I can't seem to stop crying.

I cry for my mom. For her leaving me, and my family behind.

I cry for my brothers, who have since the day I was born carried me, fed me, practically raised me alongside my father.

I cry for my father. I sob for my father. The only parent I have left. Who has loved me with everything he has, fiercely and completely. I cry for him, I cry because soon I'll be without him. I won't see his face, hear his voice, or let him hold me. I cry because I know I'm losing my dad. And that breaks me.

And lastly I cry for me. I cry for Lana. Because after everything that has happened to me, every experience I have gotten the pleasure to live through, I wouldn't change a thing. Because it led me to this moment. And it led me to him.

Racer.

I hear myself say the words. "Racer, I love you."

I raise my eyes from where I placed a kiss on his firm lips, and I find his bright, vivid blue eyes staring back at me. And for the first time I realize exactly what this man means when he says that my eyes are expressive. Because right now, his are just like that. It's like looking through a clear, crystal blue glass shimmering with stars—and I can tell that he's happy.

I can simply tell that I am loved … beyond my wildest dreams.

okay, #38

Racer

It's crunch time. Racing Abu Dhabi today. Fighting for the championship. The stakes have never been so high for me, and I've never wanted to win a race so fucking badly. Hell I love to win, but this race isn't just for me. It's for Lana and her family.

I don't sleep; don't even try to.

I feel good in the car, feel good about this.

Feel great about Lana lying in bed, sound asleep after saying she loved me last night. She's said it before—at the hospital. But somehow it counts more when she says it just because.

I dial my father once Lana wakes and steps into the shower, gazing out the window at Abu Dhabi while he answers.

"I'm fired up," Dad says.

"You watching me race?"

"We're having friends over, we're all watching. Maverick and Reese, Melanie and Greyson, Pandora and Mackenna."

I smile knowing they'll all be cheering for me.

"Racer," Dad says.

"Yeah?"

"Be careful."

"Yeah, I will."

"And Racer?"

"Yeah?"

A pause before Dad growls, "Go kill it."

"I learned from the best," I say, and hang up.

We hit the race track, and the cameras keep snapping pictures of me everywhere I go. I ignore them, focused only on what's coming ahead—and on Lana.

She's worried about me, I know.

She's lost love once—and though I know she knows we wouldn't have found each other otherwise, it hurts her and it hurts me to know she fears losing me too.

She's not gonna.

Ever.

"Nothing's going to happen to me," I tell her when I notice the look of concern in her sweet green eyes.

She opens her mouth as if to contradict me, then frowns the sweetest frown on a human being these eyes have ever seen.

I pull her closer to me by her shoulders, my voice stern. Hell, I know she can't help being fearful, but I can't help wanting to reassure her.

"Lana. Look at me. Do you believe in me?"

I give her a squeeze, willing her to know I'd never leave her. I'd fight death for my crasher. I'd fight my own monsters harder, every day, for her.

"I believe in you. It's just the other things that happen that make me fear," she says, her brow scrunching even deeper in worry.

I smile down at her, my chest soft with tenderness even as my determination doubles in steel.

I chuck her chin gently, keeping my voice low for her. "I'm doing what I love. For the person I love most. I'm the luckiest motherfucker on this planet."

I smile and pat her gorgeous ass to remind her who she belongs to before I head to the drivers' meeting. Silent. Focused. All those patches on their suits are sponsors; my goal is that after I win this thing, Lana will have to field them, vet them, pick the ones she likes.

Lana continues organizing everyone's clothes and breakfast. She takes care of us all. When this is over, I want to take care of her for a change.

I meet with Adrian to discuss strategy.

"If you've got something to give, give it now. Don't hold back," Adrian says.

"I never do."

"Good."

"Usually teams have several drivers to help each other out, to provide support and give feedback about the track. We could never afford to do that. All the track input we have will come from you and only you—"

"I got this."

"You qualified P2. Watch out for P4 and P3 on the start; they'll be trying to eat up a spot."

"P1 better watch out for me," I say.

I grab my helmet, boots, and racing suit—knowing that for this year, it's the last time I'll put these on for a race. This fucking race is for my girl. This win is for her, and for the family who believed in me enough.

It's also for me.

Because, fuck, I love this shit too much.

I change in the motorhome and search her out, sitting by her dad, when I walk down the steps.

She smiles and comes over, even more nervous than she was a few minutes ago.

"After today you won't be able to tell me I'm not the best driver in the world." I look at her meaningfully, and she presses her lips together, emotional.

"Go strut your stuff, Racer Tate," she breathes, her eyes wide, hopeful, nervous. Loving.

I take her by the back of her neck and lean downward, firmly kissing her lips.

"Watch me," I say, and smile, because it's a promise.

Lana

He walks down the track and doesn't even glance around to look at the competition. It's as if he thinks they're not worth his time, or as if he's simply in it to race—and all that is important to him right now is that car before him. I love the way he strokes it with one hand, frowning in concentration as he asks my brothers what they did to change the setting.

In racing, talent can only go so far. Talent cannot make up for the things that a car cannot do. So it is our job to be sure that we give our drivers the most capable car, set in the most capable way, for every track—which is different because of the heat, the length of the stretches, whether it rained recently or not.

He looks as hot as the devil's son would look in a racing suit, its gorgeous cut enhancing his trim waist, long legs, and wide shoulders.

On the mic, the announcers are discussing the contenders for the year, and I pick up some of what they're saying about HW Racing.

"What his team is doing is incredible. They're bringing the fight to the big guys. This team doesn't have as much resources as the others. It's a small team bringing in the right rookie, an inexperienced U.S. street racer, into the mix ... with phenomenal results!"

"You know, when Racer Tate was announced in the beginning of the season I don't think anyone expected him to ev-

er see a single podium, much less appear on most every single podium since he began ... This is one young driver with some serious *talent we're talking about here. HW Racing has never set up their cars as strongly as they do with him around. He seems to know exactly what he wants his car to do ... "*

I exhale as we all start going to do what we always do – I put my cap on, slide my ponytail through the hole in the back, and check that my dad has one too, and that he has a comfortable seat, all while my brothers and Racer focus on the cars.

I glance at them as they hover over Kelsey—who's already on the table, looking sharp and bare for one last checkup.

My eyes caress Racer's backside. From the top of his black hair, down his thick, strong neck, his wide shoulders, his narrow waist, all of that enveloped in that sexy black racing suit.

I watch the guys lower Kelsey to the ground, and Racer slide into the seat and behind the wheel, strapping down the safety harness and then gripping the wheel with his gloved hands as they start pulling him out to pits.

I cannot believe that we're at the end of the season. I cannot believe how much more racing means to me now, when the man I love is the one driving our cars—representing our team. Chasing all of our dreams.

Our eyes meet and hold for the briefest, bestest second, before his visor comes down, and Racer is full on in racing mode.

Trembling with adrenaline, I head to take my spot next to my dad. He's on his feet to get a better view, and I feel a prick of nerves as the cars shuffle out to the track.

Drake walks up and rehashes everything with Dad and me. "So if Clark doesn't finish the race, we'll win the championship if Tate at least comes in second. But if Clark finishes the race, then we need that first come hell or high water."

I exhale and nod.

Dad nods as well, his expression stubbornly determined. "We're not skimping on wheels, on anything he needs," Dad tells Drake.

"No sir, we're not," Drake assures him, patting my dad's back as we watch the cars in anticipation.

The engines flare to life.

The crowd gets restless, their excitement palpable in the air. I watch Racer's car, bright red with blue and our sponsors' logos, pull into the track, his shiny blue visor reflecting the sunlight off his helmet.

My pulse skyrockets in anticipation as my eyes stay on Kelsey. All that red on that car is pure absolute fire, home to the devil behind the wheel.

The Clarks are going to pull every stop to ensure the win, try every trick in the trade from pitting in for fresher tires to tweaking their downforce to saving fuel to more. Clark continues leading the championship, after all. I'm afraid there could be some rough driving—and my nerves are eating at me.

I take position and slide on the headset that Clay hands over. We all discussed how it should be, and though I insisted Clayton should be the one on the headset with Racer, both Clayton and Racer disagreed.

Racer wanted me here with him; and though I feel completely unprepared and am not as good at this as Clayton is, I caved in because I want to be here too.

"Let's do this," I whisper to him through the mic, and my stomach clutches as they circle several laps until finally, the green flag flashes in the wind.

And they're off!

I keep my eyes on him. When he drives past, all I see is a flash of red and dust behind him. I check the stats and the times for the drivers, wanting to keep him as informed as possible. "P2 and holding steady," I say.

He doesn't reply—we're too focused on winning here—but I almost notice his car kick up faster after P1.

The cars appear from around the curve. They zoom past the stretch, one next to the other. I glance at the stats and whisper, "0.06 after P1."

"I'm outbraking him," he mutters.

I hold my breath. To outbrake him is to brake after the other guy, so that you can pass him on a curve. It can go well, and it can go badly.

Racer outbrakes. There's screeching, and they're off, with—

"P1!" I say excitedly.

Clark is on his tail, and as both cars charge down the track, kicking up a storm, the cheers from the stands get louder and louder.

Racer

Sweat coats me under my racing suit and drips down my temples under my helmet. The heat is simmering in my body as I keep pushing for my best, still leading on P1 with my girl on the line.

I'm on eighth gear, go to second for turn 1, and exit turn 1 going up through the gears. When gear five fails, I know it's not good.

"Shit," I growl.

From fourth I have to push to sixth, but I lose engine torque, and Clark catches up.

Goddamn me. I'm going to fucking lose torque every time I move up the gears because I'm skipping a gear. I'm going to need to make up all the time I lose in every turn on the straightaway.

When you lose one gear, it's fucking dangerous. The gearbox can fail. It's hard on the gearbox and it can completely fail. I can't head to pits, it takes hours to fix. I'm on lap 52 out of 70, I'm in P1, but Clark is close behind. Too close behind. And he'll be getting the gift of catching up with me on every fucking turn.

I just hope the gearbox doesn't break down completely and I end up in the wall.

I push through around the curve and speed like the devil down the straightaway with Clark on my ass, and when I take my next turn and lose gear three too, I know I'm fucked.

"Fuck fuck FUCK!" I yell.

"What's wrong?" Lana asks.

"Put Clay on," I rasp.

"Racer, what's wrong."

"Put Clay on for just a second," I repeat, shifting to eighth on the straightaway, pushing Kelsey as hard as I've ever pushed her.

Lana

Clayton is rehashing strategy with Racer, and I keep noticing Clark is right up on Kelsey's ass on every turn.

"What's going on? I can tell something's wrong," I ask Clay.

"He's lost fifth and third gear," Clayton says, mumbling "Yeah I'll put her on" and passing me back the headset.

"Hey, baby."

I start to sob, and I remove the headset for a tiny second as I try to control my tears and keep him from listening to me. I suck in a harsh breath and force myself to put it back on, wiping my tears.

I know he needed to discuss options for him when he asked for Clay, and now I don't know why they aren't just bringing him back to pits safe and sound.

"Hey. Hey, baby," Racer says, more sternly. "I'm coming out of this car and you're going to be the first person I want there. You remember what I like to do the moment I get out of the car, you got to be there to greet me in the winner's circle. I'll be pissed if you're not there."

"Racer, please, slow down. Stop. I don't mind if you lose the race." More frantic tears fall, and I'm fearing that if I lose him, there will be only a dark black pit for me. No more life, no more love, no more good things for me.

"Don't worry about me, baby, this is for your dad, this is for you."

I can barely speak through the pikes in my throat. It's a war just to force my voice to stay level. "I love you. You have no idea how much."

"I love you like that too," he says.

I get mad the next second. "Racer Tate! People die from this! You know that?! This is not something to fuck around with, this is not street racing anymore! These are dangerous machines that you're fucking with!"

"Not me. Not today. I know this car. It's a part of me." The steel in his voice strengthens me, and I exhale as he quietly commands, "Now walk me through it. Where's Clark."

I wipe my tears and straighten my spine, trying to focus as I strain my eyes and try to lead him safely back home. *So the best driver in the world can please come safely back to me.*

Racer

Come on, girl.

I struggle with the gearbox on every turn, trying to get Kelsey back on her fastest speed on the straight-away.

I cannot disappoint my people. I can't fucking lose this—I never. Fucking. *Lose.*

I'm the best driver in the world.

Motherfucker Clark's got a better car? A better damn gearbox?

I've got more talent, and a girl to woo.

Lana

On lap 69, we're holding our collective breaths out by the tent. The announcers are going crazy speculating what is wrong with Racer's car, for it's been acting even more reckless than ever, leaving skid marks as Racer's rough, raw driving comes to show.

On lap 70, I cannot look but at the same time, I cannot take my eyes away from that red car, growling past us like a storm ...

We're down to the last lap.

Clark is trying to take the lead on every turn—attempting pass after pass—and Racer is fighting not to give it to him.

They head into the turn, almost nose to nose. Clark passes him. The crowd collectively gasps as Clark retakes the lead. They take the straightaway, and we're down to the last seconds when Tate positions Kelsey right behind Clark—using his draft to pull him forward.

Two seconds to go, Racer veers right and passes him on the straightaway.

One second to go ... and then ... the checkered flag is waving as #38, the most beautiful car in the world driven by the best fucking driver in existence, zooms past the winning line.

The announcers are going crazy.

"And it's RACER TATE, RACER TATE! The BEST rookie driver we have seen for as long as this Grand Prix has been

standing! RACER TATE takes the win in the last SECOND of the race! This is unbelievable ..."

After both the car and pilot get weighed, Racer finally steps off the scale and pulls off his helmet, swiftly scanning the crowd gathering around him.

I'm trying to push myself forward as Racer starts walking into the crowd and people start chanting,

"TATE! TATE! TATE!!"

My dad is crying like he's never cried in his life.

Racer grins as my brothers and the mechanics catch up with him and they fling him in the air, and when he lands back on his feet, his eyes lock on mine. My lungs seize up for a heart-stopping moment. Because his eyes are the most marvelous, most gorgeous blue they have ever been.

They flash primitively as he narrows them on my face, and he picks up his pace as he cuts a path toward me.

I'm frantic and breathless as I shove my way forward, needing nothing but to reach him right now. Yes, he's an amazing driver, but he is so much more than that.

He's my *guy*.

He's my guy and this is one of the most important moments of his life.

When I finally reach him, his hands take my waist and I'm tossed up in the air as if I weigh nothing. One second I squeak, and the next he catches me, and his hot mouth is on me, and I'm getting kissed as if Racer Tate means to eat me whole.

Dizzy and euphoric as he sets me back down, I laughingly press my face to his warm palm, and he shifts so that I can get closer. I slide my cheek down his arm and against his chest while he slides his arms around me and draws me closer.

He kisses my freckles. I squeeze my eyes shut and exhale.

"I love you," he growls in my ear, squeezing me.

"I love you so much I can't believe it," I admit between tears and laughter, biting down on my smile as I kiss his dimple. He groans softly and becomes hard. I lift my head, and his eyes are vivid with possessiveness—and when they drop to my lips, he presses them to mine, and I press them back to his, suddenly kissing him as if my life depends on it, and maybe it does, because right now all I know is hot, warm, hard Racer's mouth on mine, and he is my #1 in everything.

Unfortunately, I cannot kiss him forever—and soon we're caught up in the excitement of the award ceremony as I watch with a full heart as Racer gets his award and steps up to the very top of the Formula One Grand Prix podium. After a lot of cheers, a lot of crying from not only my dad, but my brothers and the mechanics, I spend the rest of the day out of the track, watching on the sidelines as Racer gets crammed with interviews and autograph requests.

p ... 1

Racer

" *thank you for the interview, Racer Tate. And that was Racer Tate! This year's Formula One champion, live with us! At the Abu Dhabi Formula One championship ... "*

I head to the motorhome to change, and I realize I've got a bazillion calls from Seattle. I shower, dress in my jeans and a plain tee, then I hop on Skype to connect with my parents.

"Racer!! My boy!" My mom is practically yelling, her face blotchy. "I am so proud I haven't stopped crying!" She seems so emotional as she presses a Kleenex to her face and buries her face in my dad's chest.

"Hey, Mom," I say, amused as shit.

My dad? He's fucking grinning ear to ear.

The pride in his eyes, the pride is basically oozing off him as he looks at me across the screen.

"You make me proud, you know that? You make me proud. If I did nothing right in this damned life, the day I die,

I'll die happy, because you and your sister? Me and your mom did you right."

I'm fucking wordless. I nod in silence, a language my dad understands well since he's not someone you'd call expressive.

I feel my jaw flex while I handle this emotion—the fucking happiness of making your parents truly proud. I end up promising to see them soon before I disconnect, then I sit there and digest shit for the next minute.

I won.

We. Fucking. WON.

I picture Lana, and her big green eyes, staring up at me in amazement. Suddenly, I want her whole damn face to be soft and wanton and her lips open as she gasps and writhes beneath me tonight, and I want my hands to run down all her sweet curves, and then my tongue, tasting and exploring every damn inch of her until I get my fill of her and fill her up with me. Yeah, and I want her fingers in my hair, or on the back of my neck, caressing my goddamn chest—I want her as turned on with me tonight as she seemed about this win. I want her sopping wet—and the mere thought of what's in store for me tonight has me throbbing in my jeans as I finally get to my feet and storm out of the motorhome.

The Heyworths drive us to a five-star restaurant nearby.

"How do you feel, champion?" Lana asks as she takes my hand and leads me to the restaurant entrance. "Do you feel hot?"

"Hot as shit." I run my eyes over her to let her know exactly what I mean.

"You amazed me today," she breathes.

"That was for you and your dad." I lift her hand and kiss the back of it.

"I would totally race back for you."

"Is that riiight?" I croon down at her as we walk inside, not certain she's the ideal person to race anything that actually moves.

"That's right," she says effusively, nodding up and down.

"I better give you some driving lessons then," I murmur, smiling as my mind begins concocting a plan.

They lead us to the back, into a large private room with a huge table set at its center. "I booked us a private room for the whole team," Lana explains.

I'm wondering why the excitement in her voice keeps mounting when she beams and signals to a sign hanging on the wall. Its background is white, and it covers the wall, side to side, and written in red, the color of both Kelsey and my mustang, are the bold letters stating:

"BEST DRIVER IN THE WORLD"

I'm damn surprised, to say the least, and a wave of satisfaction settles over me as I slide my eyes back to her wide, expectant green ones.

My hormones go out of control.

She smiles at me, and the space between us is on fire, like her eyes. Like my goddamned veins and soul.

"Surprise!" she says, motioning to the room in general and, especially, the sign.

I frown down at her and warn, "You're going to have to say it eventually."

"I know," she says with that smile of mischief.

I raise my brow as I pull out her chair and lower myself beside her, my eyes trailing over that little outfit she wears. She dropped the jeans in favor of a little red dress that reveals her legs and her tiny waist. Somehow Lana manages to make even the simplest clothes seem goddamn sexy—every piece of clothing on her makes me want to rip it off her.

She brazenly devours me with her gaze as I sit down.

"That was fucking crazy, what you did back there, crazy," Drake says as the waiters start filling our glasses with champagne.

"Pushing the car like that." Adrian's eyes are bugging out as he snatches up his glass. "You're a fucking maniac and a goddamned miracle."

"I was scared," Lana breathes, looking at me with a mix of emotions—mostly concern and lust. When she runs her little pink tongue along her bottom lip nervously and moves her head in consent, I'm fucking done for.

I lean over and whisper, "I had it, baby," and watch with pure joy as her blush runs up her neck and cheeks.

"Still. What you did was so risky … you kept going faster and faster, and I kept worrying the gearbox would fail completely."

She faces me with a look of bewilderment on her face, and I clench my fists at my sides because all I can do is sit here like an idiot while the thought of losing me seems to be tearing her apart.

"There's always risk in anything worth doing, and it's a risk I'm willing to take." My voice comes out possessive, protective, because I need her to know that for her, I'd risk anything.

She bites down on her lip and reaches out to grab part of my thigh, and her concern for me wrecks me up. I'm more wound up than a knotted rope from the need to reach out, put my hands on her waist, lift her up in the air and force her down so that her lips land hard on mine.

"Promise me you won't do that again," she pleads.

"Lana," I growl when she asks that of me.

"Promise me, Racer."

I reach out, every instinct inside me demanding me to appease her, to remind her that she's my girl—that she is mine, and that we will be in this together.

"I fucking promise I won't do it—unless I have to."

I shoot her a look that demands that she trust me. That reminds her I want something more than those damn trophies that will grace the shelves of my place in St. Pete later on.

I want her as partner, in every sense of the word. And I want her on my side, as I'll try to understand and listen to hers.

I hold her gaze—until the sheer joy takes over our faces as the reality falls on us like a light beam.

"Baby, we got P1! FUCKING GOD, WE DID IT!" I growl, pulling her up and into my arms, tossing her up in the air and catching her, and the whole damn table is yelling when Clayton yells, "To RACER FUCKING TATE GOING DOWN IN THE HISTORY BOOKS!"

"TATE, TATE, TATE!" they chant as they slam their palms to the table in tune.

"No," I say, setting down a giggling Lana onto her feet and pinning her to my side as I make eye contact with her father, brothers, and the rest of the mechanics in the room. "To

HW Racing," I say. "To HW Racing, and Mr. Heyworth!" I raise my glass to her dad.

We all guzzle down our drinks, and soon we're having dinner, talking racing and recounting the good—and bad—of the season. Lana's father soon calls it a night and returns to the hotel with Adrian, and my impatience grows from a simmer to a boil. After one last sip, I set my glass down, and mid-sip, Lana looks at me and I take her drink and set it down, too.

I lean closer to explain as succinctly as I can. "It's time for me to claim my prize," I husk out, smiling down at her.

I could fuck the wanton look she sends my way.

Whistles follow us to the door, and Lana is red, head to toe, but her dad has called it a night and I'm claiming my girl.

By the time we reach our hotel room, I'm close to busting the zipper of my jeans. My cock is so full and hard it feels like lead—hell even my balls feel like lead.

We kiss our way to the bed, and then we stop to look at each other—and hell, do I enjoy looking at this girl. My girl.

I place my hand on her hipbone, pinning her in place as I lean down and nibble a path up her neck. She squirms, and the scent of wet pussy reaches me—the sweetest scent I've ever smelled is coming from between her legs, because she fucking wants me like I want her.

I'm burning up as I shift above her, my cock grazing her thighs. The contact shoots a bolt of lightning down my spine, and I growl and pin her back down so she stops teasing me, adding fuel to a fire I can barely control.

My gut is twisted up with wanting for her as I finally reach her lips and I open them with mine, not interested in being a goddamned Casanova with her, only interested in her taste—having every goddamned inch of her mouth for me— making her move and beg and squirm and ache for me—and my kiss becomes wilder as her hands wander up the muscles of my arms and her mouth opens beneath mine.

I reach down to her wet panties and begin to tug them off, but get too impatient and rip them off instead. Lana lets out a surprised gasp, which I promptly smother with my mouth. Fitting my lips back dominatingly on hers, I tongue her deeply as I cup her pussy in my hand and begin to let my fingers wander. Desperate to explore and memorize her.

I find her clit and roll it in circles beneath the pad of my thumb, and my balls tighten in arousal when her hips start jerking upward as if on their own, as if desperate for more. I smile down at her, catching her startled, lust-crazed gaze before I bend down and lap up her taste. And for the next hour Lana knows of nothing but this. Me. Racer fucking Tate.

packing for home

Lana

We feel refreshed and hyped the next morning as we have breakfast with my family at the hotel restaurant, our luggage all ready upstairs for our flights.

Last night, in between celebratory sex and sleepy lazy sex, Racer and I debated over whether I should come back to the U.S. with him, or go back to Spain—where we usually live in between seasons—with my dad and my brothers.

He said he'd go with me if I decided to stay in Spain, and I told him it all depends on my father.

Which is true.

He looks a little more tired than the rest of us today, but there's a peace in his eyes that I'd never seen before.

"We won, Daddy," I say as I lean over my chair and hug him. "You can check that off your bucket list." I take his hand, and he smiles and glances past my shoulder at Racer.

"You love my daughter, boy?"

My brothers stop eating and look at him.

"Like crazy, sir," Racer says without missing a beat.

"I've been glad to see you two follow your hearts, but I want to make it clear once more that you have my full blessing to date my daughter."

Racer looks at him in silence, his eyes gleaming in gratefulness as he nods. "Thank you, sir."

"None of us are perfect; sometimes we fuck up. As long as there is love and loyalty, boy, anything can work, and I'm saying this to the both of you."

"Thank you, sir." Racer nods again.

My smile widens and I squeeze my dad's hand. "Thank you, Daddy."

My brothers just nod, chuckling as they rib one another.

"I told you they had it for each other from the second they walked in," Clay says, nudging Drake.

"Yeah, yeah, yeah," Drake says.

"Are you planning to race next year?" Dad asks Racer.

"Yes, sir."

"And you, Lana?"

"I'll be here. I mean"—I eye my brothers and father—"maybe in the future ... Racer will race in something closer to home. We'll be at F1 until things lead us somewhere else. Maybe closer to home. Eventually I will want a home, Daddy," I explain softly.

"You deserve it. You've been home for us all these years."

"You too, Daddy." I feel a tear slip, and I quickly wipe it away. "I want you to be okay, Daddy."

"Lainie baby," he says, drawing my eyes to his as he explains, "I didn't think getting treated would help. I didn't want to leave you alone. But now it seems you have someone to take care of you even better than I can." His lips quirk mischievously, and he looks like a young boy again.

"Daddy, I'll always be with you and you with me. I'm not going anywhere. Racer and I had been discussing me going to the U.S. with him for a while, but I'm not leaving if you—"

"What I mean is … I want to try treatment. For my cancer."

"Oh." My eyes widen, and my heart leaps. "Oh, Daddy. Really?"

"Yes, Lana. I don't want to miss this for the world." He motions to the windows and Abu Dhabi and my brothers and Racer at the table, and a tear slips down my cheek.

I wipe it away quickly even as I feel Racer's big, callused hand on my thigh, my throat still closed as I squeeze his hand in one of mine, and my father's in the other. "Yes. We're with you."

Racer leans forward. "Sir, my parents have a big home in Seattle and there's great medical care in the U.S. You're welcome to stay there if you feel like you want treatment in the States. The guys are welcome to stay there too, before the season stars. Lana can stay with me."

"I appreciate that, son."

He extracts his credit card to pay the check and once we all stand to gather our things, my dad slaps Racer's back, and Racer slaps his back in return, and they're smiling at each other, and I'm standing in one of those moments where you realize beauty is made up of a thousand tiny pieces—some pain, some bittersweetness, some hope, some love—and the end product is that life is worth *living* it.

Before we fly back to the United States, I help the team pack up the collection of trophies that we accumulated during the season, as they will travel along with our cars.

Before the cars are packed up in the trailer, I watch as Racer strokes a hand over Kelsey, then he leans over and kisses her nose. He flips a coin inside her and takes my hand to lead me out of there.

"Superstition?" I ask.

"Just don't want her to feel lonely." He smirks.

I smile. "You're lucky I'm not jealous."

"Yes you are."

"What?"

He rubs his index finger down the freckles of my nose. "If you could see the look in your eyes when the girls come over for my autograph."

I stiffen, and he chuckles, peering down at my face before pecking my lips in that fast way of his that leaves me no choice but to endure it. *Mmm.*

"I like you being jealous of me. I'm jealous of you; you're mine," he says, opening the door of his rental for me while my brothers board the SUV with my dad.

"You're mine too."

"I am. I race for you. Live for you, girl." He takes my hand and kisses the back of my knuckles, igniting the engine and driving us down to the airport for our flights to Spain, where my family and I will pack (as we agreed just recently), and then to Seattle.

best driver in the world

Lana

We're still celebrating in Seattle. My family, his family, the team mechanics, some of Racer's friends. Given the huge amount of prize money both HW Racing and our driver received, we've been splurging a little on kick-ass food and plenty of spirits (for those who drink to celebrate), and we're not one bit ashamed about it.

I've moved in with Racer. To *both* his apartments, to be exact: the one in Seattle and the one in St. Pete, which we've been visiting on and off for the past month.

I know we're moving fast, but this guy loves speed so what can I say? I adore playing house with him, fitting my clothes into the closet with his. I love us driving to nowhere during the weekends just for the hell of it, and I love it when we stay in and continue negotiating what we'll be playing on TV.

He has steep prices for whenever I plot to have my way sometimes, but it's quite the thrill because they're usually prices I'm *very* willing to pay.

We're in his parents' living room in their Seattle home now.

Racer has been talking to Henley all this time, knocking his fist onto his friend's head when he suggests he go back to street racing in his spare time.

"I've got the fastest car in the land—I race at 250 mph and it's legal. Why would I risk that for a few extra bucks?"

"For me, man," Henley says.

Racer just laughs, and my heart feels as if it literally cannot fit inside my chest.

He smirks at me, his eyes darkening a little like they do when our eyes meet—and they flood with lust, proprietariness and tenderness. God. I'm so grateful, so lucky.

"What are you thinking?" he prods as he comes up to me, pushing my hair back.

"You're the eye-reader, you tell me."

"I want you to tell me in your own words." He watches me. "That you're happy. That you're hopelessly in love with me."

I start nodding and nodding. "You made all our dreams come true. You brought love into my life ..." I press my lips trying to find more words.

He starts shaking his head, and I become puzzled. "What?" I ask.

"It's all you," he says, low, shifting closer, his gaze intent. "I always wanted to race—never in my wildest dreams did I think it would happen. I wanted a girl, never in my life did I think it would happen—and it happened the same day you crashed my car, and that day the universe brought my girl to me."

I reach out and cup his jaw in my hands, my thumb tracing his dimple. "You're the best man in the world, Racer."

He raises his brows, obviously surprised I replaced 'driver' with man. He ducks his dark head and expertly pecks my lips wearing a mischievous gleam in his eye. "Best kisser too."

"Oooh …" I playfully shake my head and tap the corner of my lips thoughtfully. "I don't know about that. You'll have to keep working on that … and I'll let you know."

He only grins in mischief.

"*So.*" I decide to ask something that's been on my mind and I haven't been able to discuss with him. "I had a special sign made that said you're the best driver in the world for your celebration. Does this mean I need to fix your car?"

"No." He seems to be relishing every moment of this, his dimple as deep as I've ever seen it. "I don't want you to fix my car or me." He pauses meaningfully and leans closer a fraction. "I want you to drive it."

"Excuse me?"

"You heard me." Something about the wicked expression on his face makes my heartbeat speed up. "You said you'd race for me. Didn't you? Was that a lie too, *Alana*?"

His eyes keep glinting and I can tell he's loving this.

"I … well I mean … no. It wasn't a lie." I stumble over my words because I hardly remember making this promise. I was so caught up in the excitement of freaking *winning.*

"So, you'll race my car for me, as promised?" He's watching me with an unreadable expression all of a sudden, and something like a challenge in those blue, blue eyes.

"Huh?" I'm confused by his words.

Racer laughs softly to himself and breathes in my neck, his eyes gleaming full of devil's intent as he gazes down at me.

"How about I give you the ultimate prize if you win for me, crasher?"

He's been giving me driving lessons daily for the past few weeks, teasing me that he's going to make me work for an engagement ring—because I've made him work for every step ahead he's gained with me. Now he kisses me and grabs my butt as Henley comes over.

Racer organized a race with me and an old lady. Like, she's literally eighty.

And it's really a race!

"Okay, you ready, Lana Tate?" Henley asks.

"It's … I'm not his sister." I shake my head at Henley, confused that he calls me Tate.

Henley smirks at Racer, and Racer just smirks back.

"Okay … remember, girls"—Henley eyes me and the old lady—"Mr. Tate here is marrying whoever wins this race."

"Racer …" I say, nervous that I might not win.

He grabs my shoulders and gazes into my eyes, the thirst for the win right there in his baby blues. "Listen to me very well, Lana," he says soberly. "It's very important that you win this race, baby. All those hours I've spent tutoring you won't be for nothing—and you're the woman I'm walking down the aisle, so make me proud."

"But Racer, what if I get too nervous—"

"I'm marrying the winner of the race, sweetheart; you'd better step on it." His eyes twinkle, and his dimple is shamelessly on full display, as he ushers me in and straps me down. "Now go and kick ass. Wait. Kiss me first."

"Oh god."

I kiss him. With tongue and everything.

Then I sit down on the seat of his mustang and look at the old lady. She's blinking behind her glasses.

I exhale, and turn on the engine.

Henley gives us the signal.

And suddenly I'm racing for my goddamn life. For my boyfriend's hand in marriage.

"I'm insane," I gasp, pushing the pedal and seeing the old lady is way, way behind. I start feeling high from the race, then brake and turn around carefully before I drive back. I pass the old lady, who literally is about ten feet from the starting line—the slowest woman I've ever seen.

I don't care. I'm high on it because my prize is …

My racer.

"Hey! You're a fucking star—come here." He reaches into the car and pulls my head to his and kisses me long and hard, and I moan when he pries his sexy, wicked mouth free. I'm so hot for him I could be the embodiment of fire right now.

"You totally paid her to go slow," I chide.

"No," he denies, eyes twinkling. "I'd rather spend my money on you."

"We just made sure her car was shit," Henley says from behind him.

"Shut up, Hen," Racer growls, turning back proudly to me. "Hell, you found her," he says.

"Who?"

"The best driver in the world."

"Who? You mean—me? You *tease*." I laugh, then look into his eyes, breathless. "Are you going to marry me or what?"

His eyes flicker possessively, as if he loves me being possessive and greedy for him too. He leans over to peck my lips and looks down at me with tender blue eyes. "You're trouble," he rasps with pride.

I nod, breathless. "Trouble likes me. Follows me wherever I go. Claims he's going to marry me."

"Let's not make a liar out of him then. *Alana*." He pulls the car door open, and as I step out, Racer folds down to his knee.

I turn to stone and blink down at him—my guy, Racer fucking Tate, on one knee, with his dimple popping out on one cheek.

There's a ring in his palm, and if it weren't for me leaning on the door of his mustang, my knees would have buckled and I'd be right there, with Racer, on the ground.

"Lana Heyworth. Marry me. Be with me. Be my girl, always. Now. Tomorrow. Forever."

I had been daydreaming about this day, secretly, for quite some time. I had been wanting a family of my own, even though I was sure I might not ever have it. I had been wanting a home, some security, and I wanted … maybe, despite my fears, to love even harder, to be loved even more.

I gaze down at the guy I will spend the rest of my life with. Whose name he wrote down on a page that I saved because for some reason, it seemed important.

Turns out, the page wasn't that important.

But it turns out, *he* was.

"Lana …" Racer prods warningly.

"Yes!" I squeak out, throwing myself into his arms and wrapping my arms around him, because I've never wanted anything more.

him

Lana

Racer wants me in white. He wants me walking down the aisle to him, in white … and he wants me to have everything I could have ever dreamed of.

We're having the whole enchilada. Church wedding, and then a reception with about 120 guests at the largest ballroom in the city's top hotel.

I wasn't the kind of girl who dreamed of her wedding when she was little. I think it's been a while since I even allowed myself to think, to hope, that I would one day be dressed in white … and the man I love with my whole being would be waiting down a long church aisle for me, ready to make me his.

My mom showed up for the wedding. We're not friends, and I know we never will be, but it's nice to have her here on my big day. She made sure my hair was perfect, and my veil was draped behind my head with no wrinkles or creases, and that I looked as beautiful as could be.

"You're a vision," she whispered when our eyes met in the mirror, and I could see she wanted to cry. All the guilt maybe of the years she has missed, of me and my brothers growing up.

"Thanks, Mom," I whisper. Because today I'm getting married and it's not a day I want to hold onto the past. I'm leaving the past in the past, where it belongs, because my future is staring right at me—and I've never loved what I see as much as I do now.

We head to the church, and my father looks dashing with his shaven head, and his gorgeous smile, and his loving brown eyes.

"The most beautiful bride ever," he says.

I am tempted to say there's no way, but I'm his only daughter, and the apple of his eye, and I know that to him, it's true. And I know that to the man who sees me now at the altar, it will be true too.

My brothers kiss my cheek. "Don't make him return you. No returns or exchanges," Drake says.

"You're the one who'll be returned as defective," I say, as he chuckles and allows Clayton and Adrian to come kiss me too.

"He's right. No exchanges," Clay says, patting the back of my head to smack a wet one on my cheek.

"Clayton! My veil!" I protest, waiting for Adrian to hug me.

"Be happy, Lana," Adrian says. He's the sweetest of my three brothers, but he speaks this as a command and it makes me laugh.

"Yes, sir."

I feel my mother fix my veil. She's not talking to my brothers, or more likely, they're not talking to her, but I know they're here—together—for me, and it just makes me value my family more.

I slip my hand into the nook of Dad's arm, and I whisper, "Thank you, Daddy."

"No need to give thanks. It's been my pleasure being my girl's dad." He chuckles and kisses the back of my hand, and we both halt at the doors, my heart hammering in my chest, my whole body buzzing because I can feel him, right behind the church doors. Waiting for me.

The music begins, and the doors swing open, and it feels like gravity is what pulls me forward. My eyes scan the length of the red carpet and look for the familiar blue of his, and when they lock together, that's where they stay.

He looks hot enough to melt the candles.

So young, so strong, and in that dark tux and crisp white shirt, still *so* him …

His dimple keeps deepening as his smile keeps widening as I approach, and a part of me even wonders why I need to say the words when I'm already his.

her

Racer

I tug restlessly on the bow tie at my neck, and I hear Henley say, "You look fine, dude."

"Thanks," I growl, impatient, my gaze glued to the church doors.

We're tying the knot before the start of the season next March. I couldn't wait, and Lana didn't want to either. But somehow these past ten minutes waiting for her up at the altar have felt about as long as waiting my whole damn life for her.

The benches are cluttered with our family and friends, and outside, we even needed to field off some reporters, interested in my wedding since I was crowned Formula One champion.

I could've swept my girl up to Vegas and got this circus over with, but I wanted to give her something she deserved—something good, and fucking memorable. Like her.

I also selfishly wanted to watch her walk up the aisle, and so here I am. Best driver in the world, sometimes selfish motherfucker, future husband and father, chomping at the bit for his bride to tie the knot with him. Yeah, I'm definitely not used to wearing suits, and I'm simmering underneath with the urge to give her my name and call her Mrs. Tate. So every minute feels like a penance for some small or large sins I've done since I was kid.

When we told my parents I'd proposed, Dad pulled me aside and told me, "I'm just going to have to ask you once because I'm your father and I care: are you certain about this?"

"Dead certain."

He'd smiled, patted my shoulder and said, "Good. I can tell she deserves you, and I know sure as fuck you deserve her."

"Don't blow smoke up my ass; you don't know her well yet."

"I saw you two at the hospital—I didn't need to see more."

The music starts ratcheting up, and when the doors of the church open and I spot Lana on her dad's arm, I blink my eyes and open them back up. I had fantasies. Watching this girl walk up to me in a white dress, her eyes screaming that she loved me.

Nothing fucking compares to the reality.

Because fuck me, I never thought something so perfect, so lovely, and so damned sweet could ever be mine. Could ever love me like she does, accept me as I am, want me back.

I run my hand over the front of my tux and hold her gaze, my insides roiling with hunger, lust, love, everything I fucking feel for this girl. Her veil is attached to the top of her head and falling down her back. She made sure not to wear it over her face; I wanted to see her face as she walked towards me, and I *see* her now and feel like someone just slammed the back of my knees.

My bride's smile is like the brightest sun on any possible galaxy out there. In her eyes is everything I need to know. Has always been there, no matter how scared, how reluctant, how much I took her by surprise.

Our families look happy about the wedding. Maybe they'd never expected us to find each other. Hell, maybe we didn't either. But we did. Now I'm not letting this girl go.

I mean to watch her sweet, lovely body swell up with my kids. Have them walk up to her, call her their mother.

I want to step out of the race track, sweaty and dehydrated, and have her always standing there to get my kiss.

And on our off days, I want to hop into my car, ignite the engine, pull us into the road with the wind in her hair, my hand on her, a song on the stereo. The road before us, our fucking love as real as the wind, sometimes soft or slow, sometimes wet and wild, always there.

She can crash my party at any time.

My smile as wide as I've ever felt it, I step off the platform and open my hand for hers. As her father hands her over to me, he gives me a steady, admiring look. "You love her hard, boy, and know that I have never seen my daughter as happy as she is with you or as in love as she is now."

I nod respectfully back at him, my hand still open as Lana's fingers slip into mine, and I grip her as tight as I can without hurting her—as tight as I plan to hold on to her, my whole damn life. We're smiling at each other as I pull her up to my side. My wife.

"You're so screwed," I rasp in her ear, a teasing tone in my voice. "I'm going to ruin you for everyone else your whole life."

"I'm counting on it," she breathes as those green eyes of hers happily caress my face.

She never once hesitates when she says her vows to me, but I notice her tear up with emotion when I say, loud and damn clear, that I, Racer Tate, take her as my wife, to have and to hold, till death do us part.

Because I mean it, and Lana knows me well enough by now to know.

We're impatient to strip when we arrive at my apartment in St. Pete. It's 3 a.m. We danced to our song—*Favorite Record* (Lana declared it ours and I fucking approve)—and then we mingled with our guests and are now ready to continue feasting in private by feasting on each other.

My girl reaches behind her to try to unzip her dress when I take her by the shoulders and gently turn her around.

On my nightstand behind me is a box with the keys to her new ride. A wedding present from me, purchased with a small part of my F1 winnings. A white Mercedes with beige interior and carbon fiber dashboard. Wheels like artwork. I want her to have the best always. But I'm not giving it to her yet. That comes later. Tomorrow. Now I need my fucking hands on her. My tongue on her. My damn smell.

"Allow your husband," I say, relishing calling myself that name for the first time as I devilishly tug the zipper down her back and place a long, wet kiss on the back of her neck, the skin exposed because her hair is still up.

As her dress starts coming down, I slide my hands down her bare arms. She shivers, and my gut coils tight with need and desire. "Racer, I'm so happy right now."

She's whispering.

"I know."

And I'm whispering too. I don't know why, as we're alone. But this moment feels fucking holy, and words are almost too superfluous for a moment like this. I turn Lana back around to face me.

She's already breathing hard, and her heart is beating rapidly in that little pulse point at her throat. I drink her in, slowly, wanting to memorize this moment for as long as I live.

My wife in a flimsy strapless bra and an even flimsier white lace thong, in garters, hose that reach up to mid-thigh, and heels that she's able to step out of as she takes a step closer to me.

Ivory skin, freckled nose, her hair still up with that veil, my gut coils back like a spring.

I want this girl like crazy. Not only with every atom, pore, and cell of my body. I want this girl heart and soul. I stare into those wide green eyes, flooded with love for me, and I watch them carefully as I start to work her lovely white lace bra open to reveal her gorgeous breasts.

I look at her, eye contact holding as I lean down, holding as I bring my tongue out to lick one puckered nipple, and my dick throbs mercilessly in my pants as her eyes flare wide and her pupils dilate even more.

I turn my head and torture the other nipple, slow and easy, making it stand up and quiver when I breathe on it.

"They're always up when I'm with you," she whispers as she leans her head to nuzzle my ear, and I raise my brows and straighten, my wife's gaze mischievous and still shy. I don't know why she continues to feel shy with me sometimes, but I like it. I like everything about her to the point she's got me all jacked up just standing here with her wedding dress pooled at her feet and that fucking lace garter looking sexy as shit on her slim legs.

There's a blue rose pin attached to her garter, and I finger it as I trail my eyes over her body. "What's this?"

"Reese gave it to me." Like a greedy siren who won't wait for more, Lana's unknotting my tie and pushing my jacket off my shoulders. "Something borrowed and something blue."

I ease my arms out of my jacket and toss it into the air, then slide my fingers up the inside of her thigh as she undoes the buttons of my shirt.

"How about something hot and wet for the groom," I murmur, easing my fingers into her white lace panties.

She groans on contact, and a more animalistic sound comes from me at the same time, and Lana presses a kiss to my neck, then starts slowly kissing the skin of my chest as she unbuttons down my shirt and pushes it off my chest.

"Girl, I love you so much," I rasp, taking her mouth beneath mine, suddenly growing a little rougher and more desperate.

Lana's tongue comes out to play with mine, and we stumble our way into the bedroom of my pad, where we'll be living for the summer months before taking off again for next year's F1 season.

My gut is churning from my need of her. My slacks are near bursting from the length and width of my damned greedy dick, and when Lana caresses it with that magic hand of hers, I growl and roll her to her back, the kiss turning more desperate.

Her panties are so flimsy I grab them to pull them down her legs and, instead, end up tearing them off her. Something I've started to do lately. My bride gasps in delight and I smile and look down at her, all bare for me except for that garter.

I like it.

Licking my teeth, I run my hands down her body, watching her pant, her breasts rising and falling, her pupils dilating.

"Racer, I need you," she breathes.

I shake my head no, smirking, as I continue exploring her very slowly, and she sits up on the bed and suddenly straddles me.

I don't complain when she drops her pussy to my hard dick and rubs against it, the only thing separating us the slacks of my tux, which I'm still wearing.

She looks at me, and I look at her, and I'm hot enough to explode as I grab her face in one hand, and tease my tongue along her lips again. "What do you want, wife?" I croon, licking her slowly, side to side, then I tease the tip of my tongue inside.

"Give me you," she breathes, reaching between our bodies to stroke my hard dick.

She turns me on like a brand-new radio when she gets greedy for me like that.

"All of me," I growl, as if that's the only condition of her getting a piece of me: it's all or nothing and that's the way it is. She's humming with anticipation as I lower her back down and then step back to remove my slacks.

She watches me—eyes running over my muscled chest, my hard abs, then down my happy trail, taking in my fully elongated dick, and my hard legs and thighs. Her breathing quickens, and she eyes me like I'm fucking perfection when the only perfect thing in this room is looking at me.

"All of me," I repeat as I crawl over her.

She licks her lips in anticipation, then raises her head and kisses me on the mouth and drops her head, smiling up at me.

I raise my brows. The look she's giving me is a full on, love-me-fuck-me look. Hell, I'm so game my adrenaline is pumping, my body straining for the release I can only find in her.

My cock continues throbbing as I grab the base and tease the head up and down her folds. I lean forward and whisper something naughty in her ear, that I'm going to fill her with my cum, and she laughs and takes a bite out of my chin and rocks her hips up to my dick to lure me.

I nearly lose control.

I crush her mouth beneath mine, holding her face tenderly in my hand as we taste each other. I can barely keep my head straight as I run my hands down her sides, cupping her lovely breasts, her smooth skin, her abdomen.

I caress my hands along her sides and squeeze her ass, my tongue and hers mating like mad, her nipples brushing against my chest, heaving up and down 'cause she's worked up so bad by what I'm doing to her. Her whispers that she loves me only make my cock throb harder and I can barely see straight. My eyes lock with hers, and hers look heavy lidded and watchful.

Growling softly, I lick my way up her throat, to her mouth, kissing her everywhere as I start to drive inside her.

It's as if the world stops and doesn't start moving again until I'm fucking embedded, balls deep, inside her. Inside my wife.

For the first time with no condom. Nothing between us. Just her.

She feels so damn perfect I'm straining every muscle in my body to make this moment last.

I move, deliberately deep. "Every piece of me," I thickly murmur down at her, moving and moving, wanting to flood her, to fucking fill her with me until there's nothing else.

She's tight, hot and wet for me, and I'm driving harder and harder in the danger zone, her heart beating with mine. I never want to pull out, to come out of here—out of her. Fucking *her*. I cup her cheek and ease back to glance down at her stomach.

"I want your belly growing, Lana. I want your body swelled up because of me, and a baby you and I are going to make right there, inside you. A baby that I put there." I kiss her to show her I mean it, moving faster and faster.

Lana is clawing at my back, her nails sliding down to grip my ass and dig into my tattoo. "RACER!" she's crying out.

My fucking wife, taking me, my seed, everything I want to give her and giving me everything back.

I come inside her with a harsh growl, and Lana detonates when the spurts of my cum shoot up inside her walls. She trembles beneath me, her eyes rolling to the back of her head as she arches up, clutching me as her lifeline.

She tucks her face into my neck when we're done, and I run my nose along her hair, smelling and kissing her as I whisper that I love her.

"I love you," she says, gripping my jaw and looking deeply into my eyes, tears glistening in hers. "Thank you for coming into my life. Thank you for being you. For showing me how to love again, and how to love like this …"

"Crasher," I rasp, stroking my knuckles down her cheeks, "you're the one who showed me how to love. And I'm never going to love anything or anyone the way I love you."

It's a vow. Like the ones we spoke in church, this one in a moment of intimacy when my wife's sweet, malleable body is entwined with my larger one and is still gripping me inside her. Her cheeks are flushed, and I peck her lips every few minutes as we caress each other, relaxed and in fucking love.

Since Belgium, my BP seems stabilized, something I'm thankful for. Sometimes it's like a shadow that's with me wherever I go, there but not quite touching me. Others, it feels like it's one that I can outrun. I'm learning to live with it, and so is she.

At some point in my life, I thought I was fucked by getting stuck with bipolar.

All I knew was that somewhere, somehow, some asshole had fucked me over in the health department. Taking something crucial for a normal man and making me less than what any normal man in the world was. I fought to be more. Better. Faster. Smarter. If only to fucking feel good enough. I managed well, thanks to the support of my family. And their acceptance. But it was her who changed my idea of this shit.

It's easy for people to like you when you're fine, when you're fun, when you're on top. But when you're down and shit gets hard, only the true stuff remains. Who you are to the bone, not a lot of people can appreciate it, some of that shit can only be seen by someone with eyes that can really look deep. And see you. None of the other stuff.

This BP only makes me realize that the connection she and I have, the fucking love, the trust, the highs, and even the lows, what we have—isn't for sissies. But Lana and me ... What we have.

This love is real.

DEAR READERS,

Thanks so much for picking up *Racer.*

I always had a soft spot for Remy and Brooke's son, and though I wasn't sure when or how I would write his book, he took care of things quite easily. One morning he popped into my imaginary world, and from that moment on, just like his dad, he never let me go. I really hope you enjoyed his and Lana's story as much as I did writing it.

XOXO,

Katy

acknowledgments

Although writing is a personal thing and sometimes quite a lonely profession, publishing is a whole other beast, and I couldn't do it without the help and support of my amazing team. I'm grateful to you all.

To my family, I love you!

Thank you Amy and everyone at Jane Rotrosen Agency.

Thank you CeCe, Lisa, Anita, Nina, Kim, Angie, and Monica.

Thank you Nina, Jenn, and everyone at Social Butterfly PR …

Thank you Melissa,

Gel,

S&S Audio,

and my fabulous foreign publishers.

Special thanks to Sara at Okay Creations for the beautiful cover

and Julie for her wonderful formatting,

to bloggers for sharing and supporting my work throughout the years,

and readers—I'm truly blessed to have such an enthusias-
tic, cool crowd of people to share my books with. You are the
greatest, for real!. ☺

Katy

about

New York Times, *USA Today*, and *Wall Street Journal* bestselling author Katy Evans is the author of the Real, Manwhore, and White House series. She lives with her husband, two kids, and their beloved dogs. To find out more about her or her books, visit the sites below. She'd love to hear from you.

Website:
www.katyevans.net

Facebook:
https://www.facebook.com/AuthorKatyEvans

Twitter:
@authorkatyevans

Sign up for Katy's newsletter:
http://www.katyevans.net/newsletter/

titles by katy evans